Series: Arden High

Title: *Twelfth Grade Night*

Authors: Molly Horton Booth and Stephanie Kate Strohm

Illustrator: Jamie Green

Imprint: Hyperion

In-store date: October 11, 2022

Paperback ISBN: 978-1-368-06465-1

Hardcover ISBN: 978-1-368-06239-8

Price: US $14.99 / CAN $19.99; US $24.99 / CAN $30.99

E-book ISBN: 978-1-368-06383-8

Trim size: 6 x 9

Page count: 160

Ages: 12–18

Grades: 7–12

ATTENTION, READER:

This is an uncorrected galley proof. It is not a finished book and is not expected to look like one. Errors in spelling, page length, format, etc. will be corrected when the book is published several months from now. Direct quotes should be checked against the final printed book.

We are pleased to send this book for review.

Please send two copies of any review or mention to:

Disney Publishing Worldwide

Attn: Children's Publicity Department

77 West 66th Street, 3rd Floor

New York, NY 10023

dpw.publicity@disney.com

ARDEN HIGH

Twelfth GRADE Night

Written by Molly Horton Booth
and Stephanie Kate Strohm

Illustrated by Jamie Green

HYPERION

Los Angeles   New York

First Edition, October 2022

10 9 8 7 6 5 4 3 2 1

FAC-034274-22238

Printed in the United States of America

This book is set in CCScoundrel/Fontspring; with hand-lettering by Jamie Green

Illustrated by Jamie Green
Lettering by Chris Dickey
Designed by Tyler Nevins

Library of Congress Cataloging-in-Publication Data
Names: Booth, Molly, author. • Strohm, Stephanie Kate, author. • Green,
   Jamie (Illustrator), illustrator. • Shakespeare, William, 1564-1616.
   Twelfth night.
Title: Twelfth grade night / by Molly Booth and Stephanie Kate Strohm ;
   illustrated by Jamie Green.
Description: New York : Disney/Hyperion, 2022. • Series: Arden High ; book
   1 • Audience: Ages 12-18. • Audience: Grades 10-12. • Summary: New
   student Vi finds herself falling for Orsino, even though he wants Vi's
   help asking Olivia to the school dance.
Identifiers: LCCN 2021042567 • ISBN 9781368062398 (hardcover) • ISBN
   9781368064651 (paperback) • ISBN 9781368063838 (ebook)
Subjects: CYAC: Graphic novels. • Love—Fiction. • Twins—Fiction. •
   Brothers and sisters—Fiction. • High schools—Fiction. •
   Schools—Fiction. • LCGFT: Graphic novels.
Classification: LCC PZ7.7.B664 Tw 2022 • DDC 741.5/973—dc23
LC record available at https://lccn.loc.gov/2021042567
Reinforced binding

Visit www.hyperionteens.com

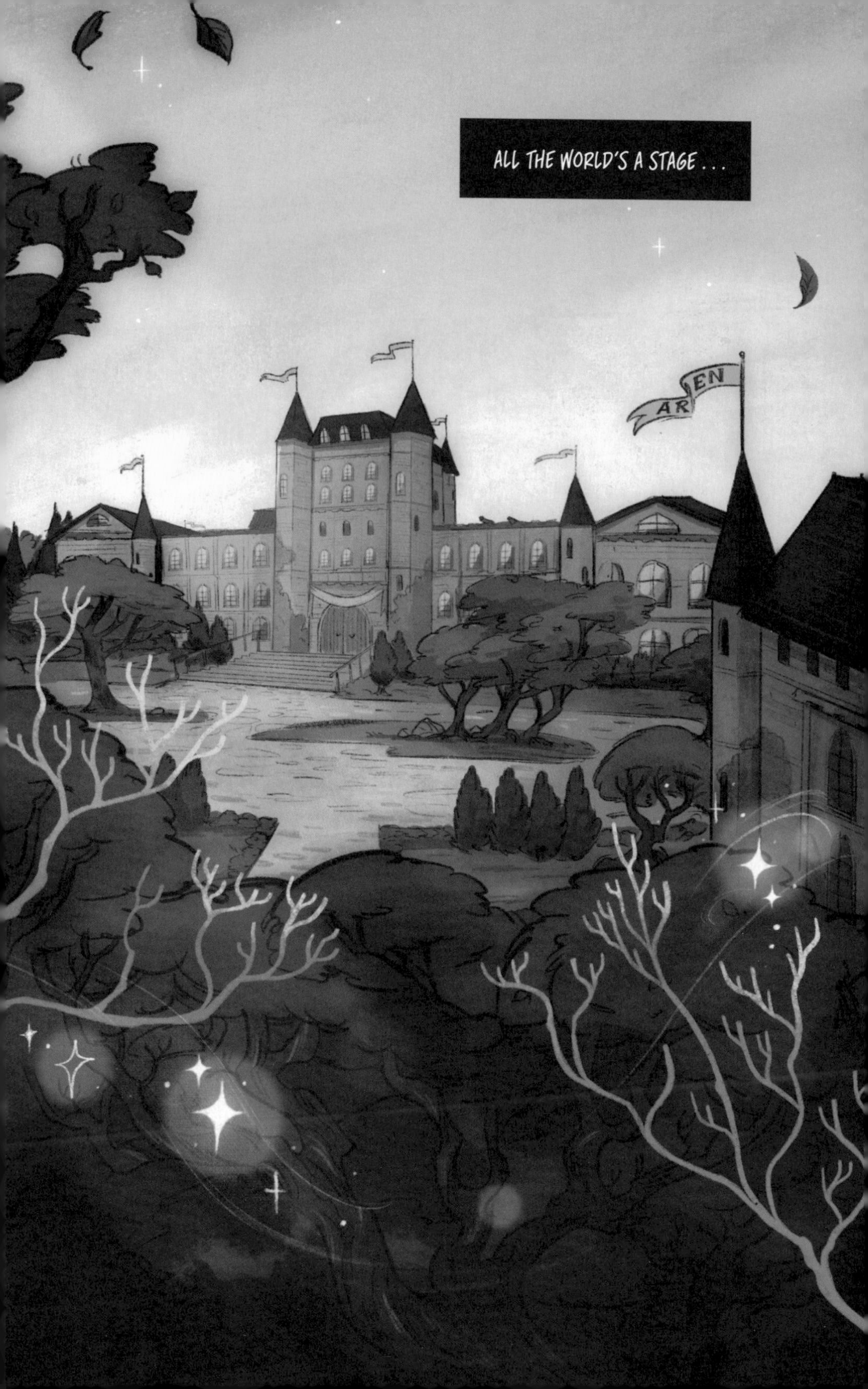
ALL THE WORLD'S A STAGE . . .
AR EN

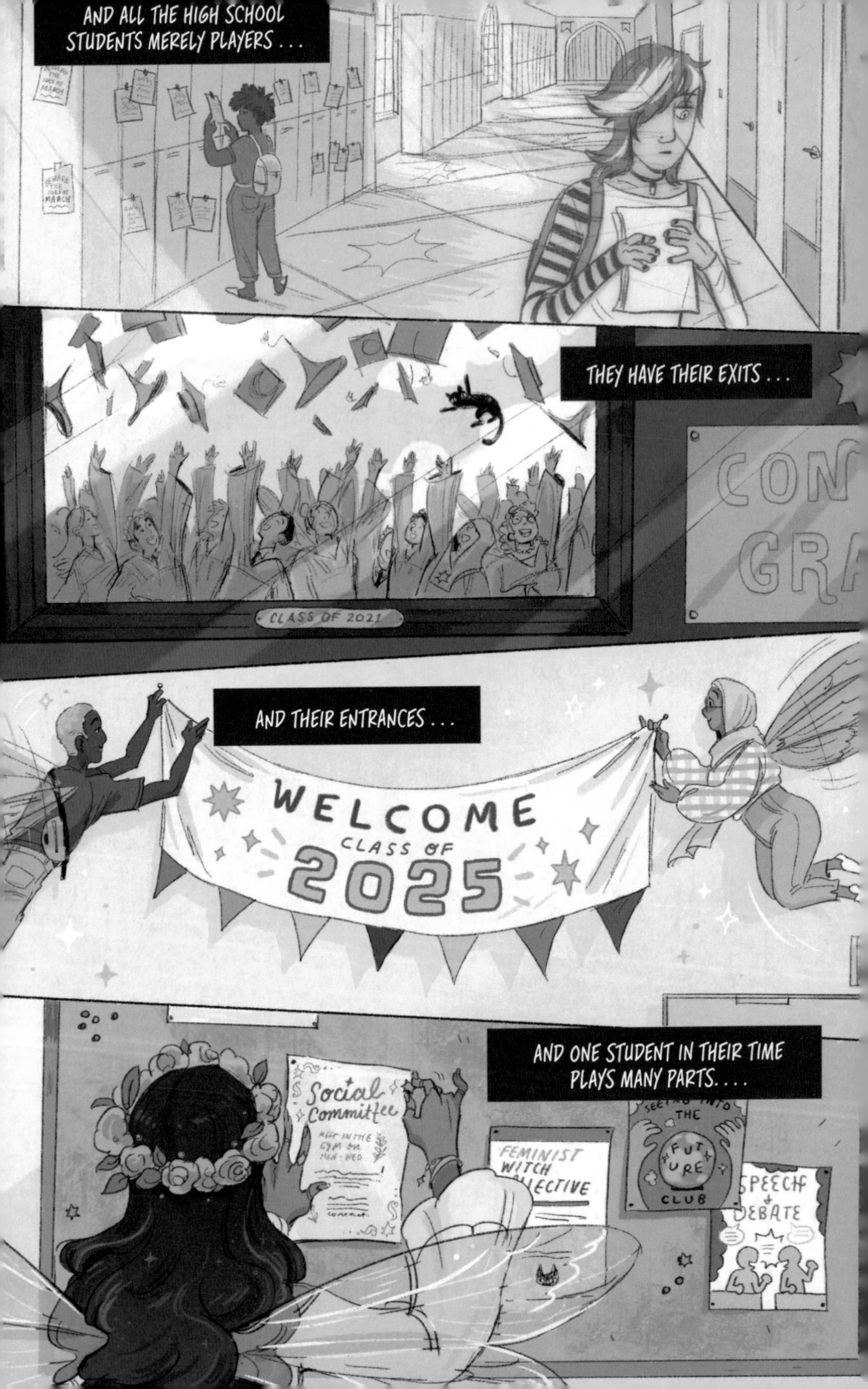
AND ALL THE HIGH SCHOOL STUDENTS MERELY PLAYERS . . .
THEY HAVE THEIR EXITS . . .
CLASS OF 2021
AND THEIR ENTRANCES . . .
WELCOME CLASS OF 2025
AND ONE STUDENT IN THEIR TIME PLAYS MANY PARTS. . . .
Social Committee
FEMINIST WITCH
THE FUT URE CLUB
SPEECH & DEBATE

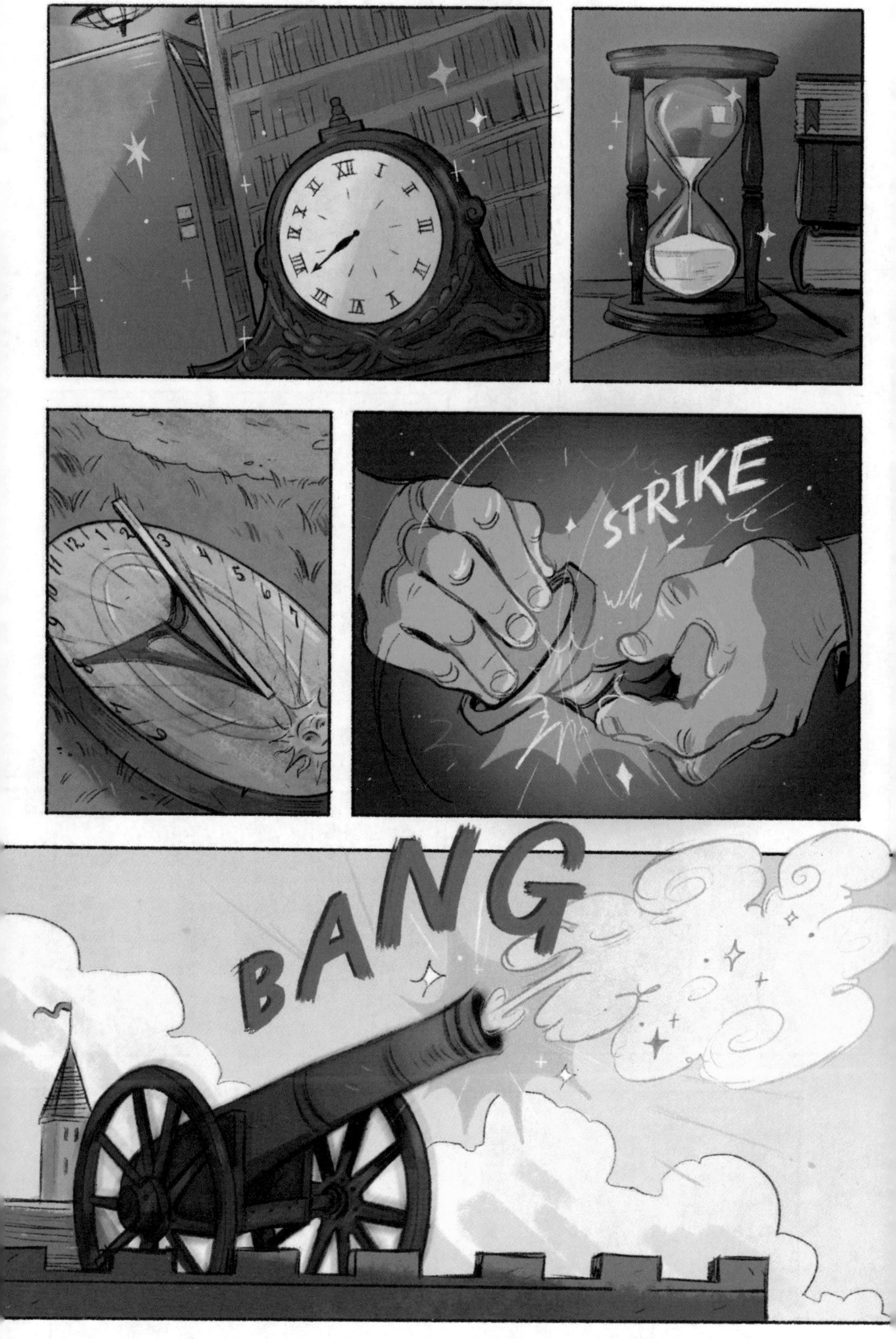
STRIKE
BANG

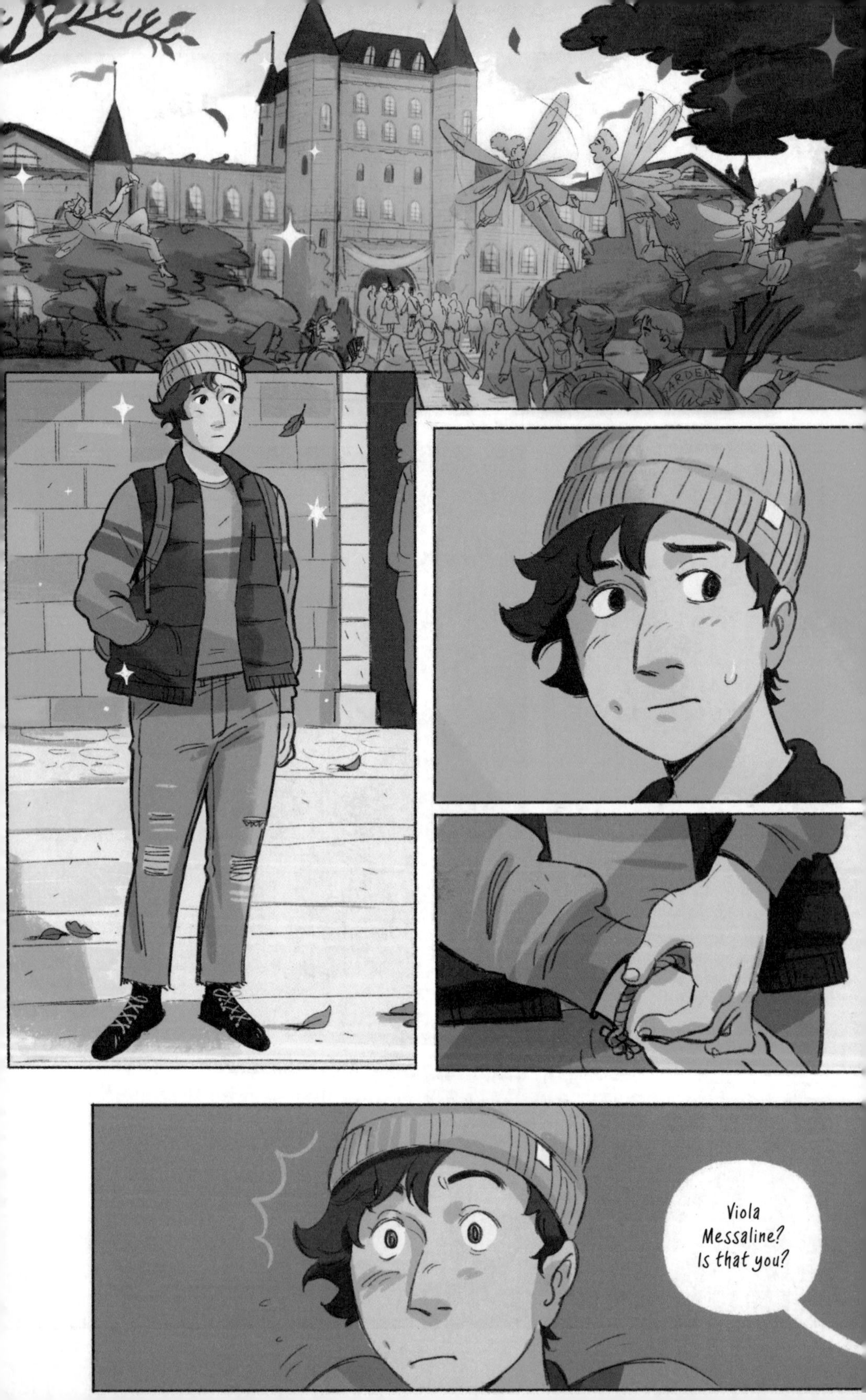
Viola Messaline? Is that you?

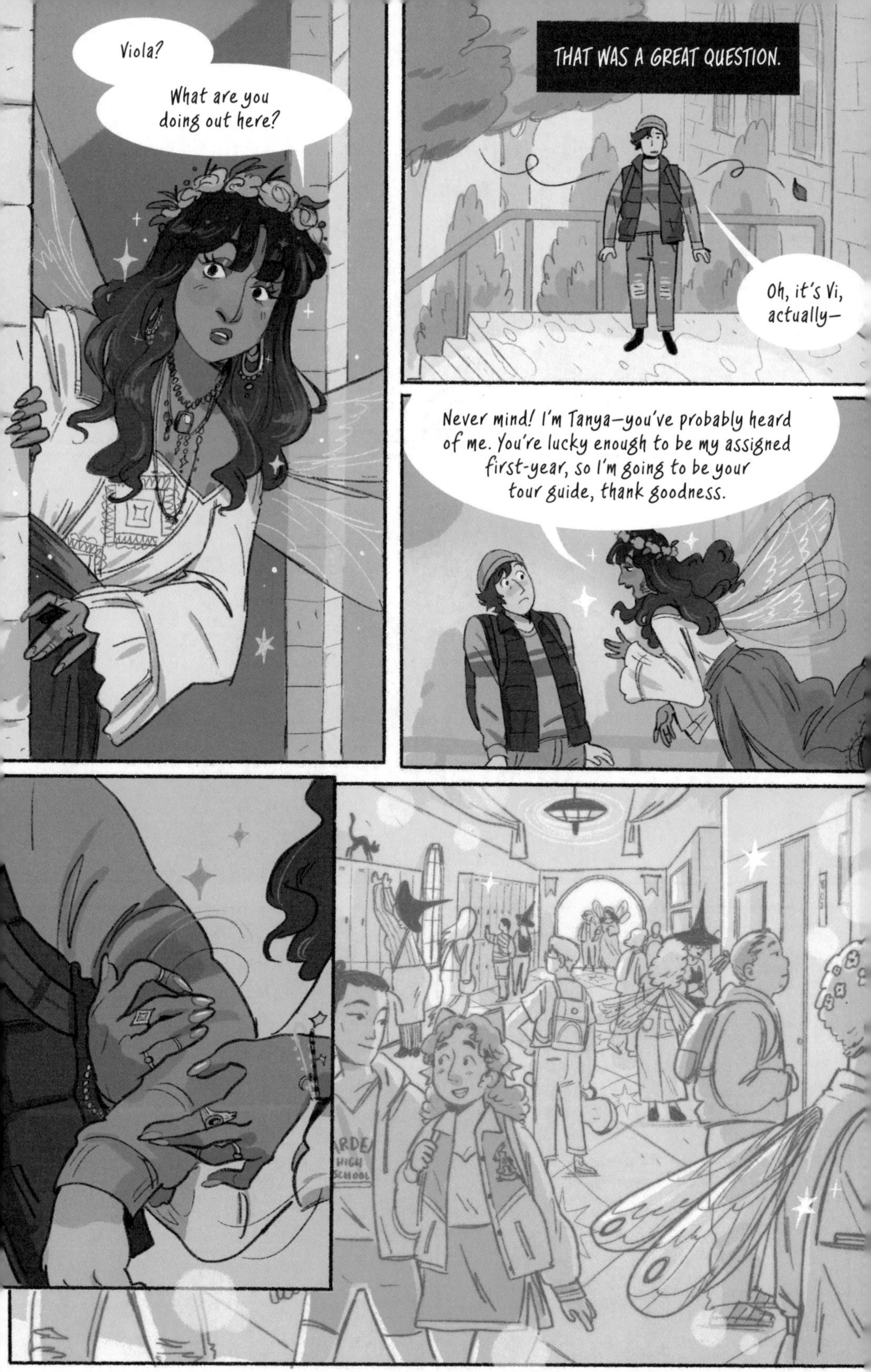
Viola?
What are you doing out here?
THAT WAS A GREAT QUESTION.
Oh, it's Vi, actually—
Never mind! I'm Tanya—you've probably heard of me. You're lucky enough to be my assigned first-year, so I'm going to be your tour guide, thank goodness.

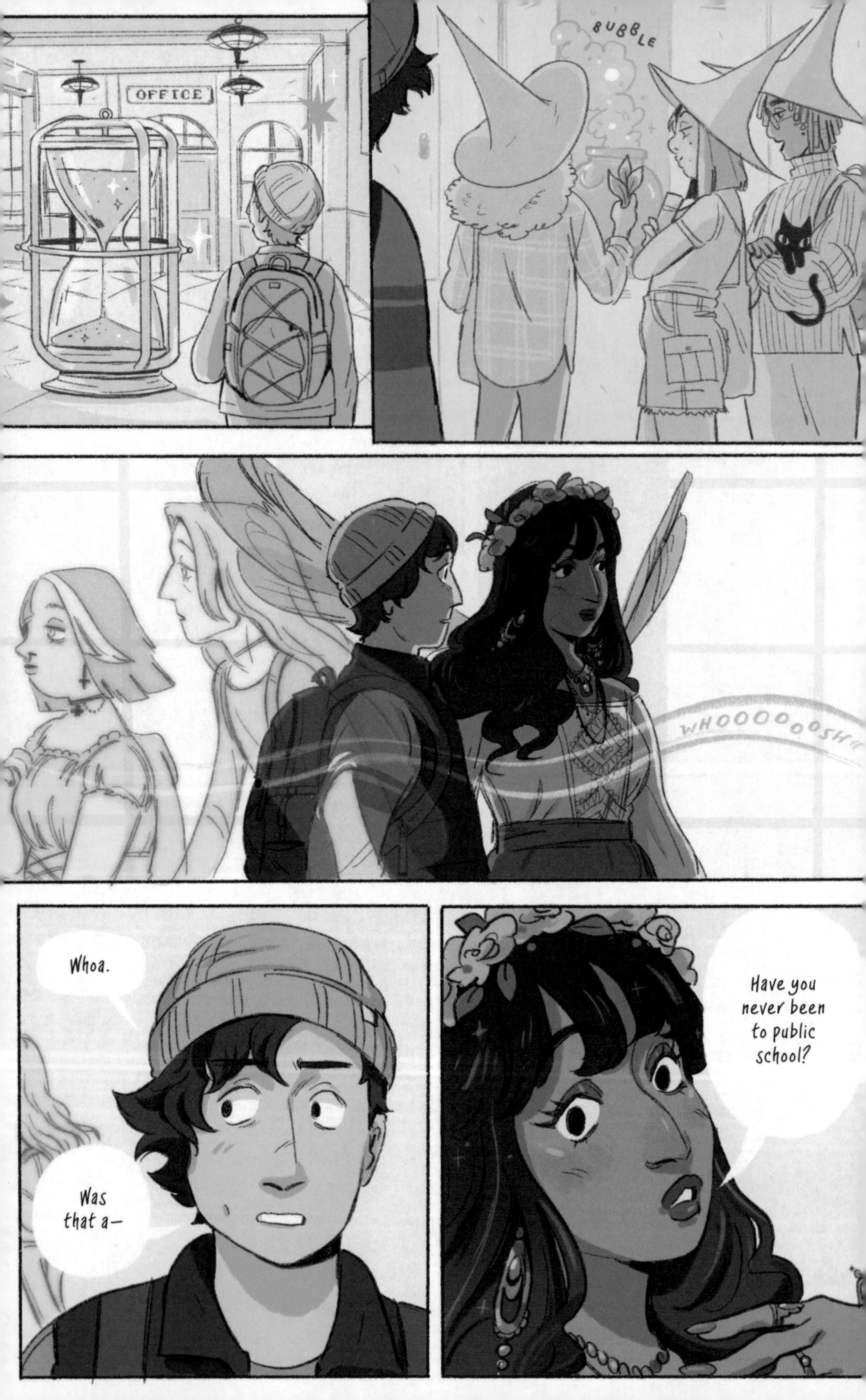
OFFICE
BUBBLE
WHOOOOOOSHH
Whoa.
Was that a—
Have you never been to public school?

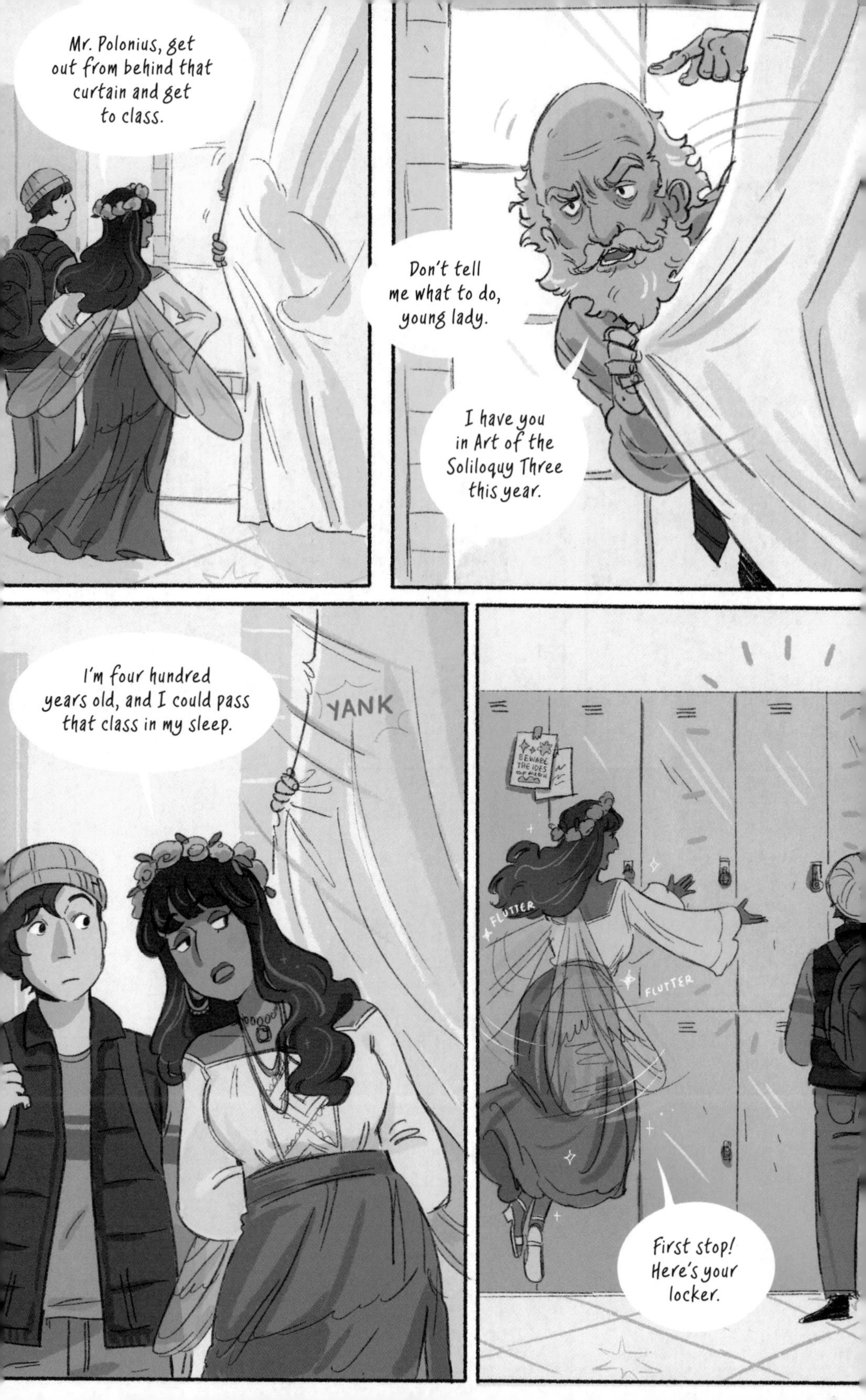
Mr. Polonius, get out from behind that curtain and get to class.
Don't tell me what to do, young lady.
I have you in Art of the Soliloquy Three this year.
I'm four hundred years old, and I could pass that class in my sleep.
YANK
FLUTTER
FLUTTER
First stop! Here's your locker.

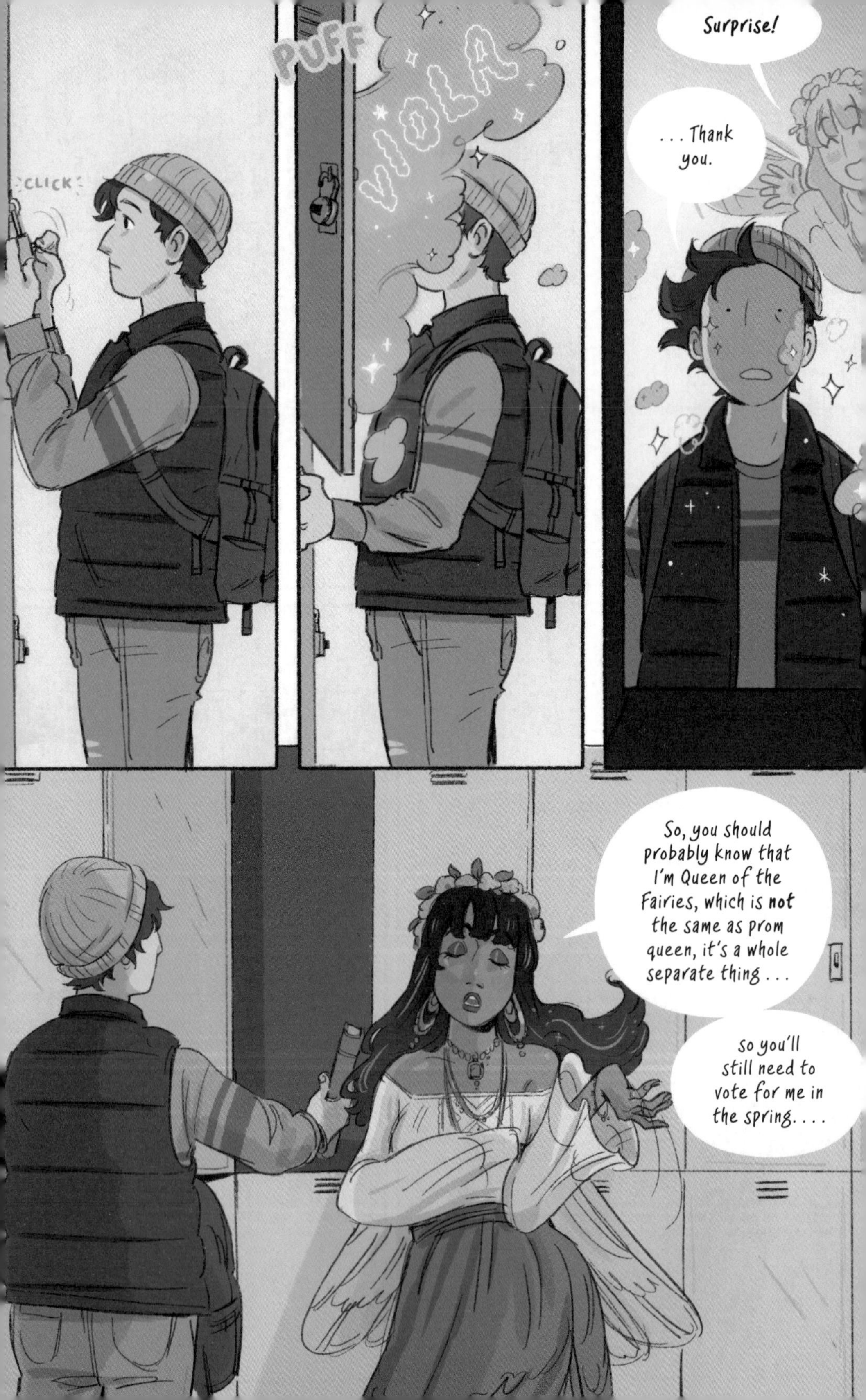
CLICK
PUFF
VIOLA
Surprise!
. . . Thank you.
So, you should probably know that I'm Queen of the Fairies, which is **not** the same as prom queen, it's a whole separate thing . . .
so you'll still need to vote for me in the spring. . . .

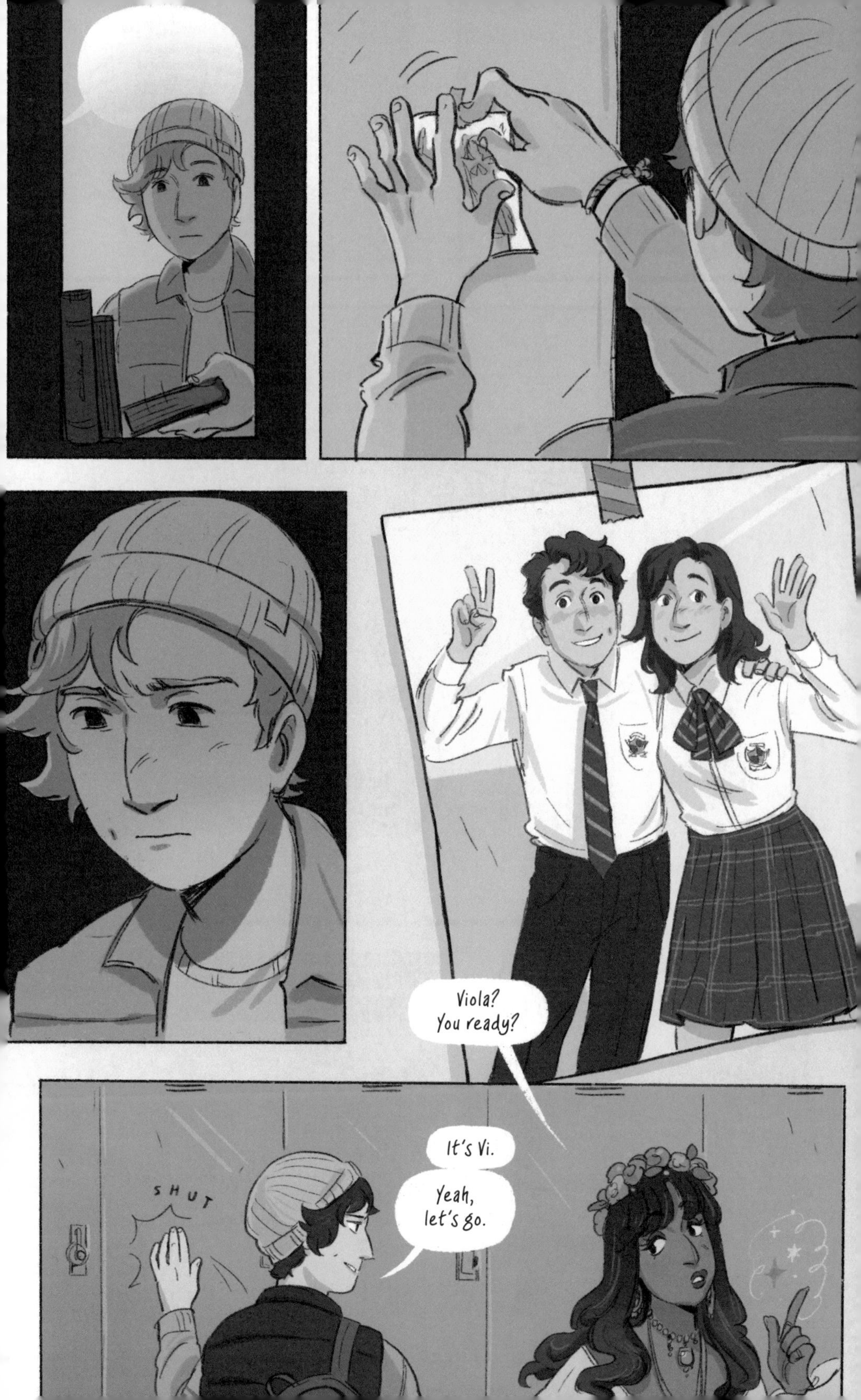
Viola?
You ready?
It's Vi.
Yeah,
let's go.
SHUT

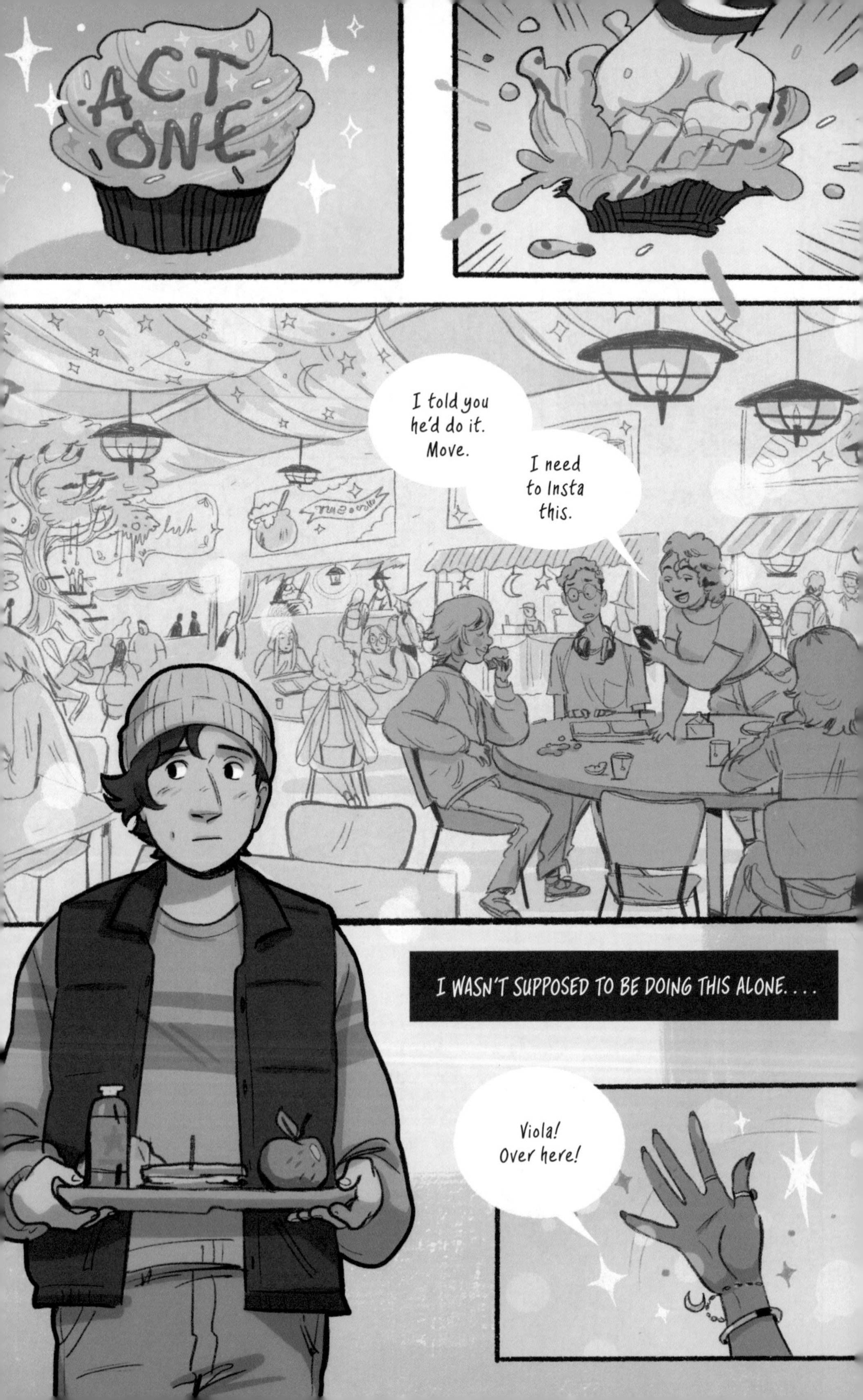
ACT ONE
I told you he'd do it. Move.
I need to Insta this.
I WASN'T SUPPOSED TO BE DOING THIS ALONE. . . .
Viola! Over here!

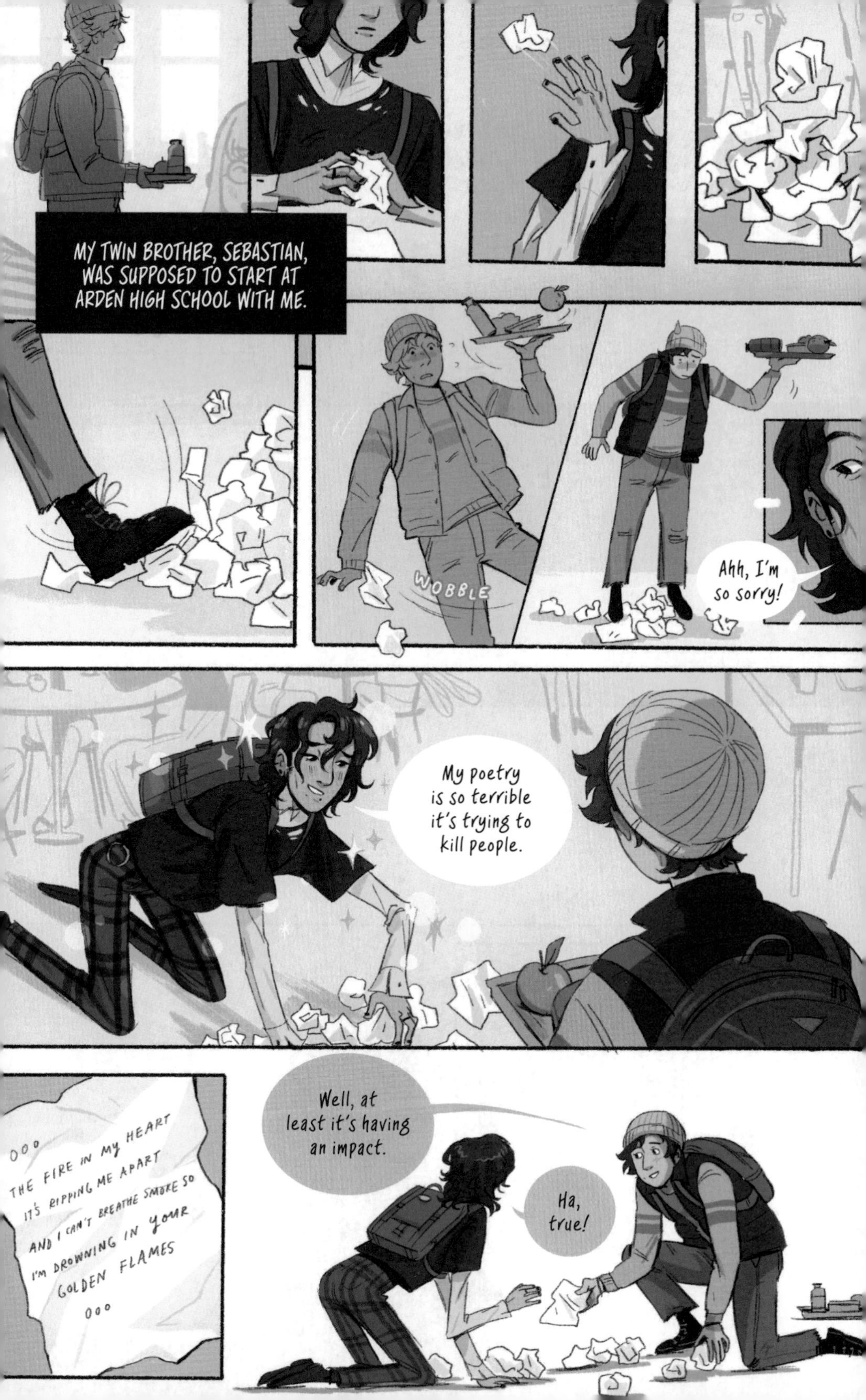
MY TWIN BROTHER, SEBASTIAN, WAS SUPPOSED TO START AT ARDEN HIGH SCHOOL WITH ME.
WOBBLE
Ahh, I'm so sorry!
My poetry is so terrible it's trying to kill people.
ooo THE FIRE IN MY HEART IT'S RIPPING ME APART AND I CAN'T BREATHE SMOKE SO I'M DROWNING IN YOUR GOLDEN FLAMES ooo
Well, at least it's having an impact.
Ha, true!

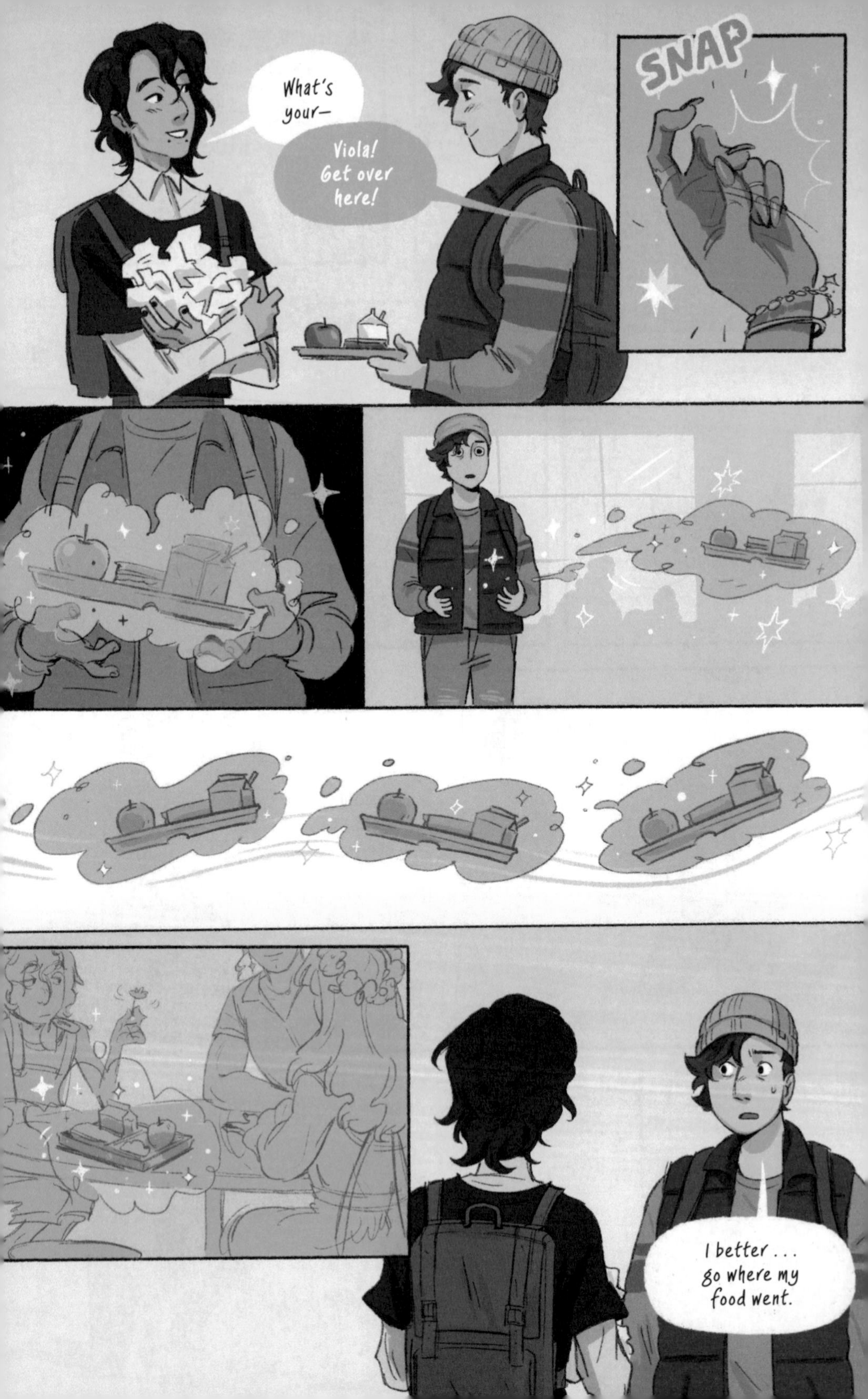
What's your—
Viola! Get over here!
SNAP
I better . . . go where my food went.

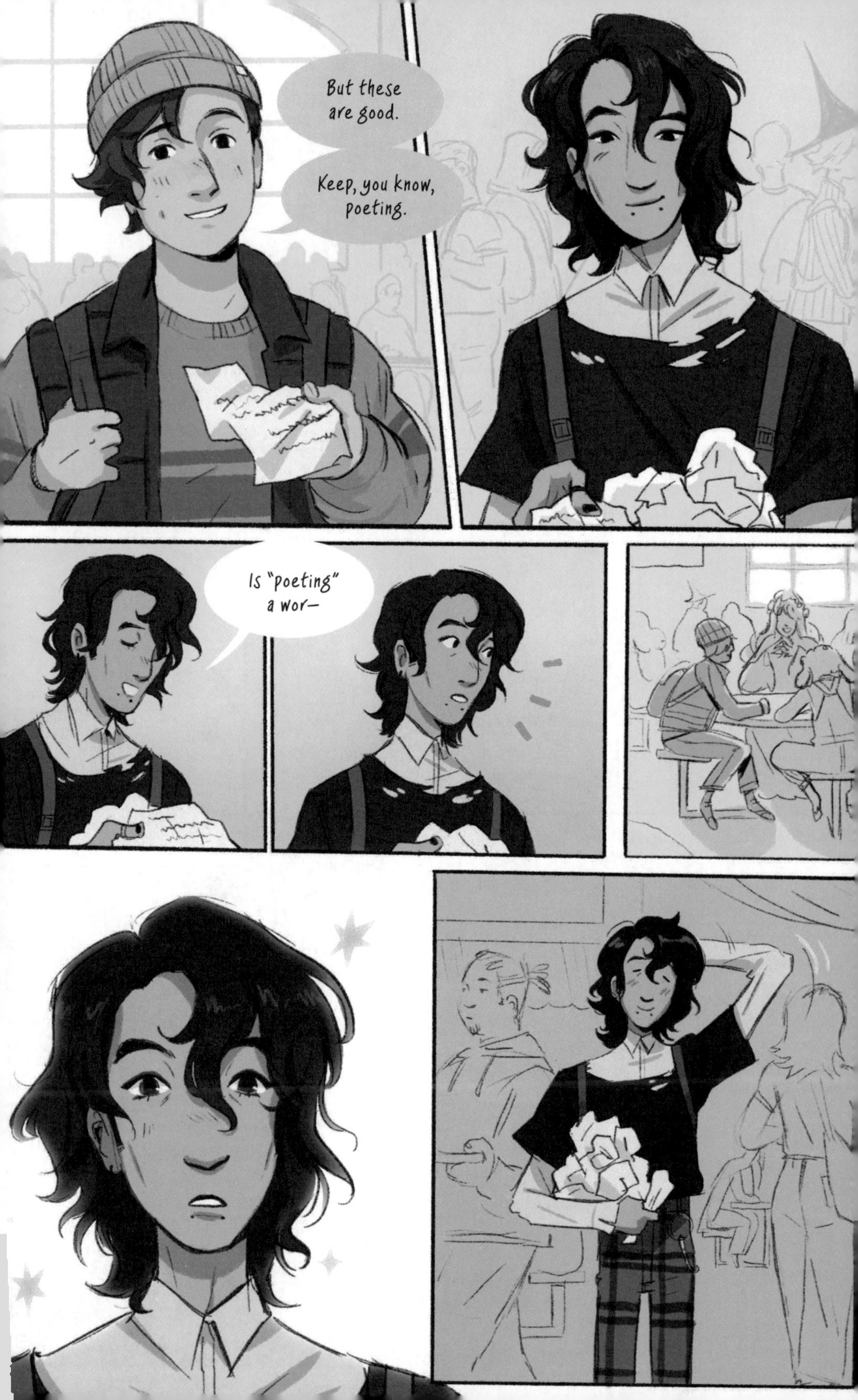
But these are good.
Keep, you know, poeting.
Is "poeting" a wor—

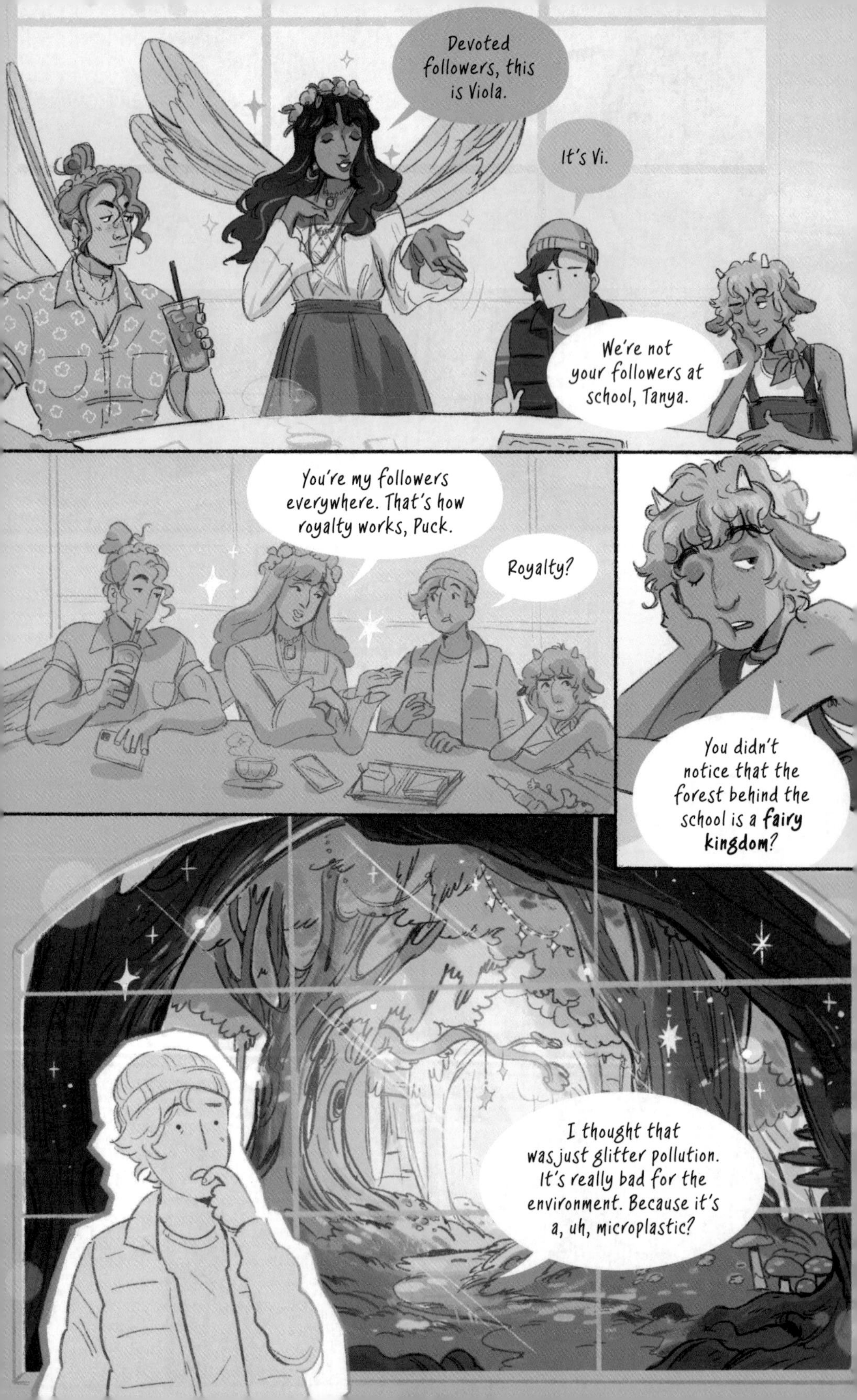
Devoted followers, this is Viola.
It's Vi.
We're not your followers at school, Tanya.
You're my followers everywhere. That's how royalty works, Puck.
Royalty?
You didn't notice that the forest behind the school is a **fairy kingdom**?
I thought that was just glitter pollution. It's really bad for the environment. Because it's a, uh, microplastic?

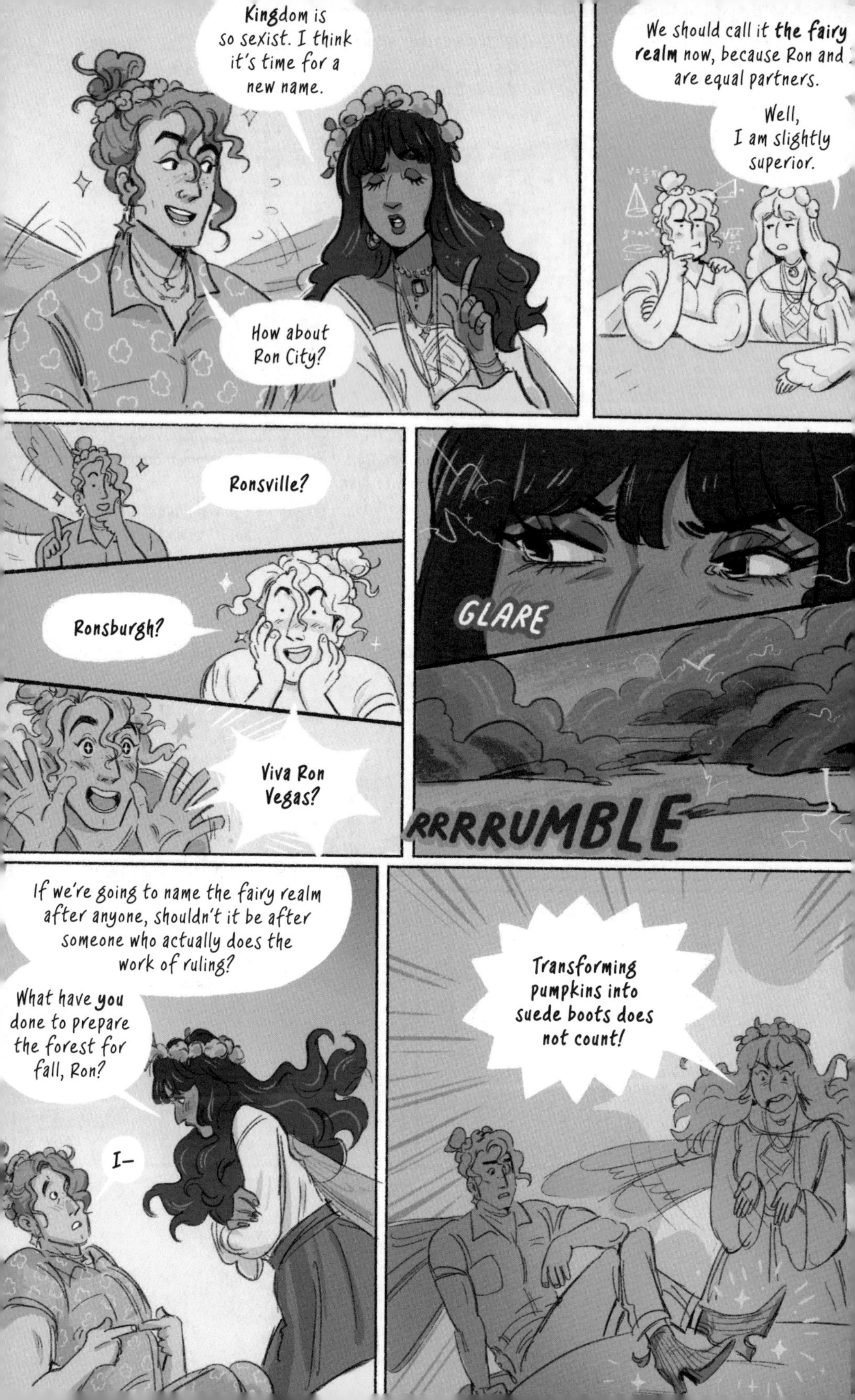
Kingdom is so sexist. I think it's time for a new name.
How about Ron City?
We should call it **the fairy realm** now, because Ron and I are equal partners.
Well, I am slightly superior.
Ronsville?
Ronsburgh?
Viva Ron Vegas?
GLARE
RRRRUMBLE
If we're going to name the fairy realm after anyone, shouldn't it be after someone who actually does the work of ruling?
What have **you** done to prepare the forest for fall, Ron?
I—
Transforming pumpkins into suede boots does not count!

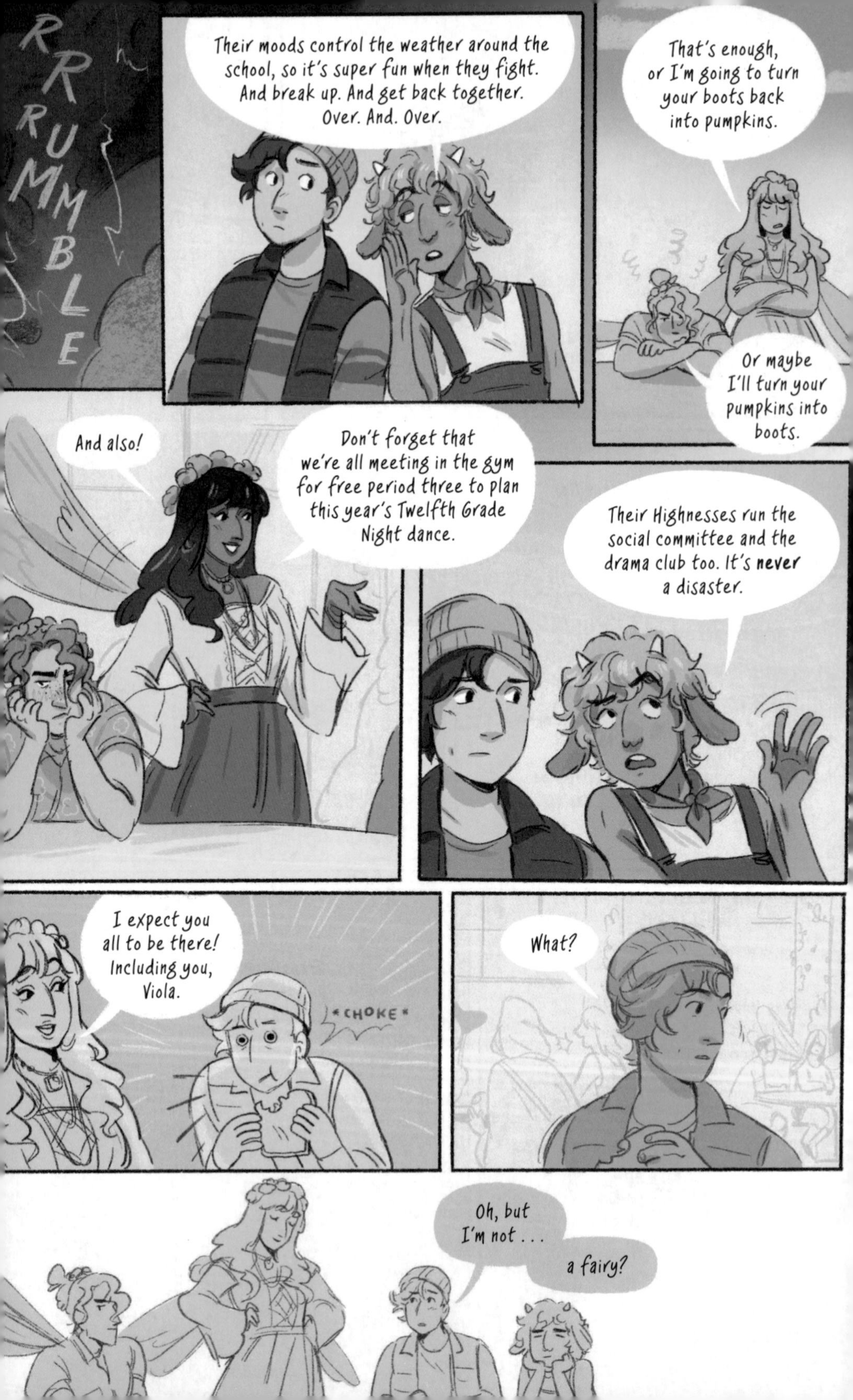
RRRUMMBLE
Their moods control the weather around the school, so it's super fun when they fight. And break up. And get back together. Over. And. Over.
That's enough, or I'm going to turn your boots back into pumpkins.
Or maybe I'll turn your pumpkins into boots.
And also!
Don't forget that we're all meeting in the gym for free period three to plan this year's Twelfth Grade Night dance.
Their Highnesses run the social committee and the drama club too. It's **never** a disaster.
I expect you all to be there! Including you, Viola.
CHOKE
What?
Oh, but I'm not . . .
a fairy?

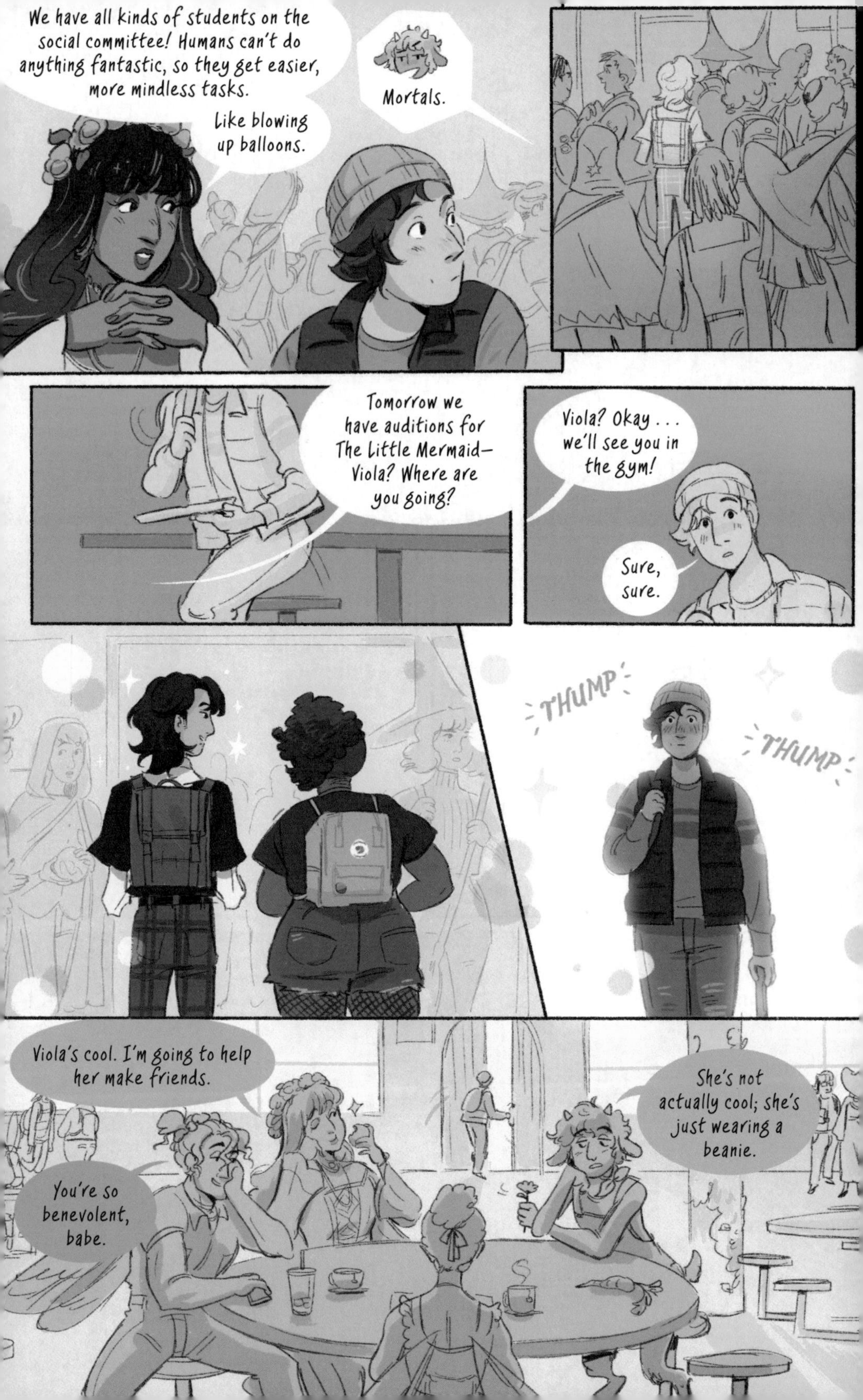
We have all kinds of students on the social committee! Humans can't do anything fantastic, so they get easier, more mindless tasks.
Like blowing up balloons.
Mortals.
Tomorrow we have auditions for The Little Mermaid—Viola? Where are you going?
Viola? Okay . . . we'll see you in the gym!
Sure, sure.
THUMP
THUMP
Viola's cool. I'm going to help her make friends.
You're so benevolent, babe.
She's not actually cool; she's just wearing a beanie.

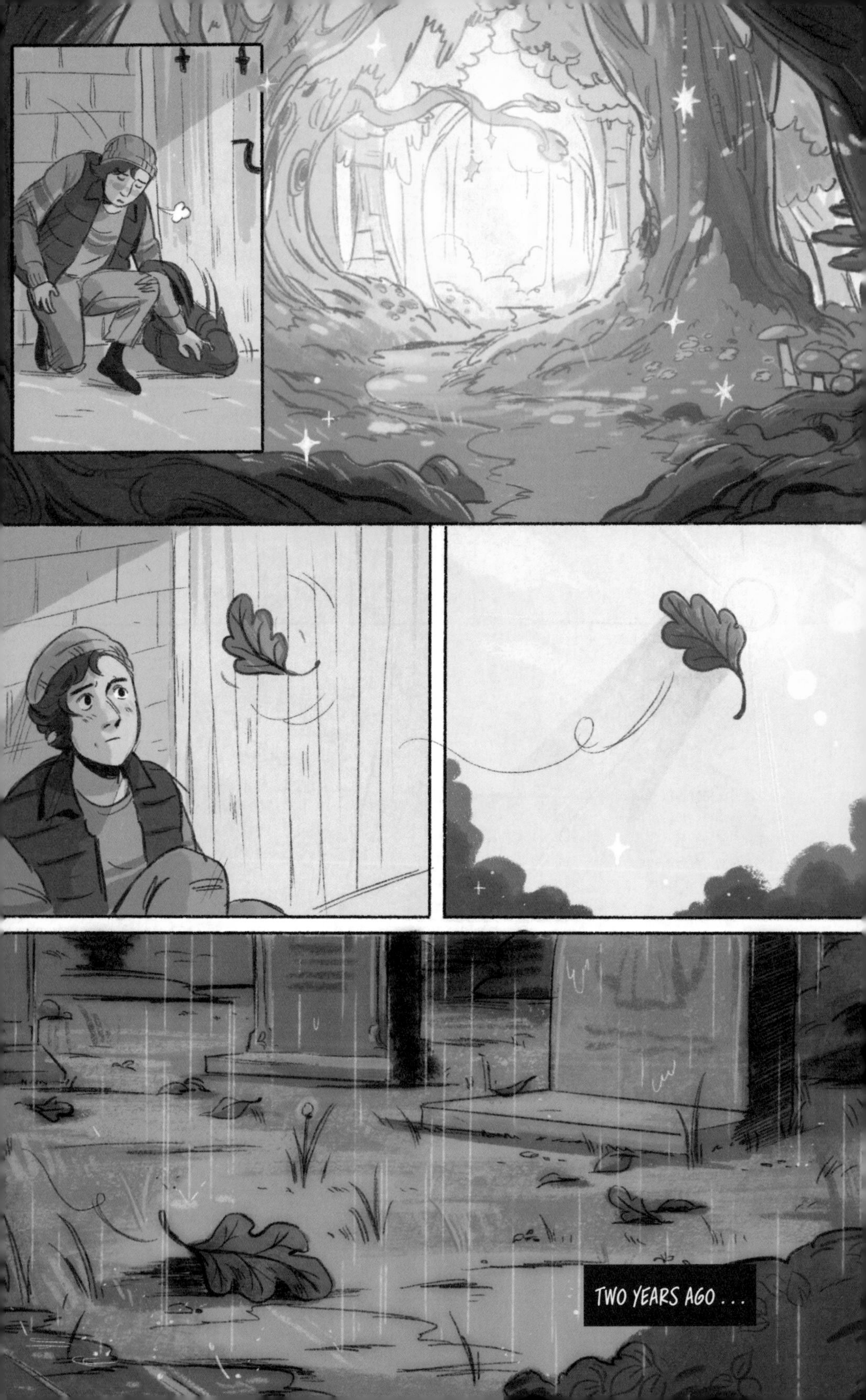
TWO YEARS AGO . . .

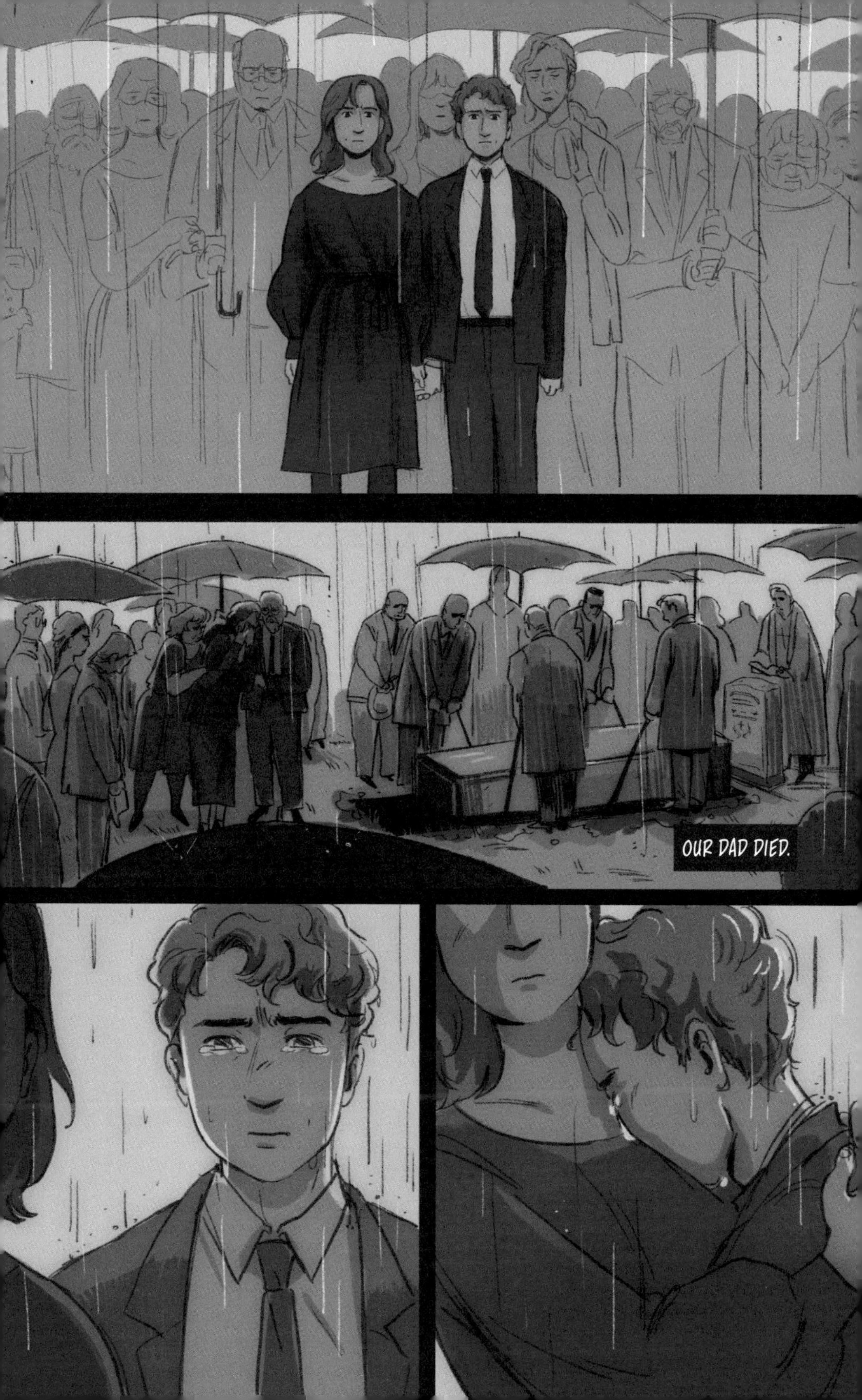
OUR DAD DIED.

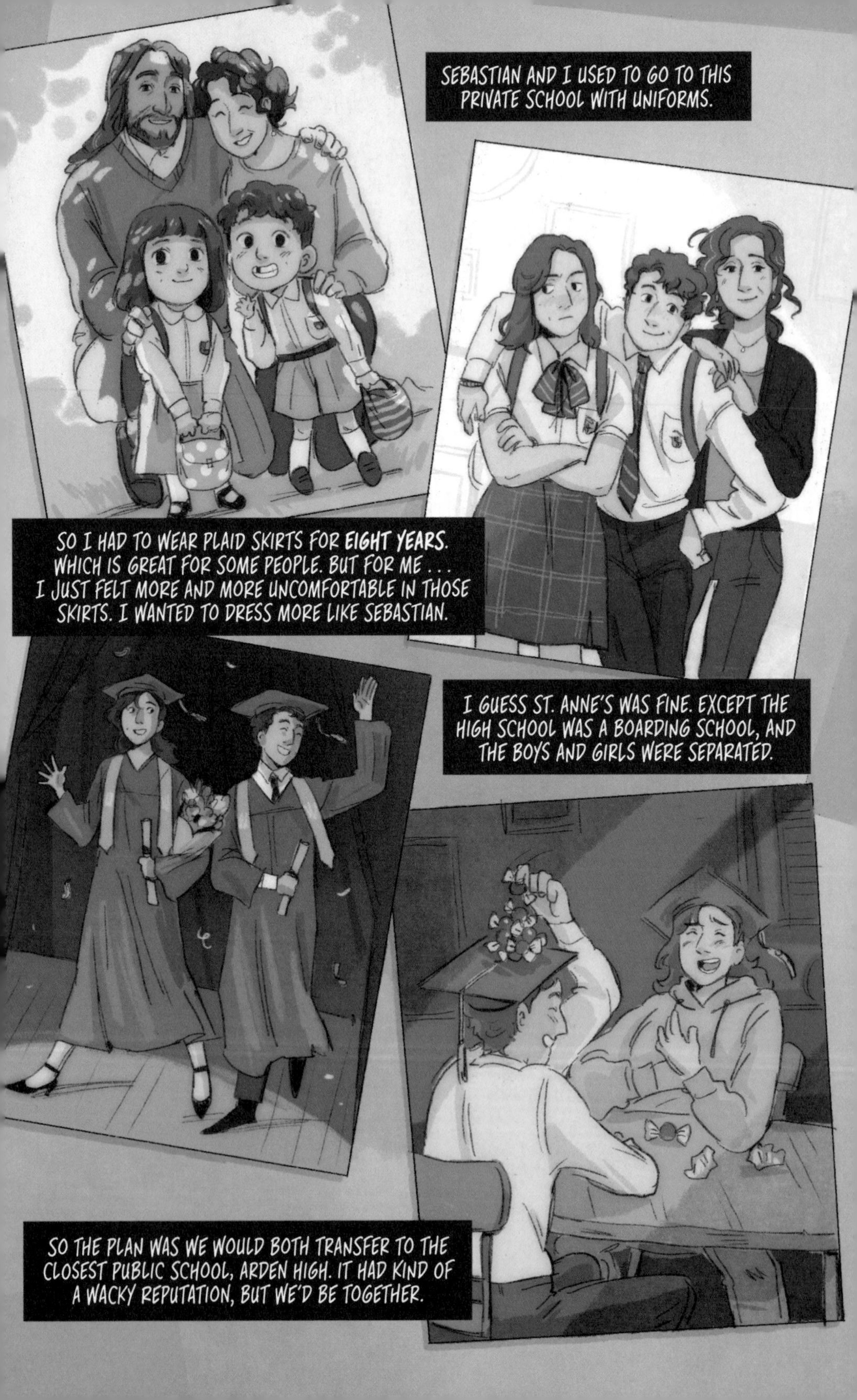
SEBASTIAN AND I USED TO GO TO THIS PRIVATE SCHOOL WITH UNIFORMS.
SO I HAD TO WEAR PLAID SKIRTS FOR **EIGHT YEARS.** WHICH IS GREAT FOR SOME PEOPLE. BUT FOR ME . . . I JUST FELT MORE AND MORE UNCOMFORTABLE IN THOSE SKIRTS. I WANTED TO DRESS MORE LIKE SEBASTIAN.
I GUESS ST. ANNE'S WAS FINE. EXCEPT THE HIGH SCHOOL WAS A BOARDING SCHOOL, AND THE BOYS AND GIRLS WERE SEPARATED.
SO THE PLAN WAS WE WOULD BOTH TRANSFER TO THE CLOSEST PUBLIC SCHOOL, ARDEN HIGH. IT HAD KIND OF A WACKY REPUTATION, BUT WE'D BE TOGETHER.

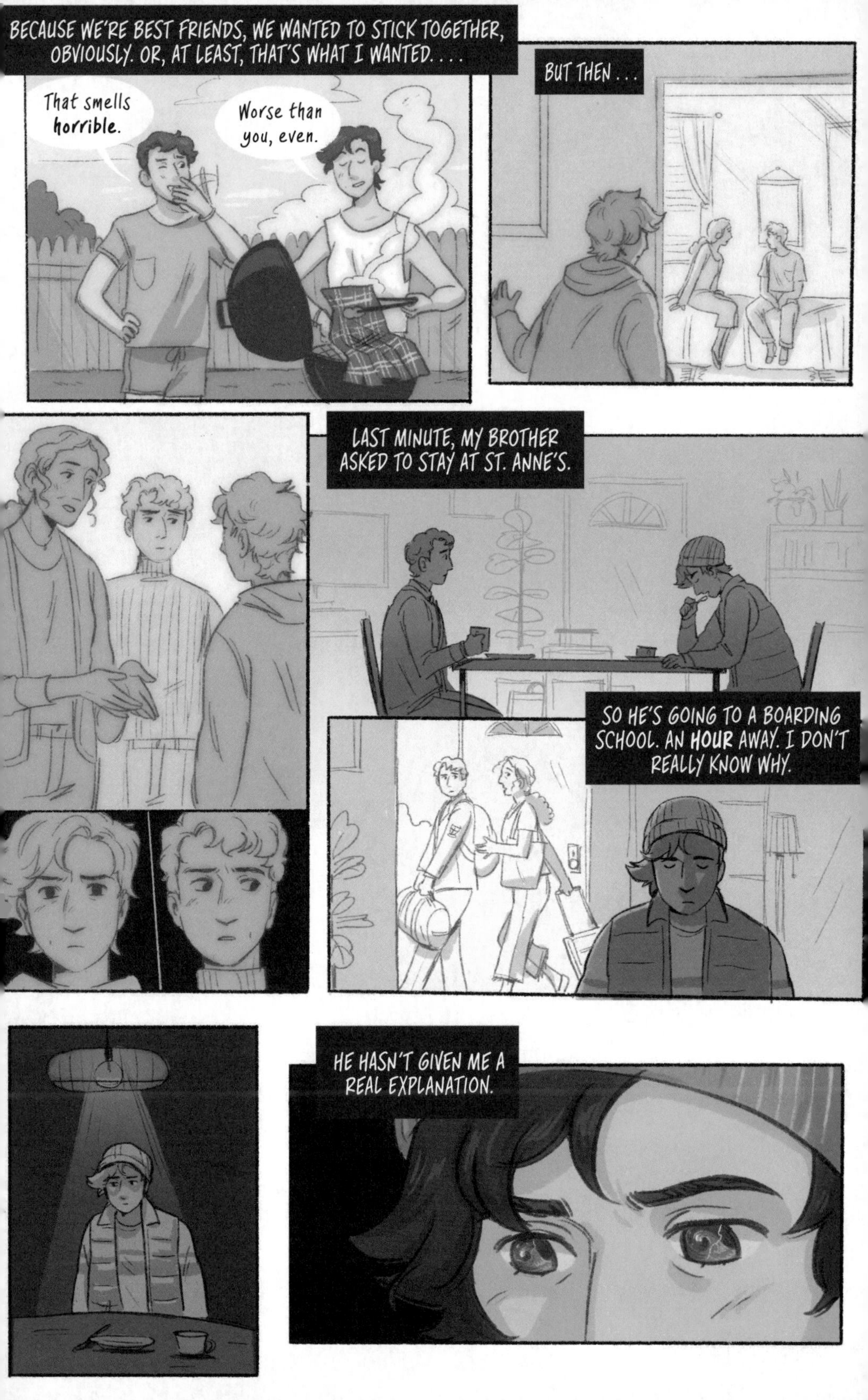
BECAUSE WE'RE BEST FRIENDS, WE WANTED TO STICK TOGETHER, OBVIOUSLY. OR, AT LEAST, THAT'S WHAT I WANTED. . . .
That smells **horrible**.
Worse than you, even.
BUT THEN . . .
LAST MINUTE, MY BROTHER ASKED TO STAY AT ST. ANNE'S.
SO HE'S GOING TO A BOARDING SCHOOL. AN **HOUR** AWAY. I DON'T REALLY KNOW WHY.
HE HASN'T GIVEN ME A REAL EXPLANATION.

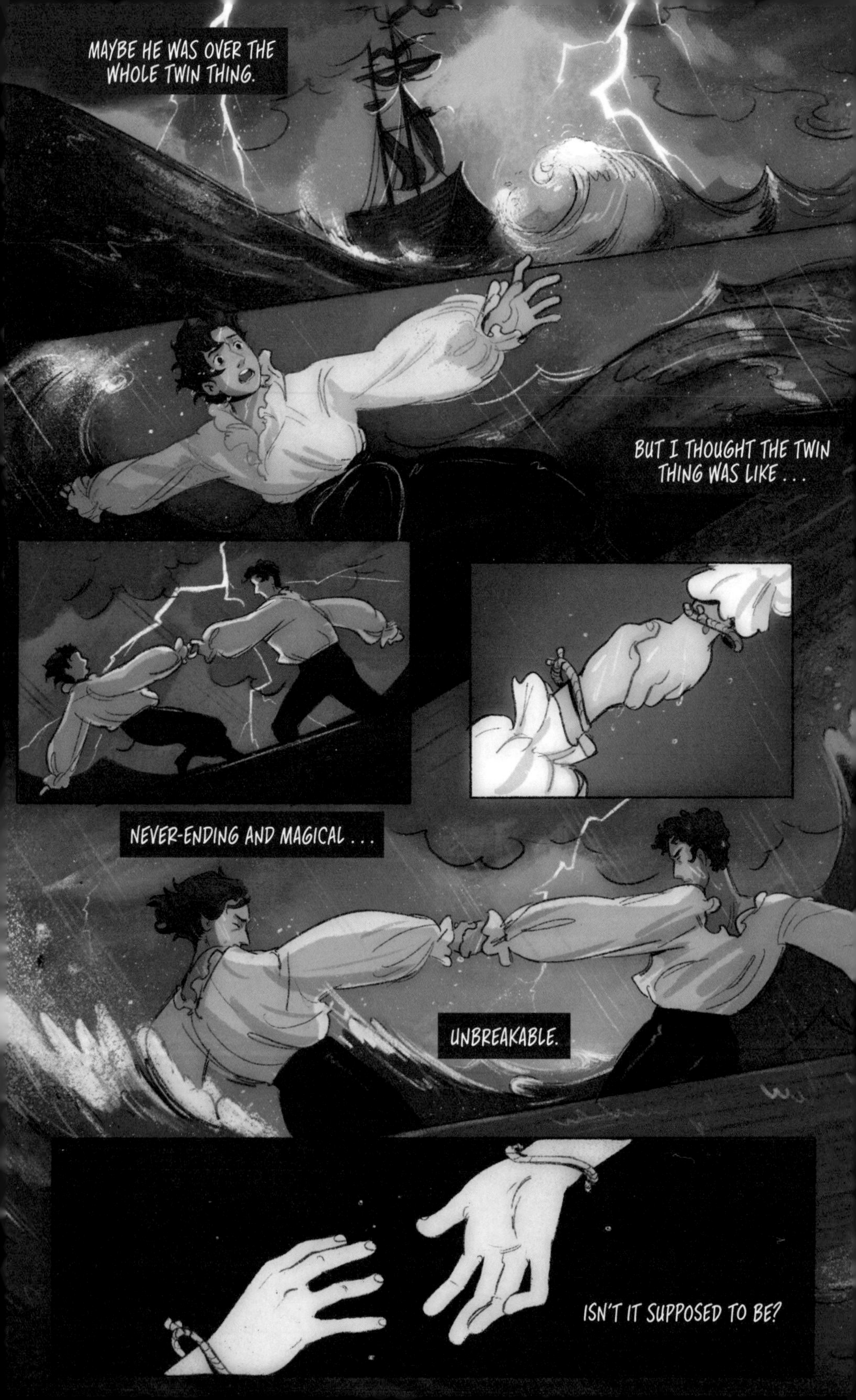
MAYBE HE WAS OVER THE WHOLE TWIN THING.
BUT I THOUGHT THE TWIN THING WAS LIKE . . .
NEVER-ENDING AND MAGICAL . . .
UNBREAKABLE.
ISN'T IT SUPPOSED TO BE?

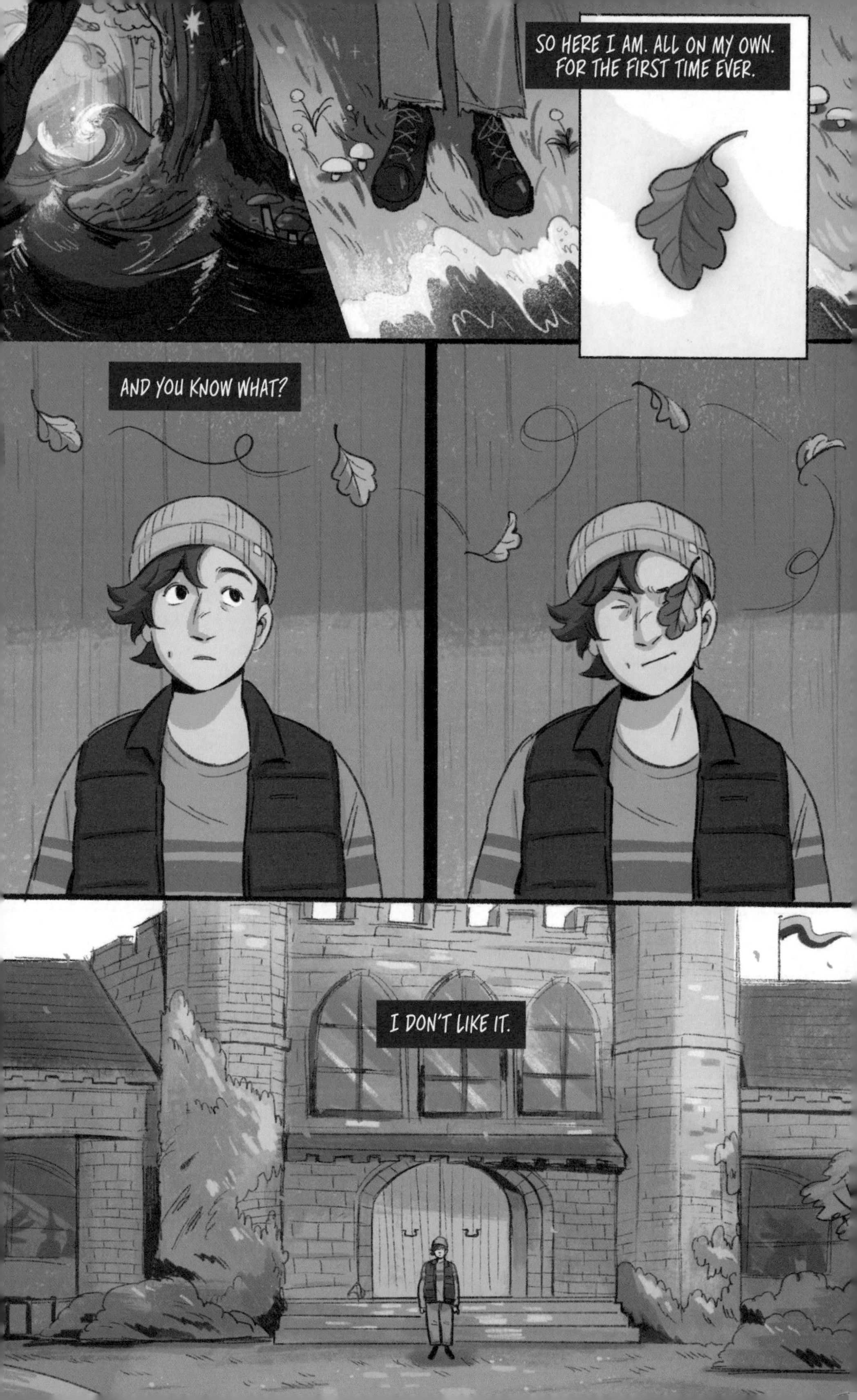
SO HERE I AM. ALL ON MY OWN. FOR THE FIRST TIME EVER.
AND YOU KNOW WHAT?
I DON'T LIKE IT.

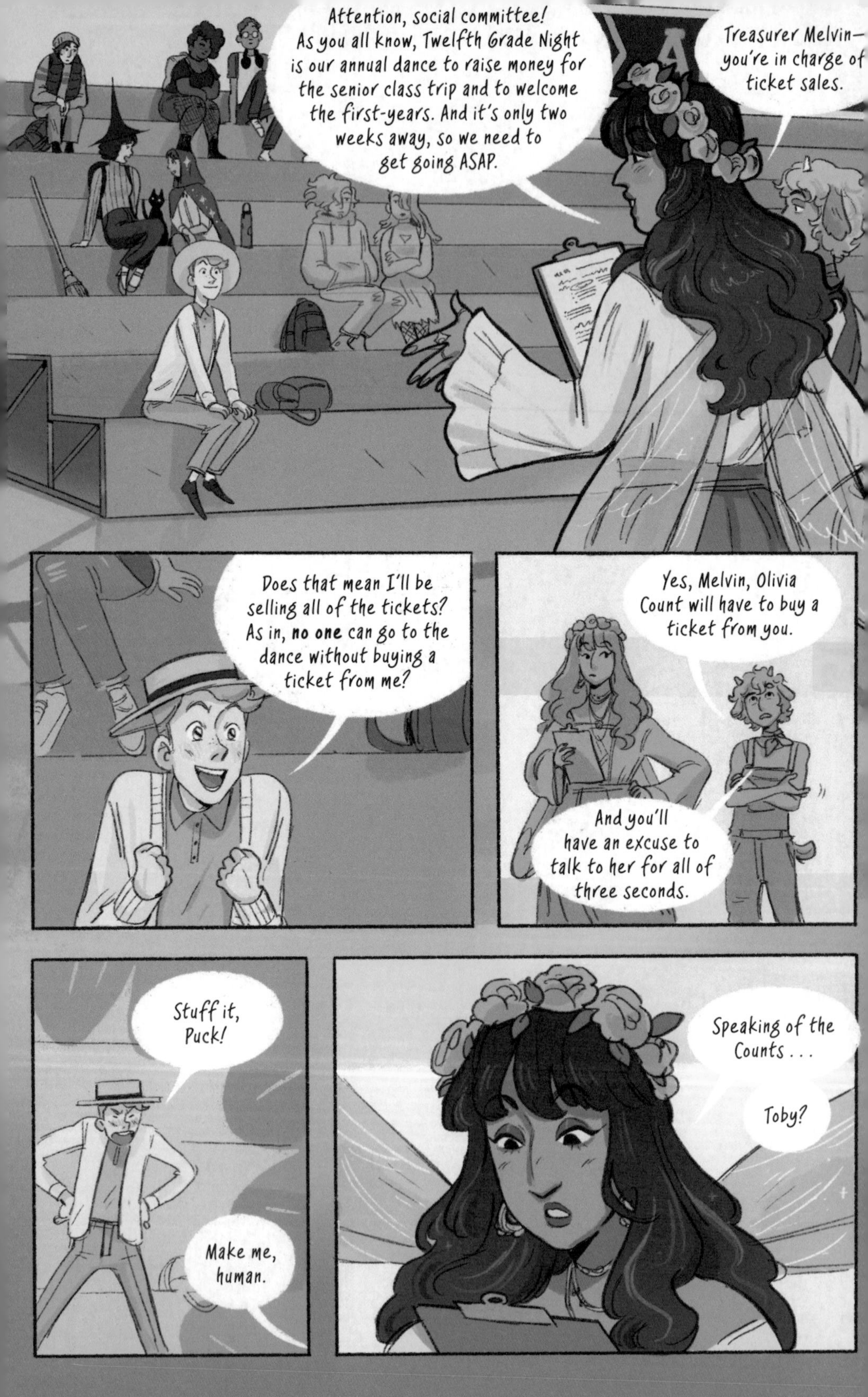
Attention, social committee! As you all know, Twelfth Grade Night is our annual dance to raise money for the senior class trip and to welcome the first-years. And it's only two weeks away, so we need to get going ASAP.
Treasurer Melvin—you're in charge of ticket sales.
Does that mean I'll be selling all of the tickets? As in, **no one** can go to the dance without buying a ticket from me?
Yes, Melvin, Olivia Count will have to buy a ticket from you.
And you'll have an excuse to talk to her for all of three seconds.
Stuff it, Puck!
Make me, human.
Speaking of the Counts . . .
Toby?

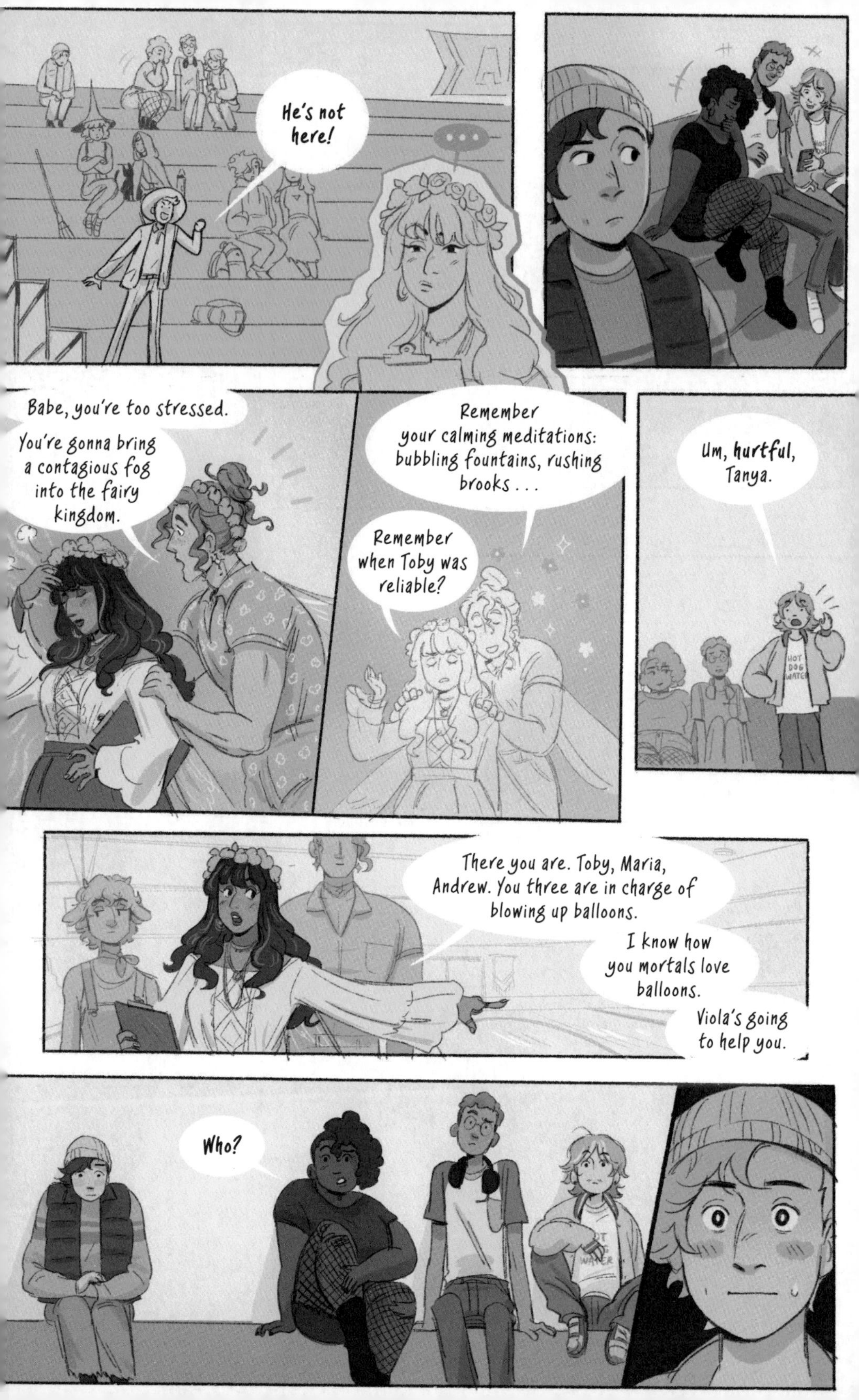
He's not here!
...
Babe, you're too stressed.
You're gonna bring a contagious fog into the fairy kingdom.
Remember your calming meditations: bubbling fountains, rushing brooks . . .
Remember when Toby was reliable?
Um, **hurtful**, Tanya.
HOT DOG WATER
There you are. Toby, Maria, Andrew. You three are in charge of blowing up balloons.
I know how you mortals love balloons.
Viola's going to help you.
Who?

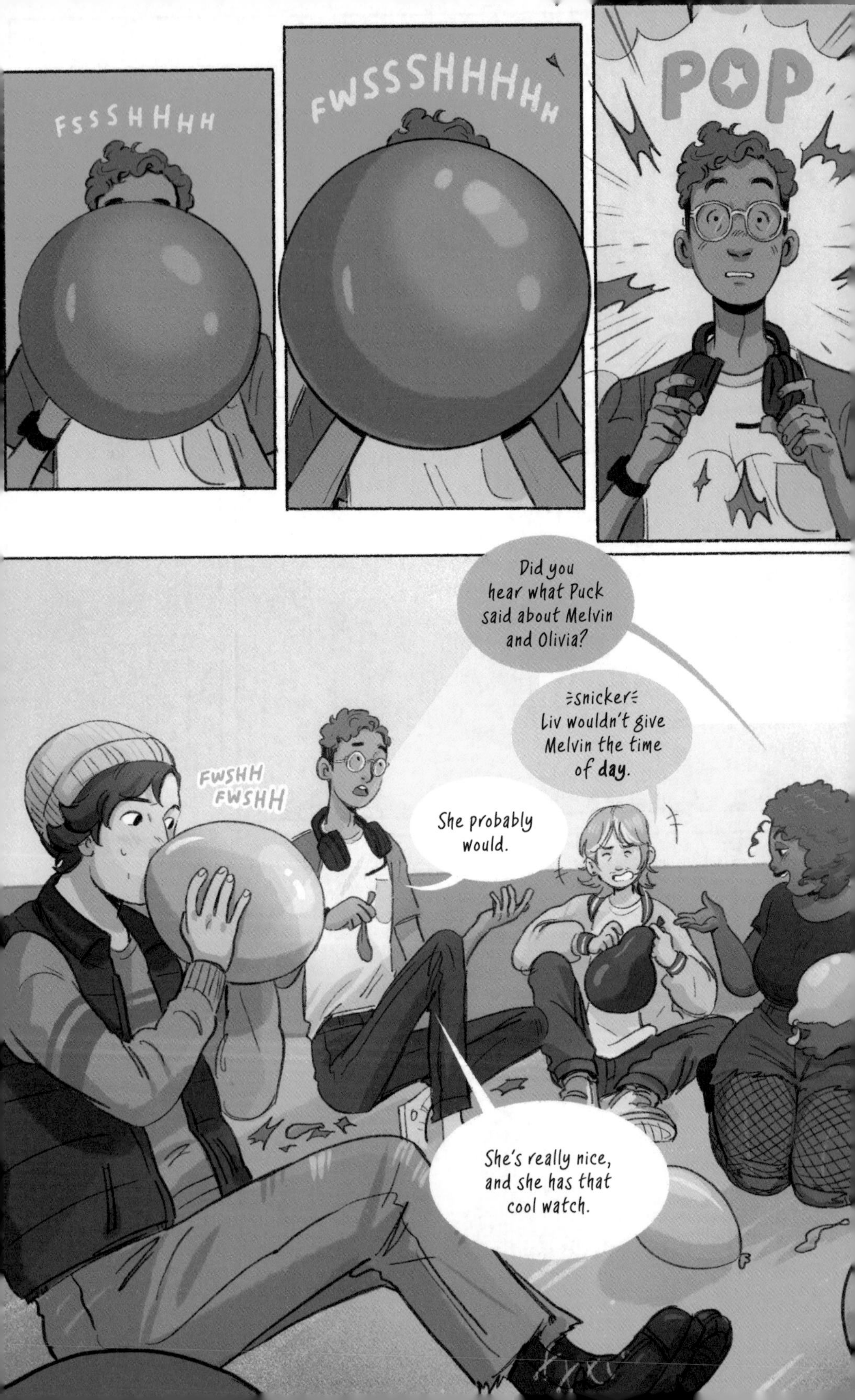
FSSSHHHHH
FWSSSHHHHHH
POP
Did you hear what Puck said about Melvin and Olivia?
≈snicker≈ Liv wouldn't give Melvin the time of day.
FWSHH FWSHH
She probably would.
She's really nice, and she has that cool watch.

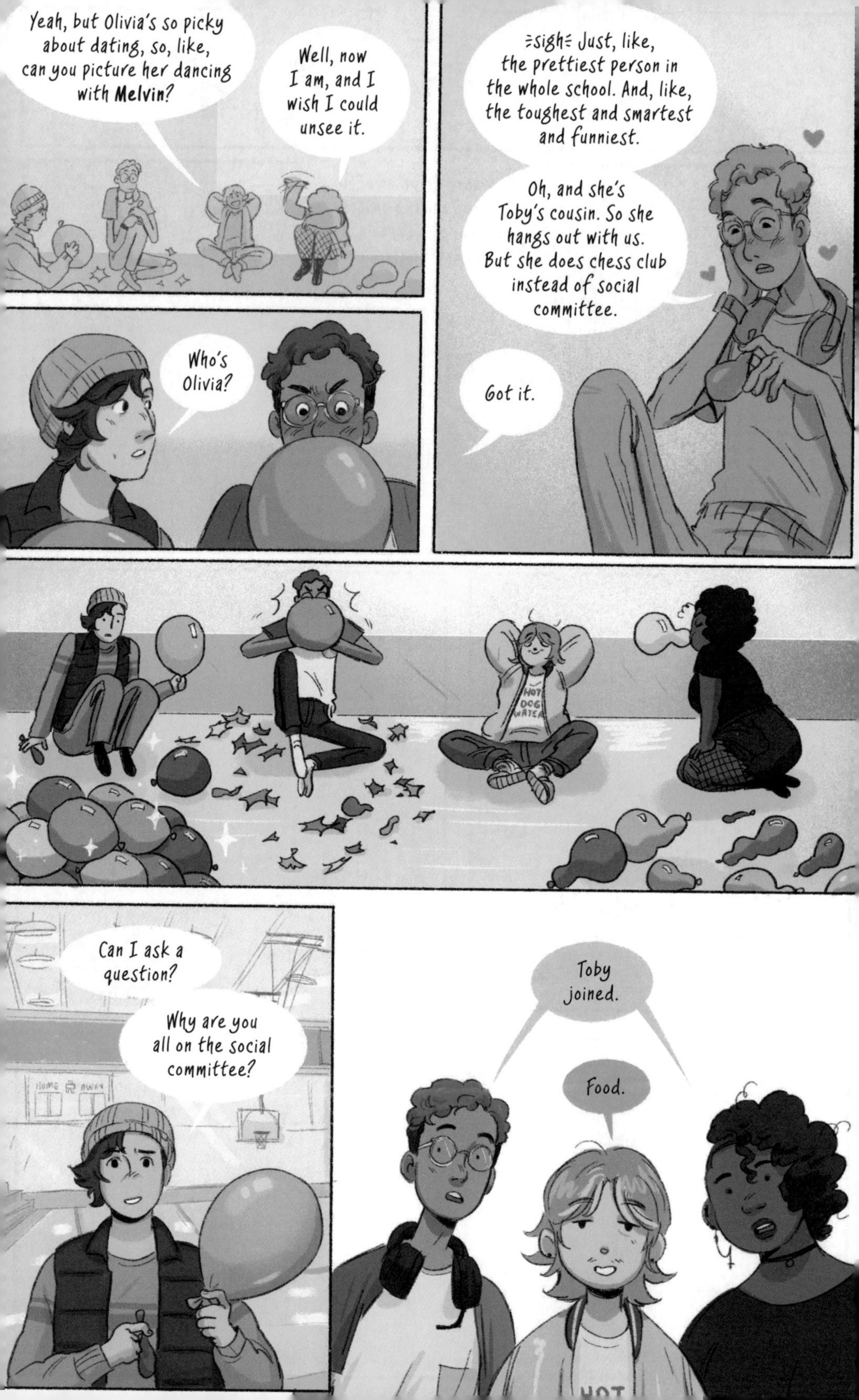
Yeah, but Olivia's so picky about dating, so, like, can you picture her dancing with **Melvin**?
Well, now I am, and I wish I could unsee it.
≈sigh≈ Just, like, the prettiest person in the whole school. And, like, the toughest and smartest and funniest.
Oh, and she's Toby's cousin. So she hangs out with us. But she does chess club instead of social committee.
Who's Olivia?
Got it.
Can I ask a question?
Why are you all on the social committee?
HOME AWAY
Toby joined.
Food.

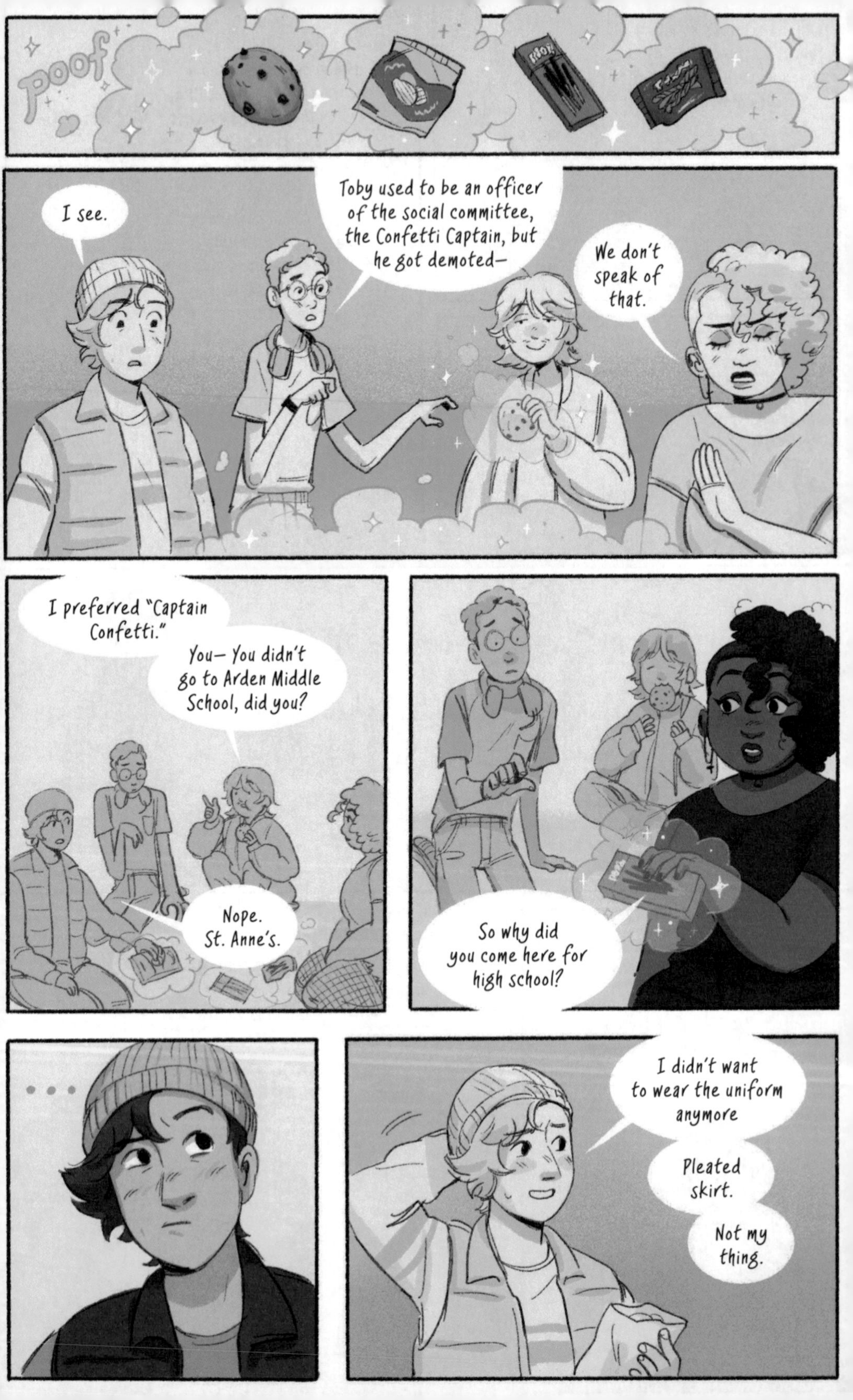
poof
I see.
Toby used to be an officer of the social committee, the Confetti Captain, but he got demoted—
We don't speak of that.
I preferred "Captain Confetti."
You— You didn't go to Arden Middle School, did you?
Nope. St. Anne's.
So why did you come here for high school?
• • •
I didn't want to wear the uniform anymore
Pleated skirt.
Not my thing.

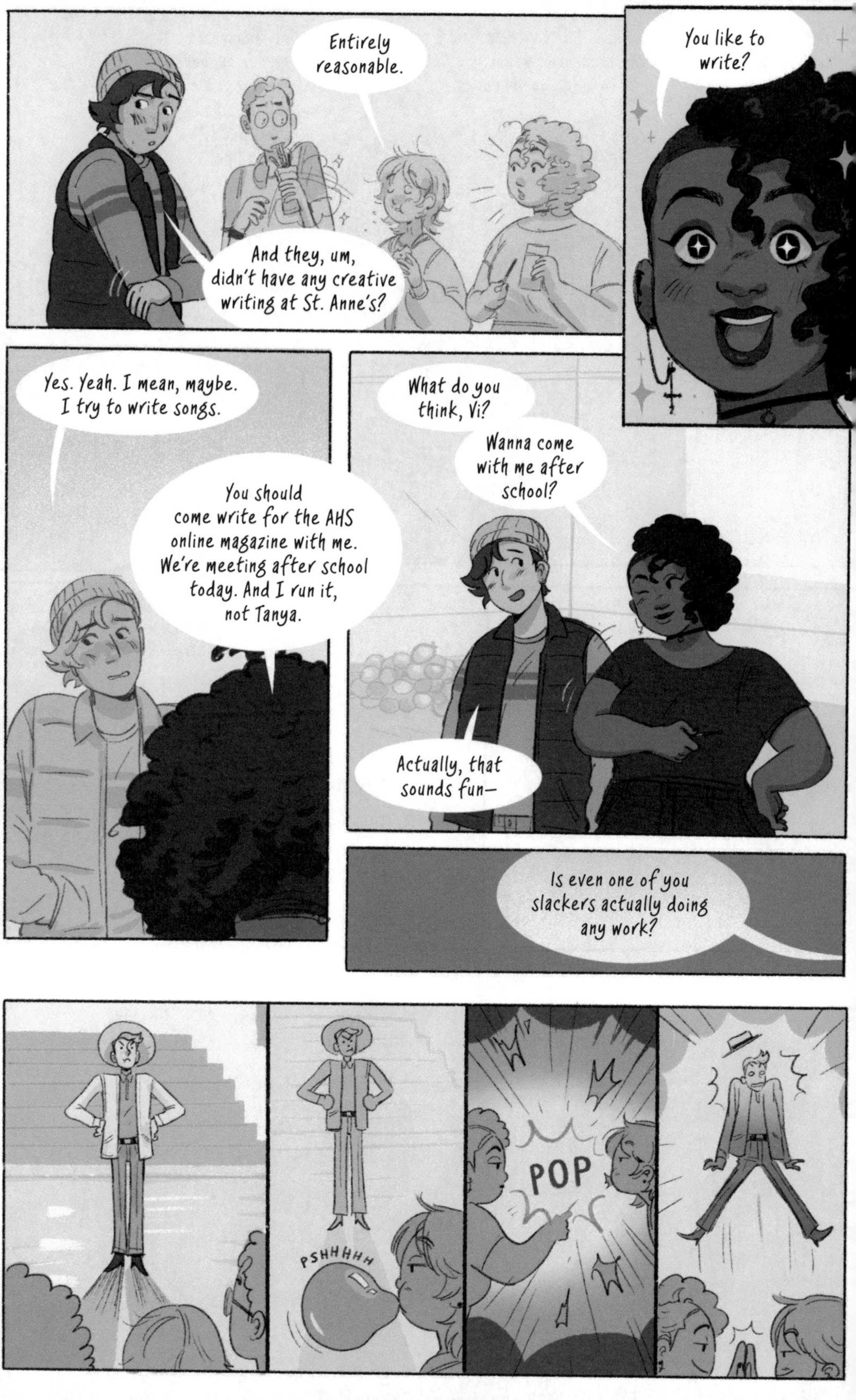

Entirely reasonable.
And they, um, didn't have any creative writing at St. Anne's?
You like to write?
Yes. Yeah. I mean, maybe. I try to write songs.
You should come write for the AHS online magazine with me. We're meeting after school today. And I run it, not Tanya.
What do you think, Vi?
Wanna come with me after school?
Actually, that sounds fun—
Is even one of you slackers actually doing any work?
PSHHHHH
POP

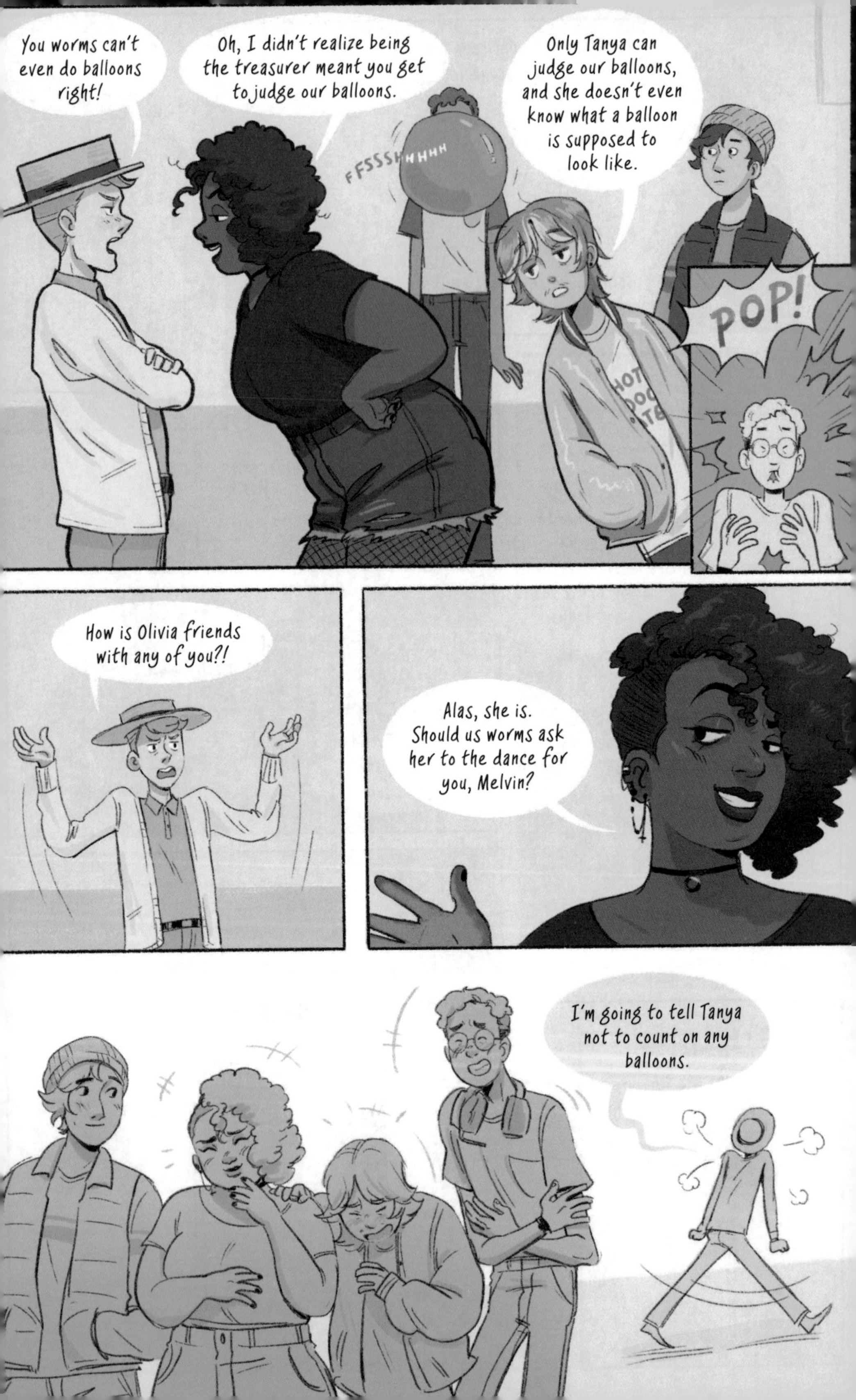
You worms can't even do balloons right!
Oh, I didn't realize being the treasurer meant you get to judge our balloons.
FFSSSHHHHH
Only Tanya can judge our balloons, and she doesn't even know what a balloon is supposed to look like.
POP!
How is Olivia friends with any of you?!
Alas, she is. Should us worms ask her to the dance for you, Melvin?
I'm going to tell Tanya not to count on any balloons.

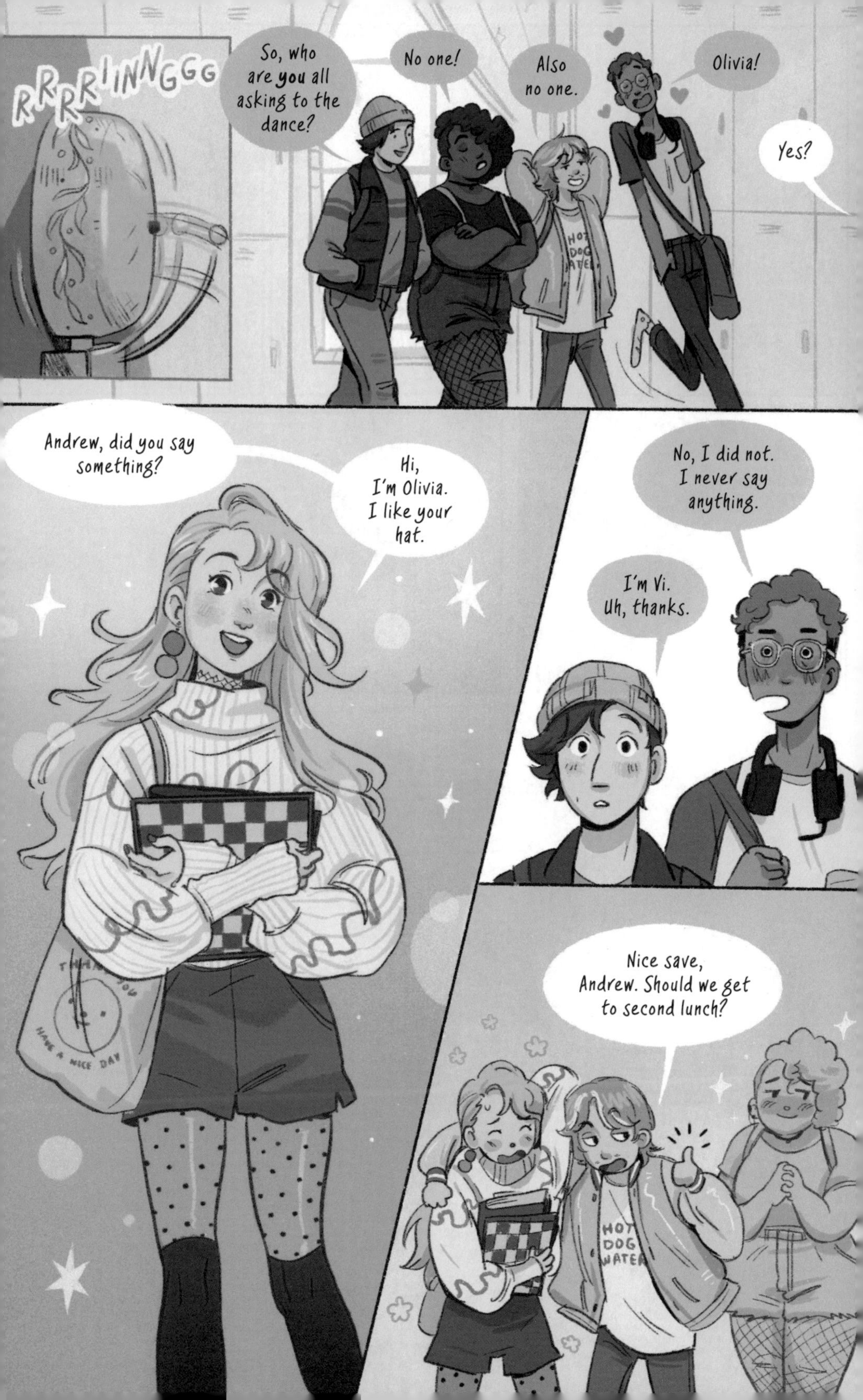
RRRRIINNGGG
So, who are you all asking to the dance?
No one!
Also no one.
Olivia!
Yes?
HOT DOG WATER
Andrew, did you say something?
Hi, I'm Olivia. I like your hat.
No, I did not. I never say anything.
I'm Vi. Uh, thanks.
HAVE A NICE DAY
Nice save, Andrew. Should we get to second lunch?
HOT DOG WATER

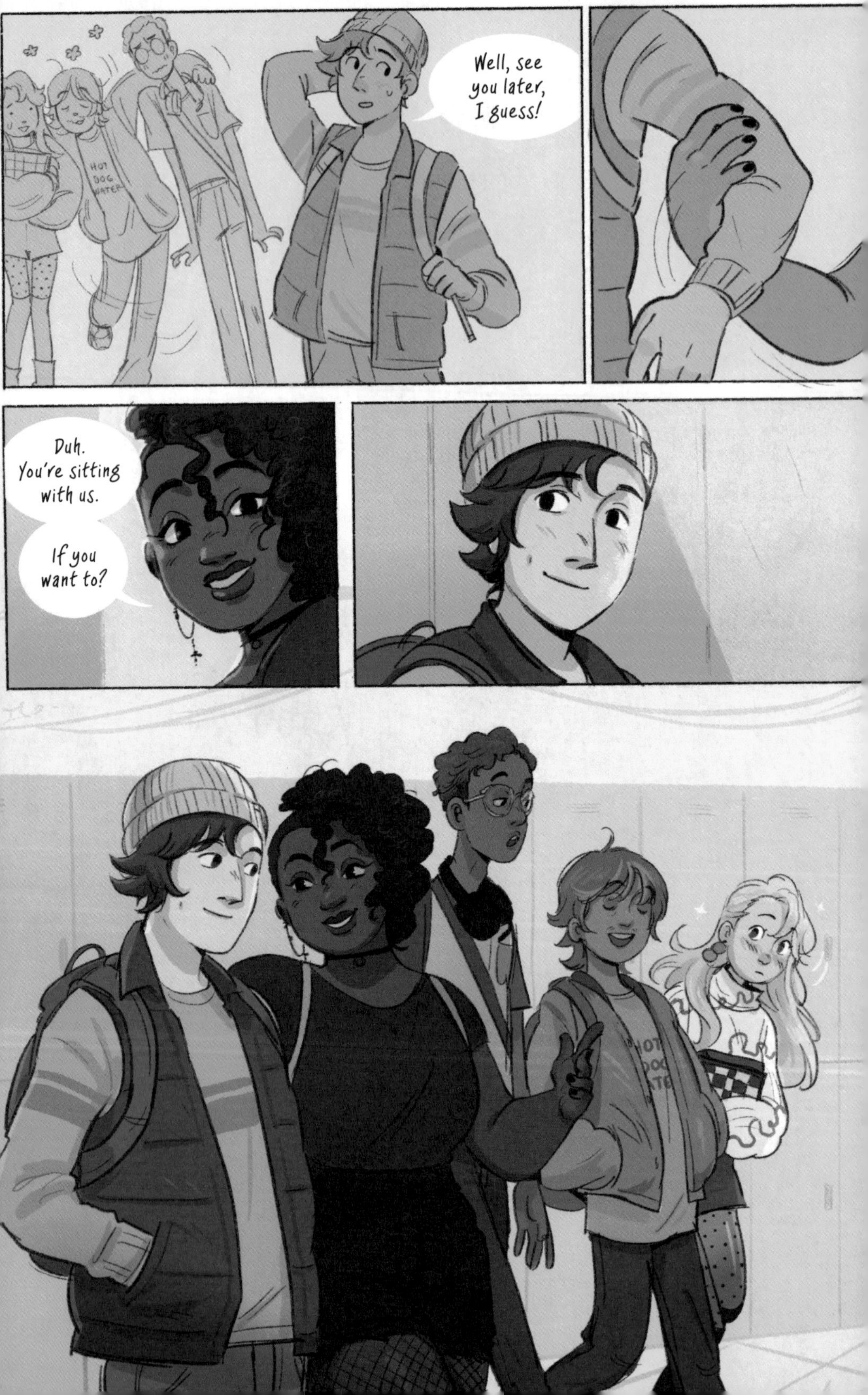
HOT DOG WATER
Well, see you later, I guess!
Duh. You're sitting with us.
If you want to?
HOT DOG WATER

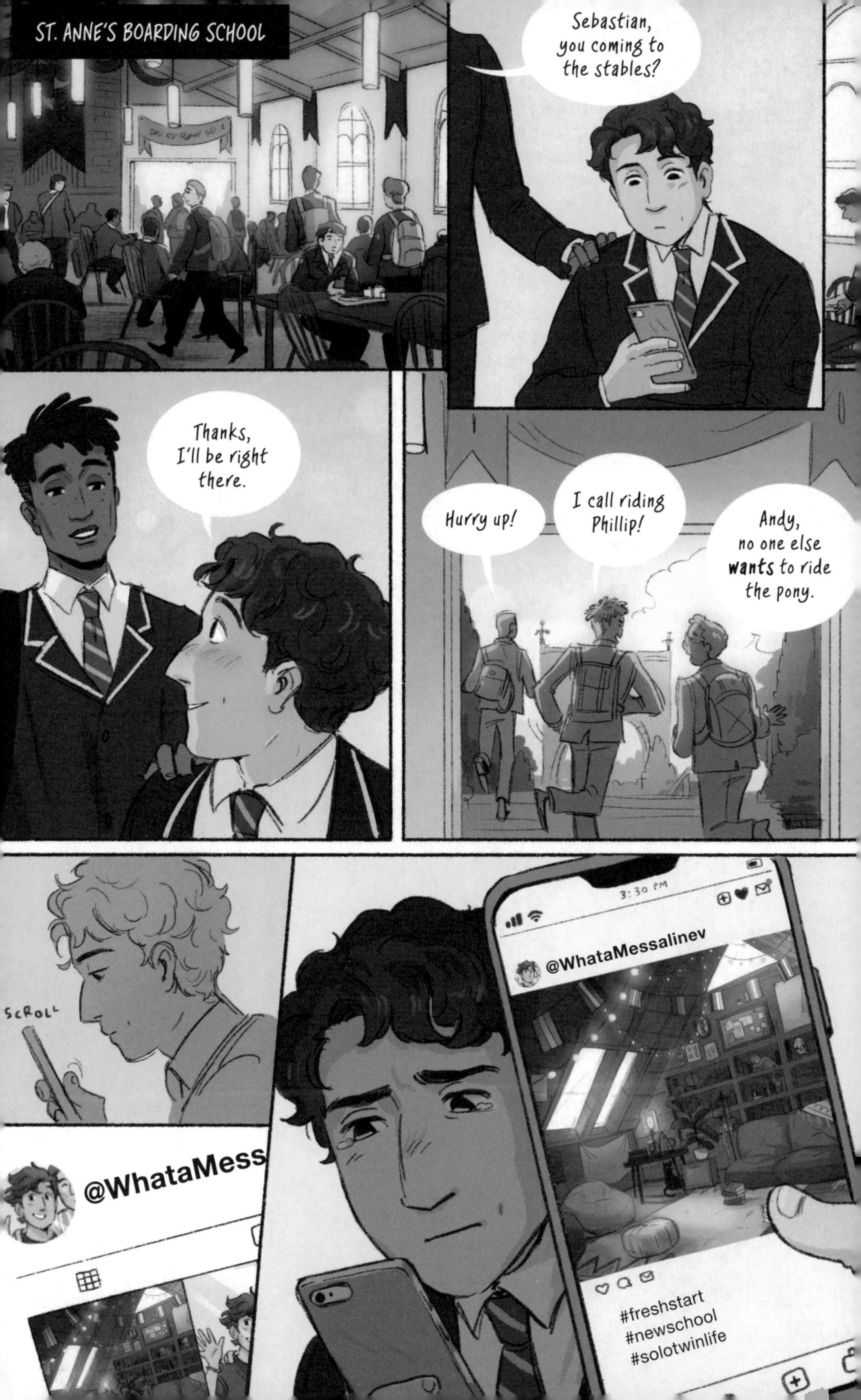

ST. ANNE'S BOARDING SCHOOL
Sebastian, you coming to the stables?
Thanks, I'll be right there.
Hurry up!
I call riding Phillip!
Andy, no one else **wants** to ride the pony.
SCROLL
3:30 PM
@WhataMessalinev
#freshstart
#newschool
#solotwinlife
@WhataMess

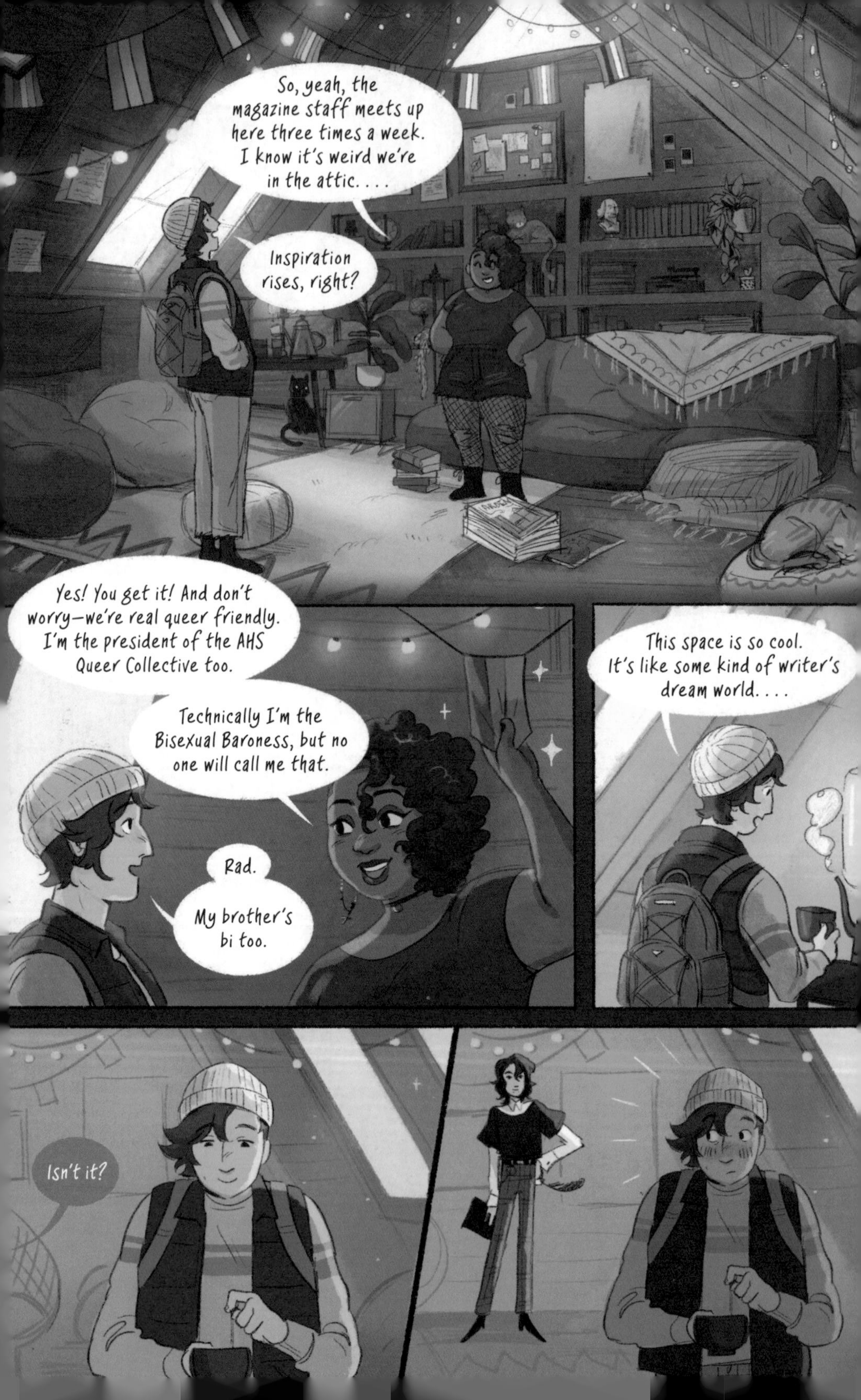
So, yeah, the magazine staff meets up here three times a week. I know it's weird we're in the attic. . . .
Inspiration rises, right?
Yes! You get it! And don't worry—we're real queer friendly. I'm the president of the AHS Queer Collective too.
Technically I'm the Bisexual Baroness, but no one will call me that.
Rad.
My brother's bi too.
This space is so cool. It's like some kind of writer's dream world. . . .
Isn't it?

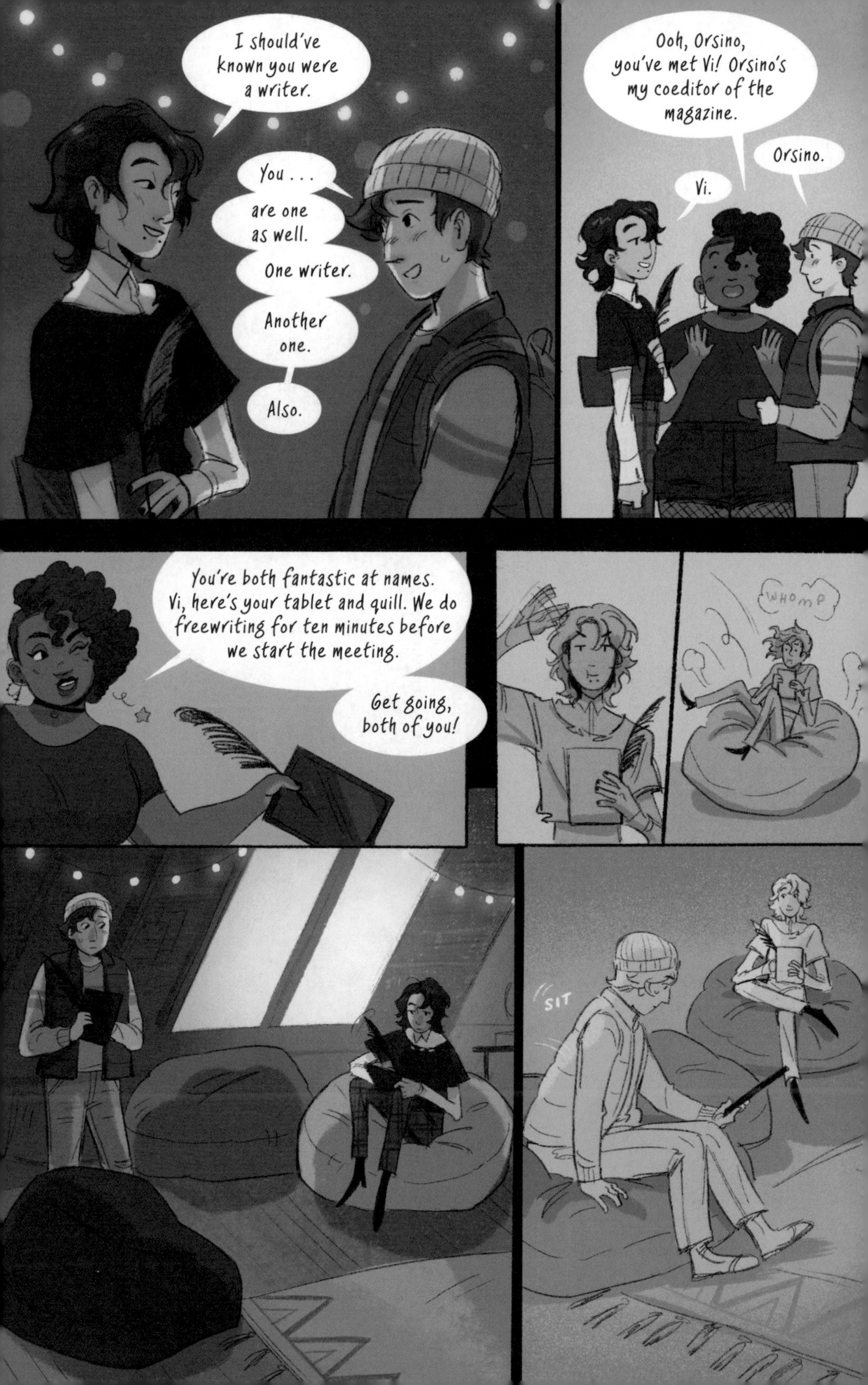

I should've known you were a writer.
You . . .
are one as well.
One writer.
Another one.
Also.
Ooh, Orsino, you've met Vi! Orsino's my coeditor of the magazine.
Vi.
Orsino.
You're both fantastic at names. Vi, here's your tablet and quill. We do freewriting for ten minutes before we start the meeting.
Get going, both of you!
WHOMP
SIT

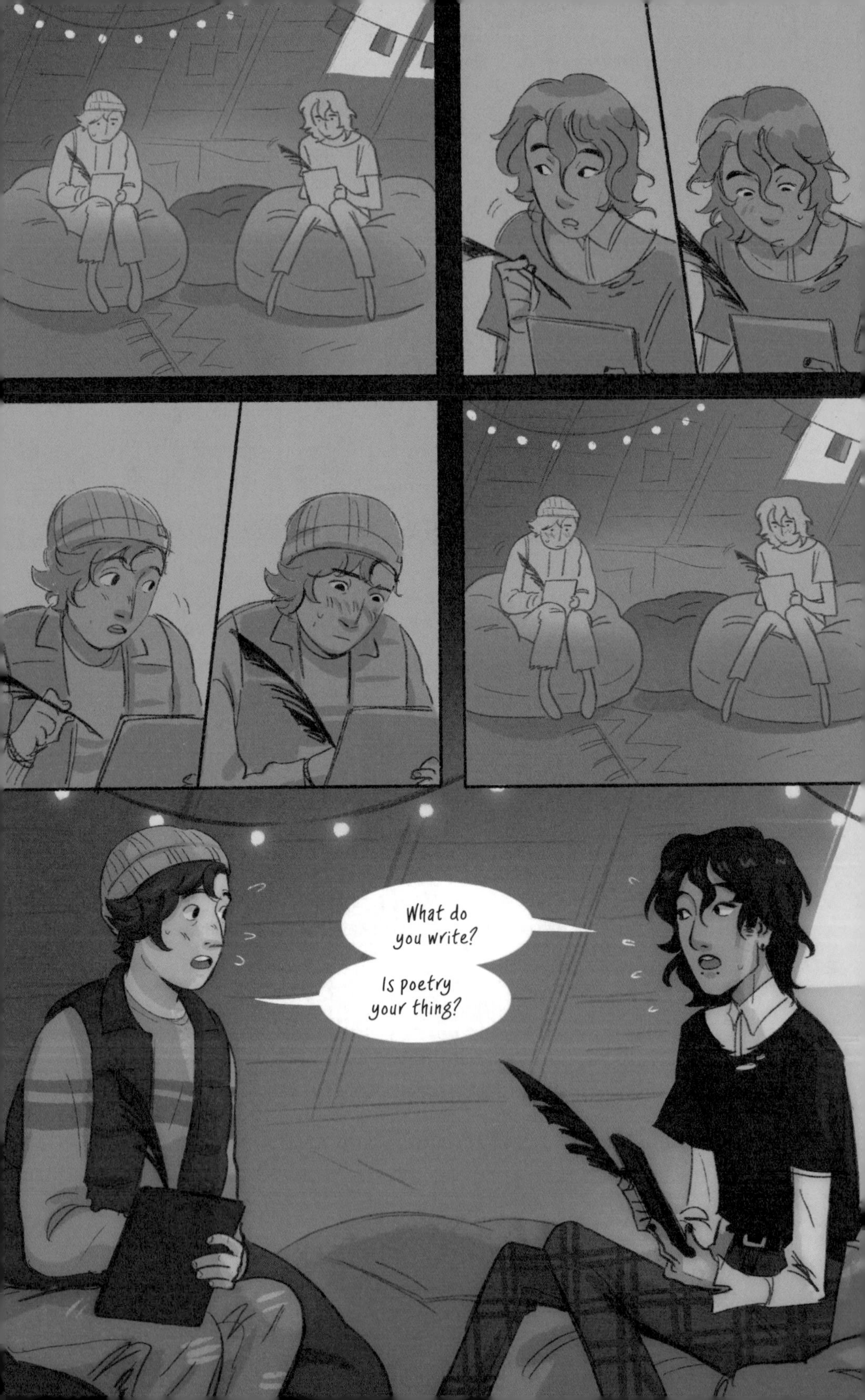
What do you write?
Is poetry your thing?

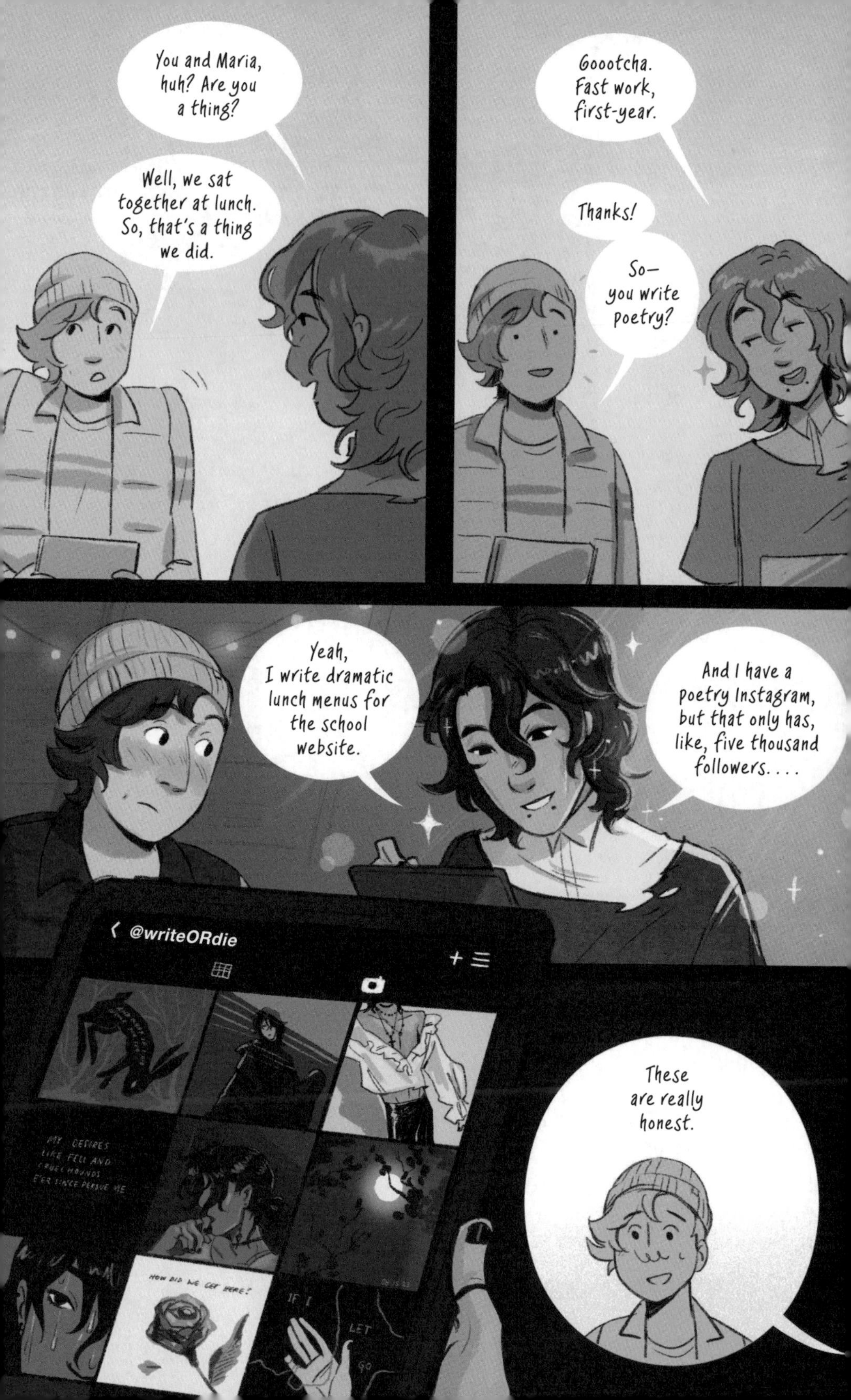
You and Maria, huh? Are you a thing?
Well, we sat together at lunch. So, that's a thing we did.
Goootcha. Fast work, first-year.
Thanks!
So—you write poetry?
Yeah, I write dramatic lunch menus for the school website.
And I have a poetry Instagram, but that only has, like, five thousand followers. . . .
@writeORdie
HOW DID WE GET HERE?
IF I LET GO
These are really honest.

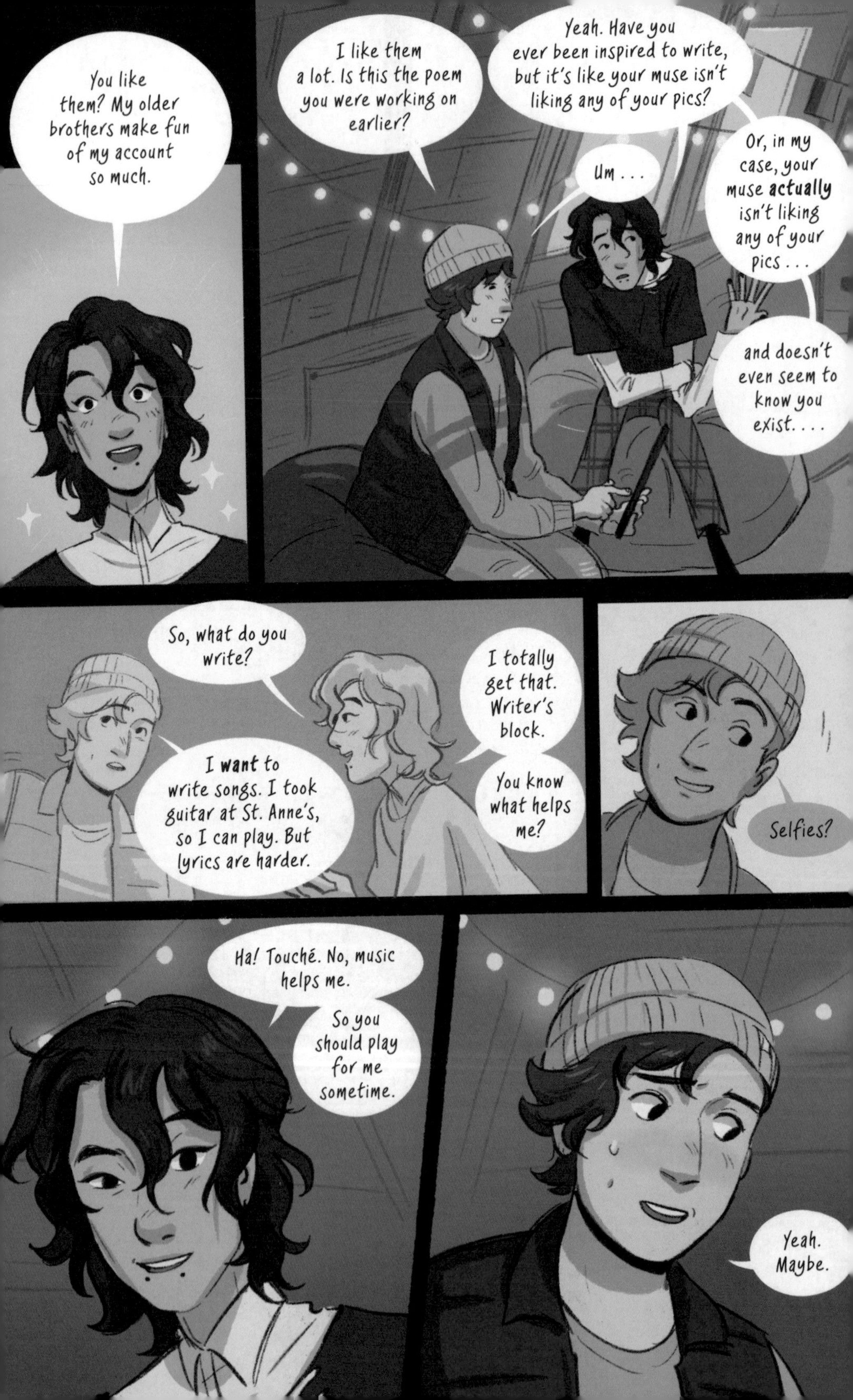

You like them? My older brothers make fun of my account so much.
I like them a lot. Is this the poem you were working on earlier?
Yeah. Have you ever been inspired to write, but it's like your muse isn't liking any of your pics?
Um . . .
Or, in my case, your muse **actually** isn't liking any of your pics . . .
and doesn't even seem to know you exist. . . .
So, what do you write?
I **want** to write songs. I took guitar at St. Anne's, so I can play. But lyrics are harder.
I totally get that. Writer's block.
You know what helps me?
Selfies?
Ha! Touché. No, music helps me.
So you should play for me sometime.
Yeah. Maybe.

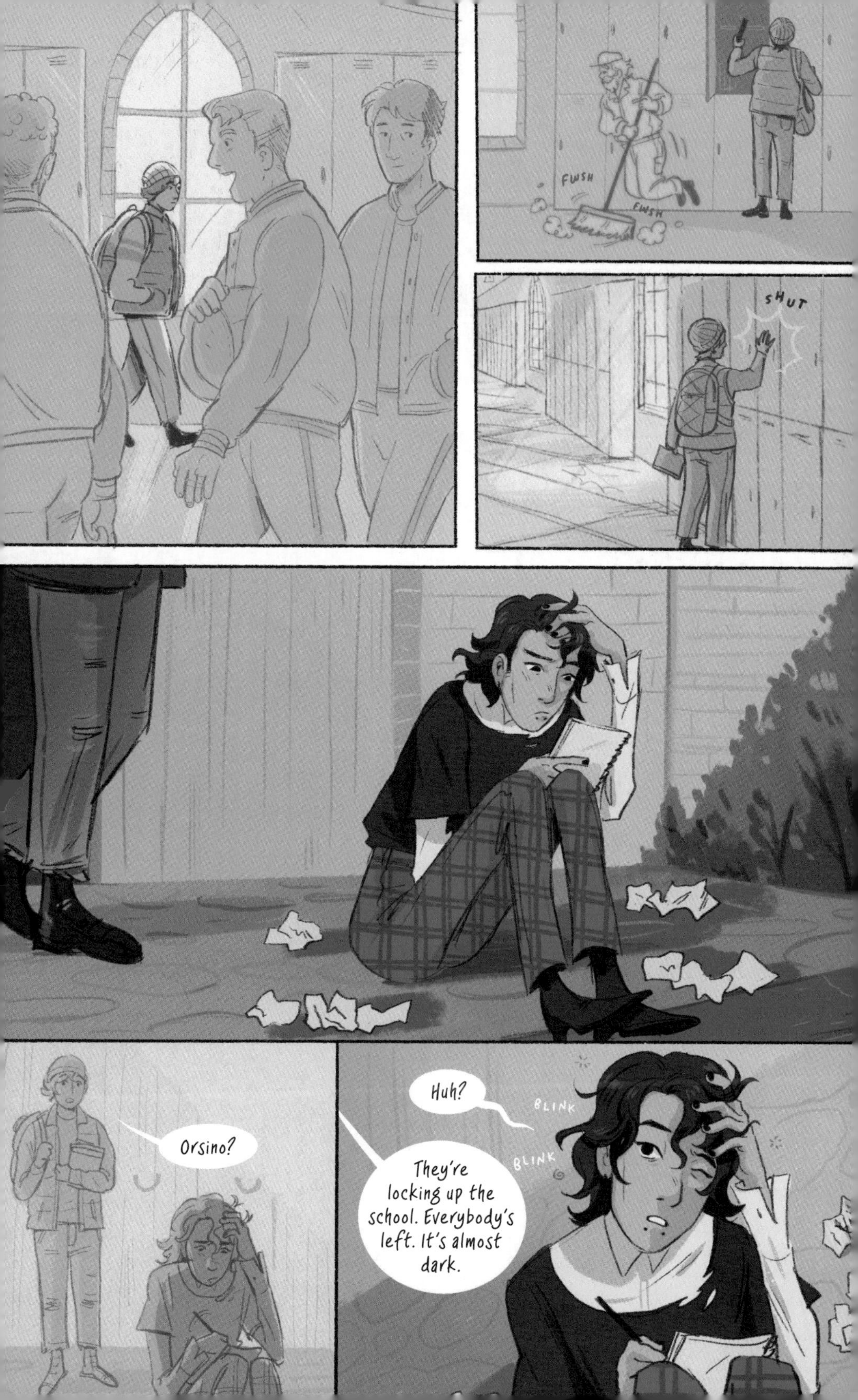
FWSH
FWSH
SHUT
Orsino?
Huh?
BLINK
BLINK
They're locking up the school. Everybody's left. It's almost dark.

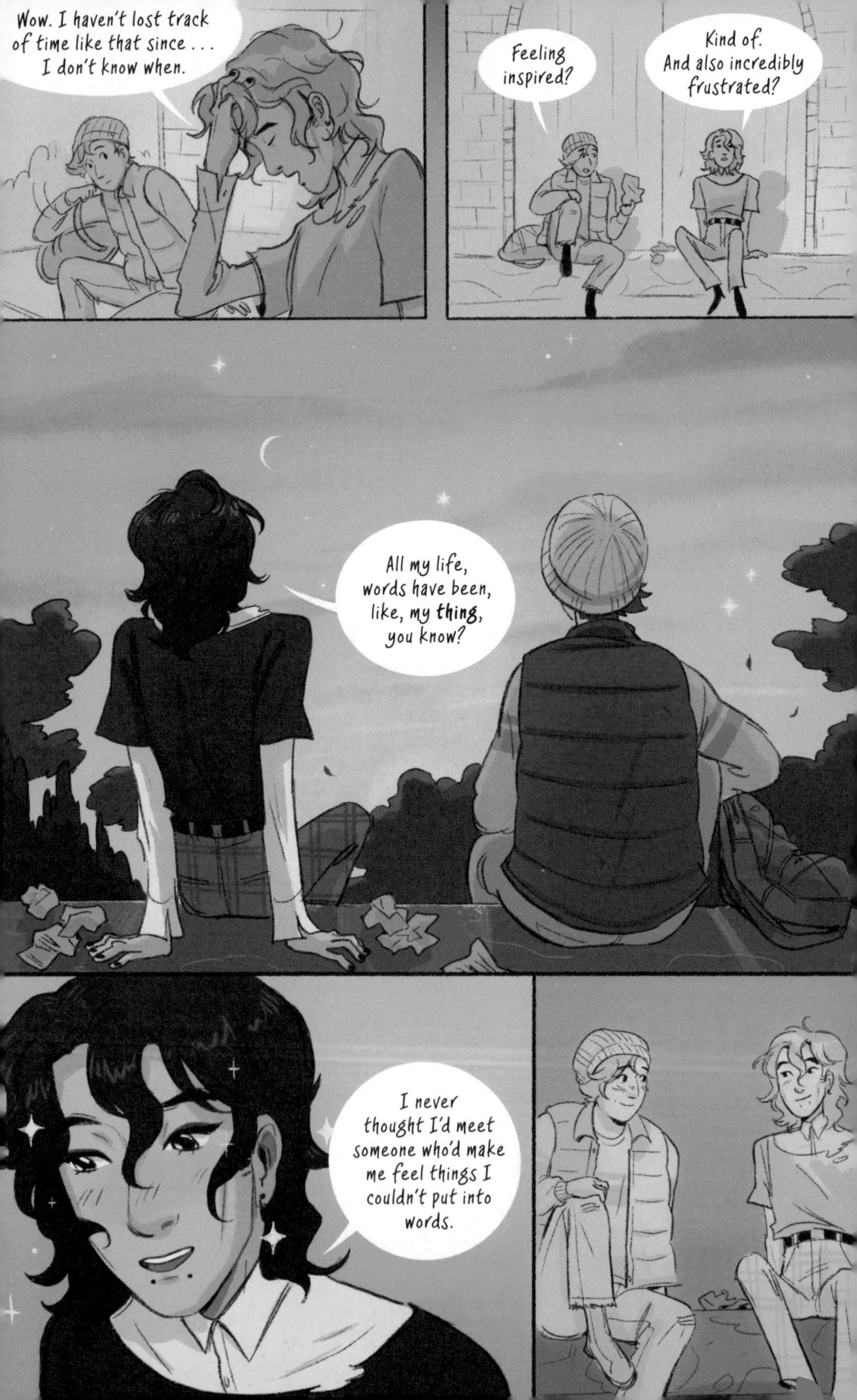
Wow. I haven't lost track of time like that since . . . I don't know when.
Feeling inspired?
Kind of. And also incredibly frustrated?
All my life, words have been, like, my **thing**, you know?
I never thought I'd meet someone who'd make me feel things I couldn't put into words.

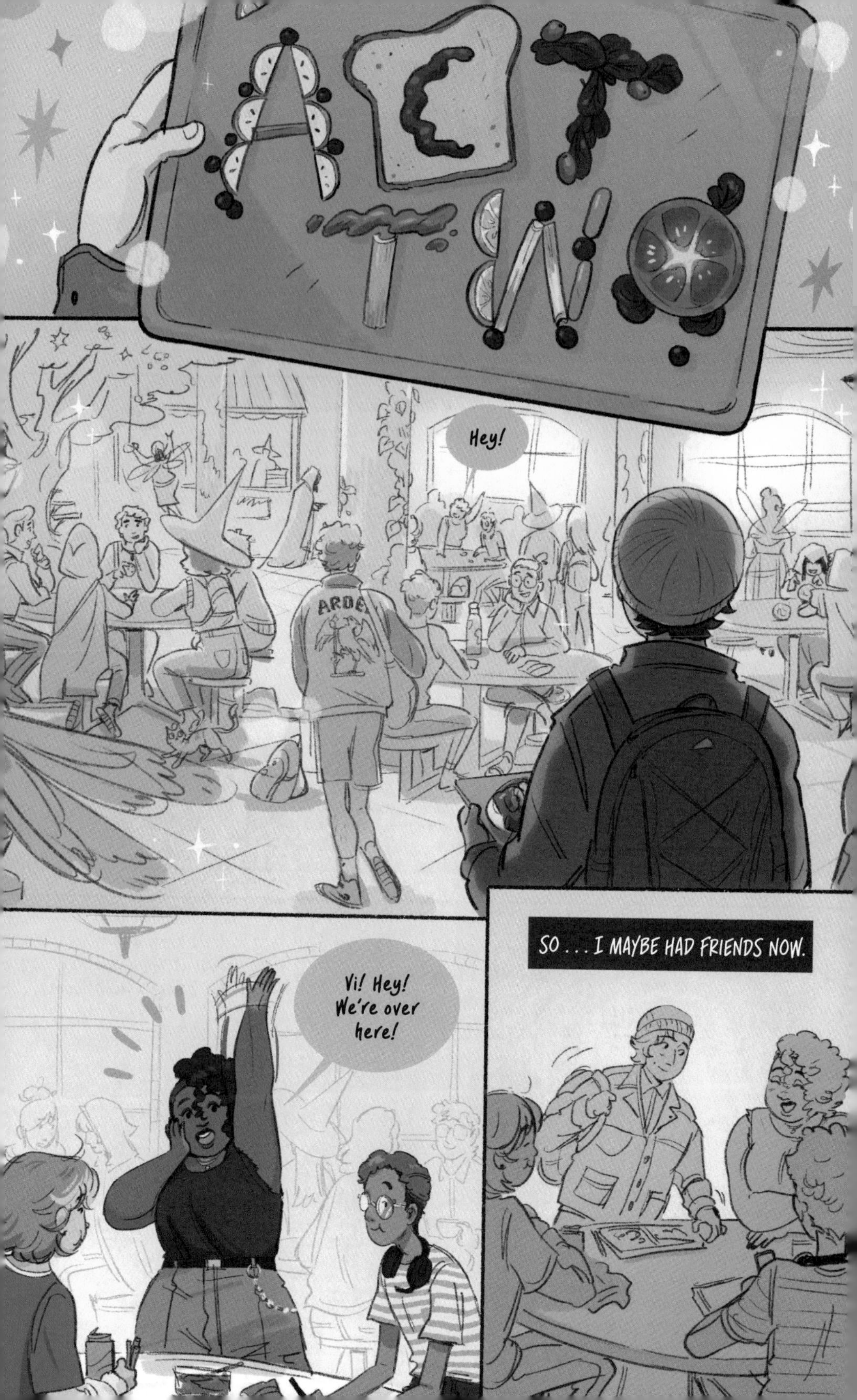
ACT TWO
Hey!
Vi! Hey! We're over here!
SO . . . I MAYBE HAD FRIENDS NOW.

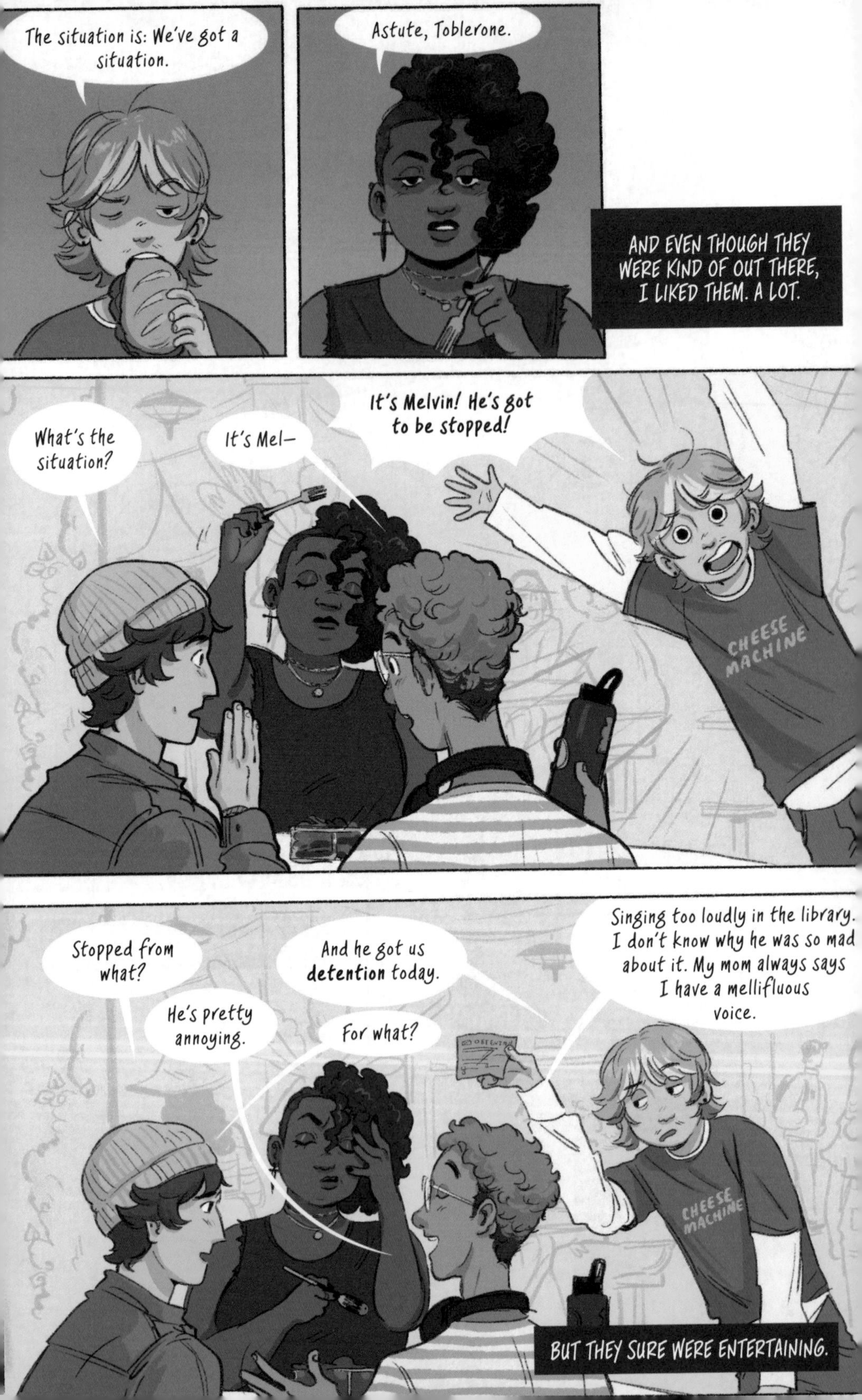
The situation is: We've got a situation.
Astute, Toblerone.
AND EVEN THOUGH THEY WERE KIND OF OUT THERE, I LIKED THEM. A LOT.
What's the situation?
It's Mel—
It's Melvin! He's got to be stopped!
CHEESE MACHINE
Stopped from what?
He's pretty annoying.
And he got us detention today.
For what?
Singing too loudly in the library. I don't know why he was so mad about it. My mom always says I have a mellifluous voice.
CHEESE MACHINE
BUT THEY SURE WERE ENTERTAINING.

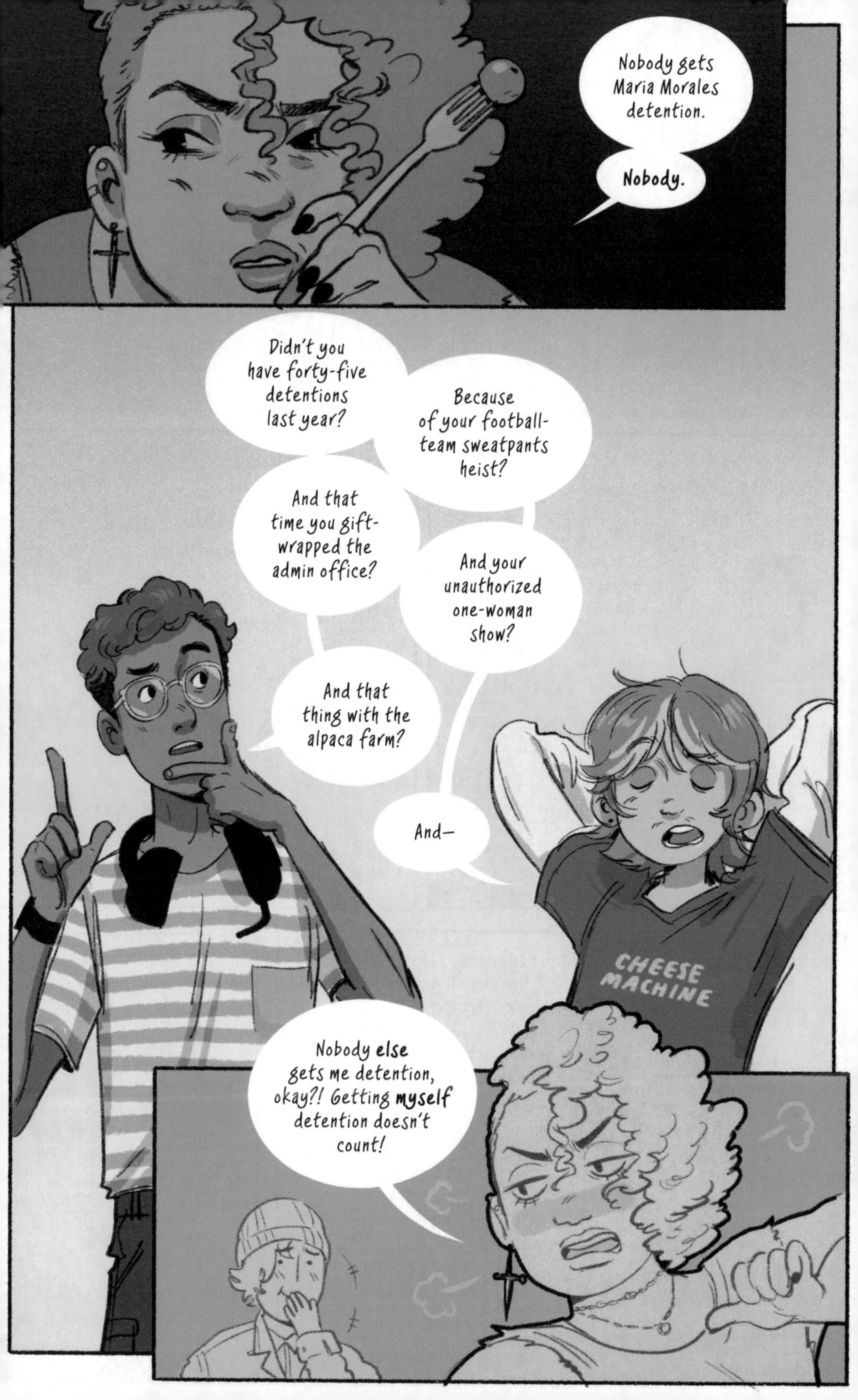
Nobody gets Maria Morales detention.
Nobody.
Didn't you have forty-five detentions last year?
Because of your football-team sweatpants heist?
And that time you gift-wrapped the admin office?
And your unauthorized one-woman show?
And that thing with the alpaca farm?
And—
CHEESE MACHINE
Nobody else gets me detention, okay?! Getting myself detention doesn't count!

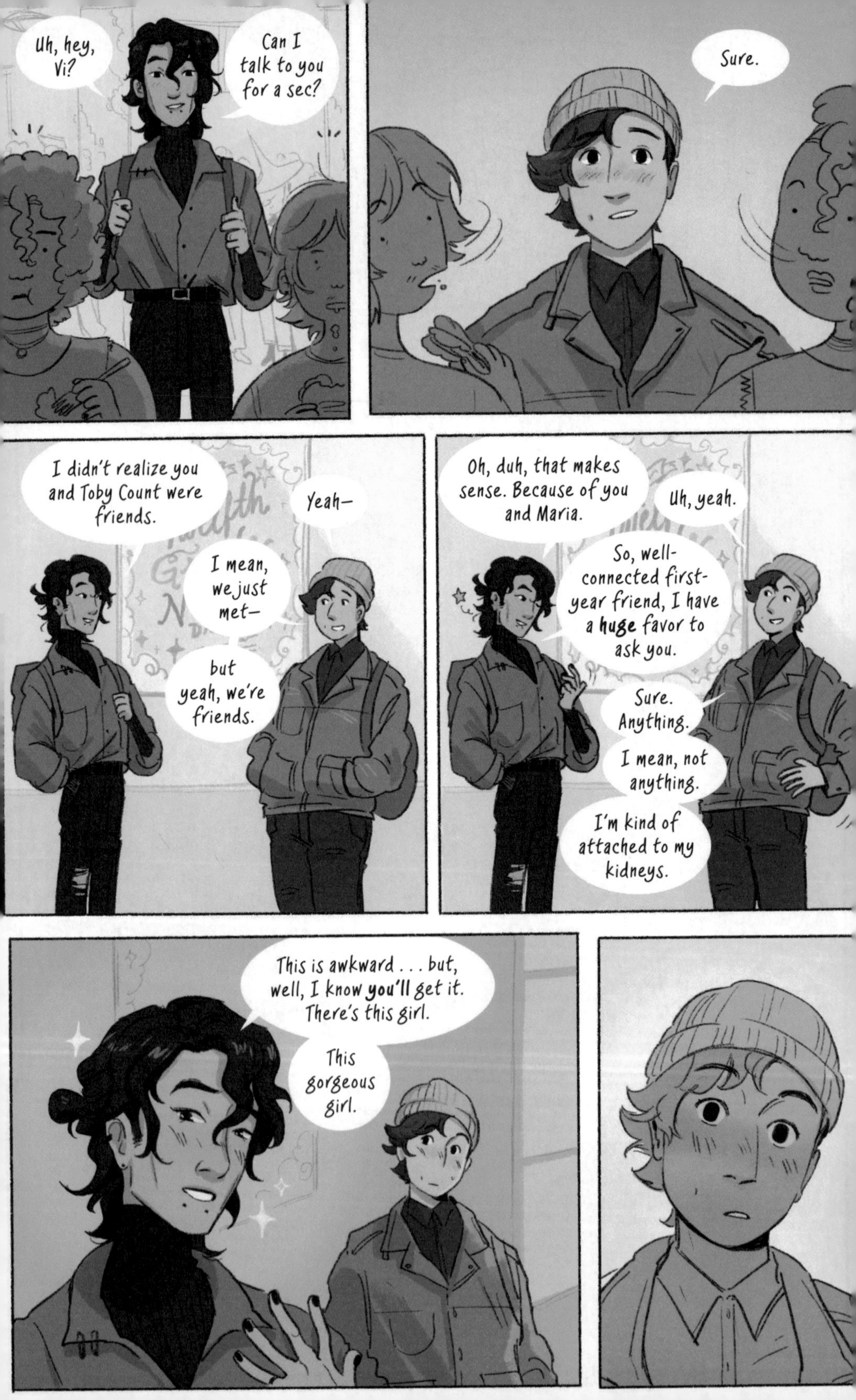
Uh, hey, Vi?
Can I talk to you for a sec?
Sure.
I didn't realize you and Toby Count were friends.
Yeah—
I mean, we just met—
but yeah, we're friends.
Oh, duh, that makes sense. Because of you and Maria.
Uh, yeah.
So, well-connected first-year friend, I have a **huge** favor to ask you.
Sure. Anything.
I mean, not anything.
I'm kind of attached to my kidneys.
This is awkward . . . but, well, I know **you'll** get it. There's this girl.
This gorgeous girl.

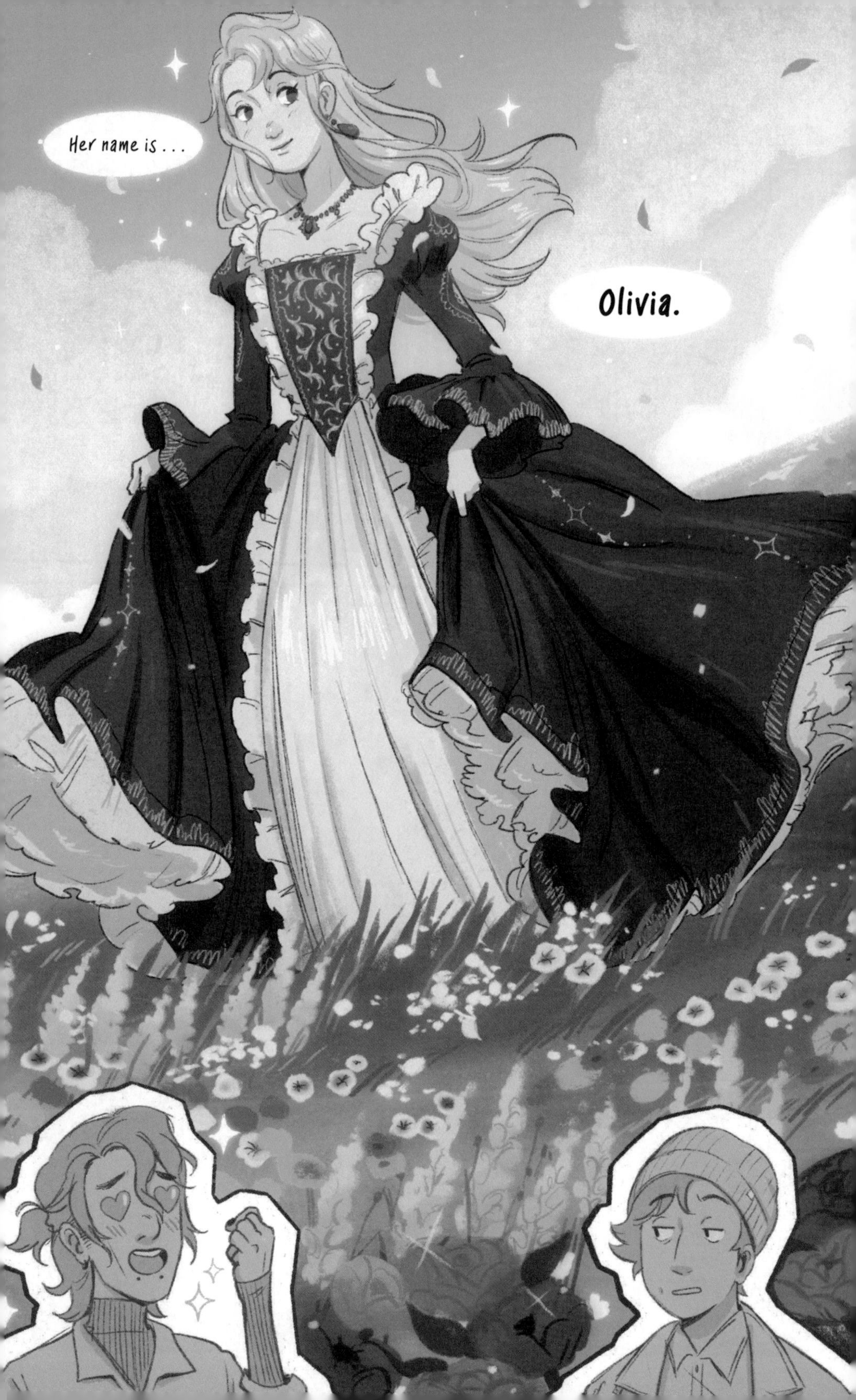
Her name is . . .
Olivia.

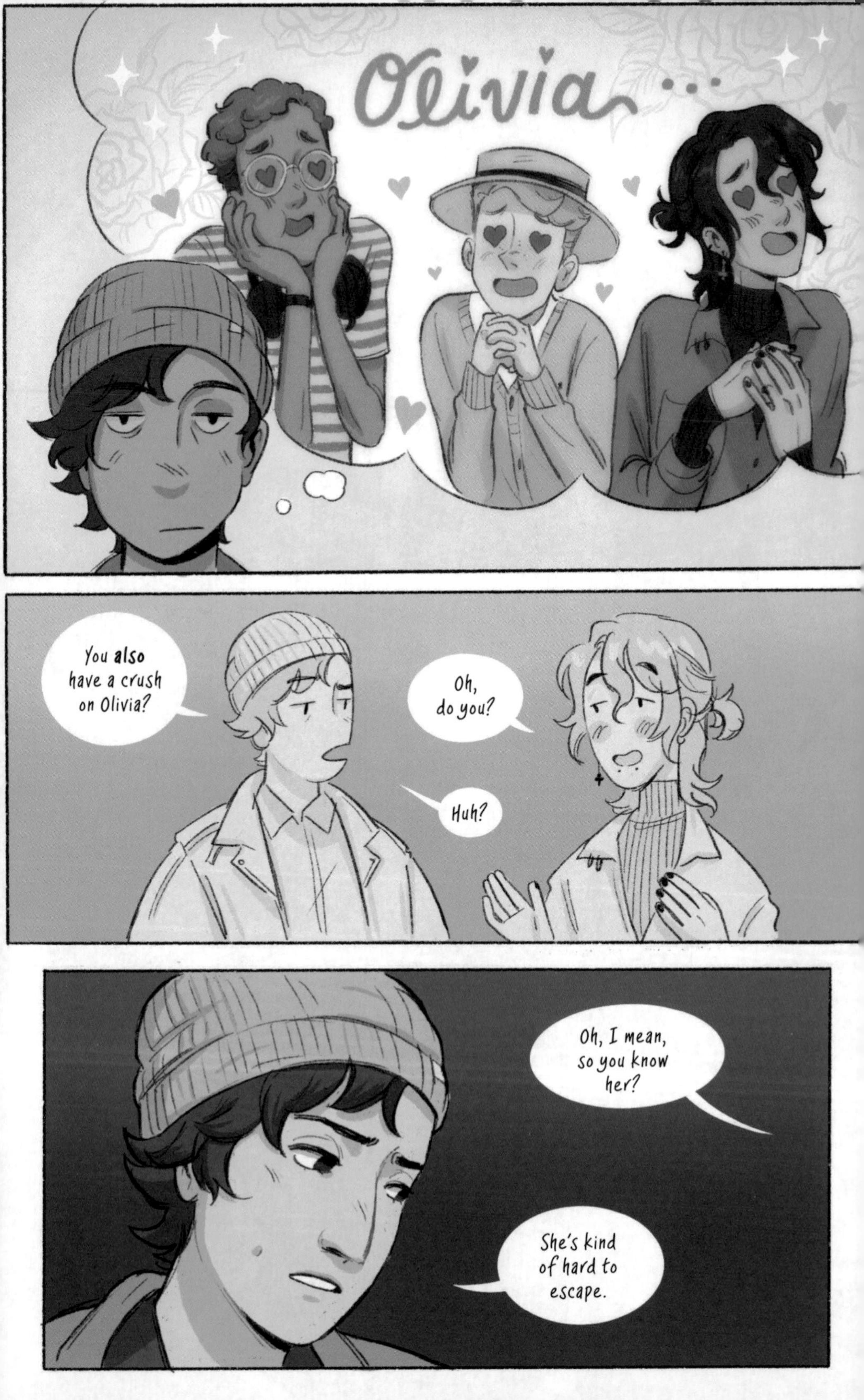
Olivia...
You also have a crush on Olivia?
Oh, do you?
Huh?
Oh, I mean, so you know her?
She's kind of hard to escape.

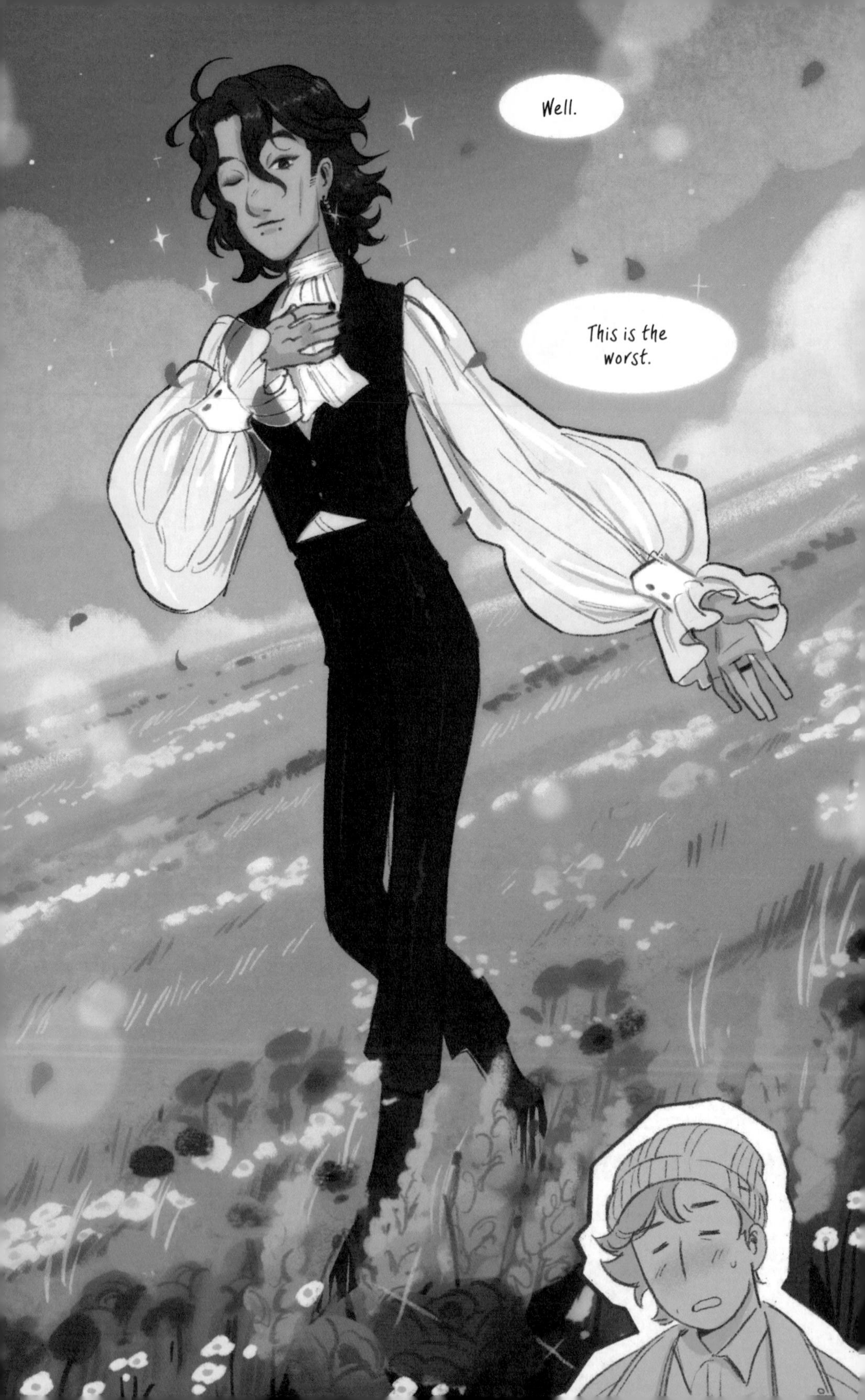
Well.
This is the worst.

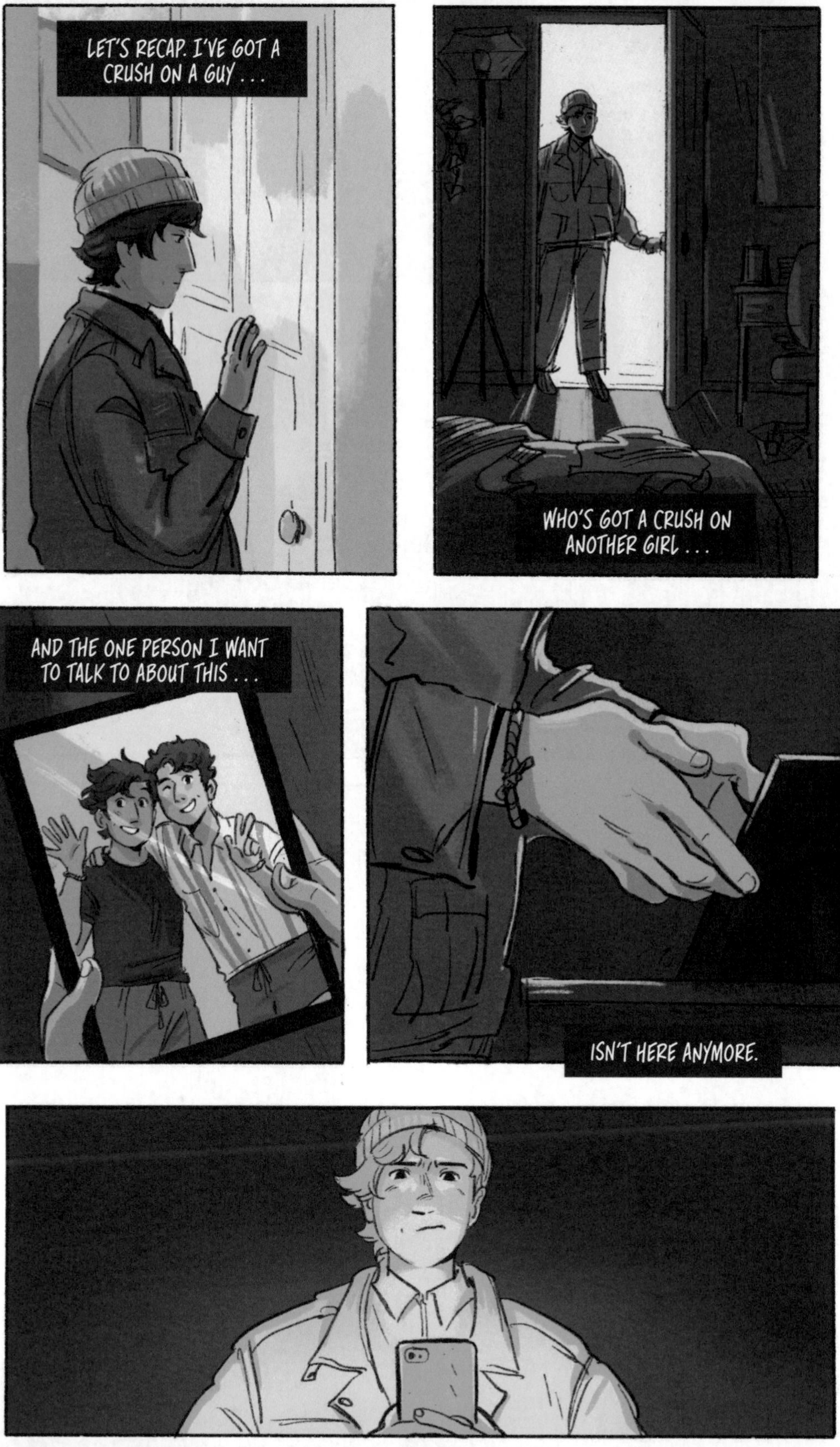
LET'S RECAP. I'VE GOT A CRUSH ON A GUY . . .
WHO'S GOT A CRUSH ON ANOTHER GIRL . . .
AND THE ONE PERSON I WANT TO TALK TO ABOUT THIS . . .
ISN'T HERE ANYMORE.

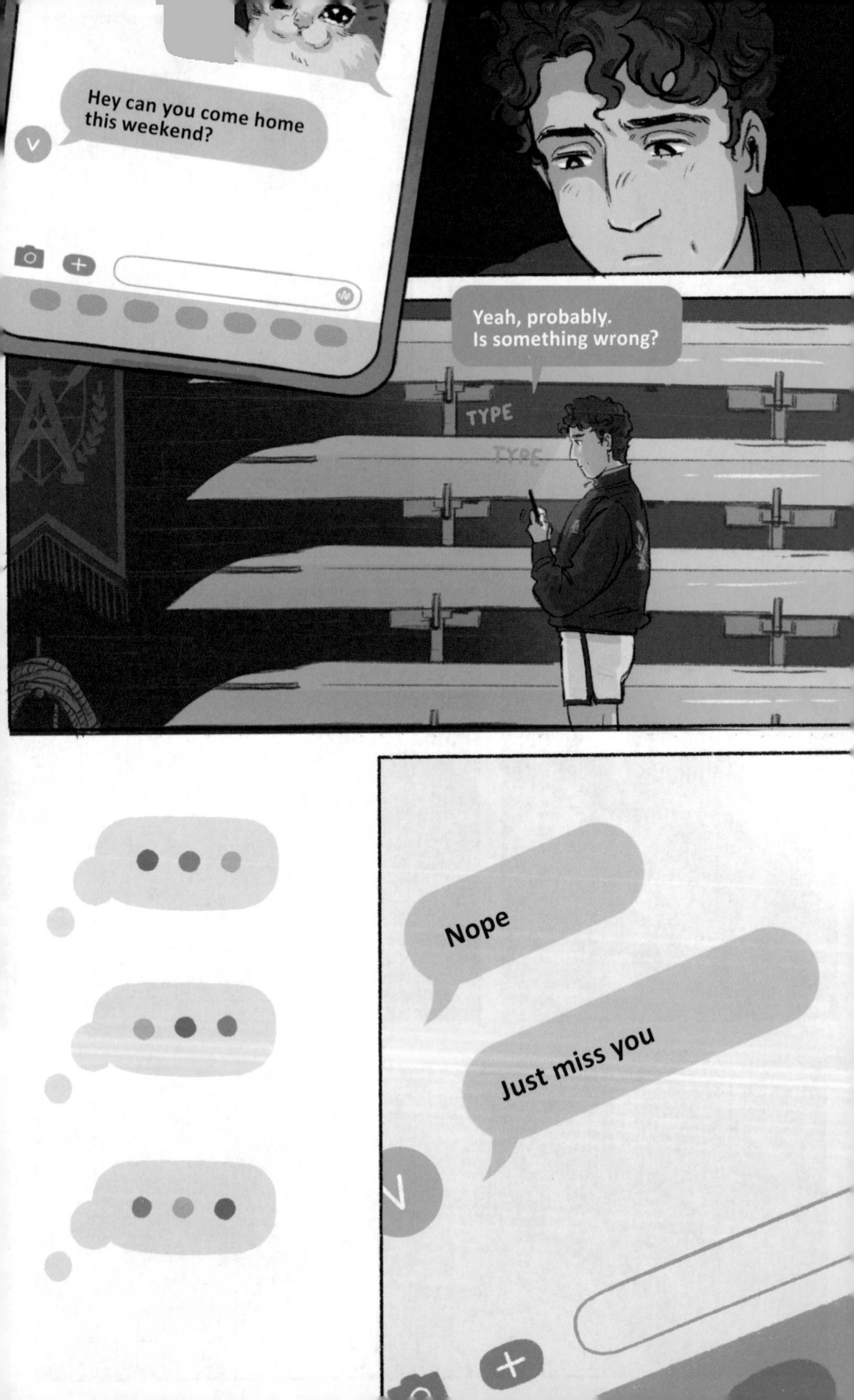
Hey can you come home this weekend?
Yeah, probably. Is something wrong?
TYPE
TYPE
Nope
Just miss you

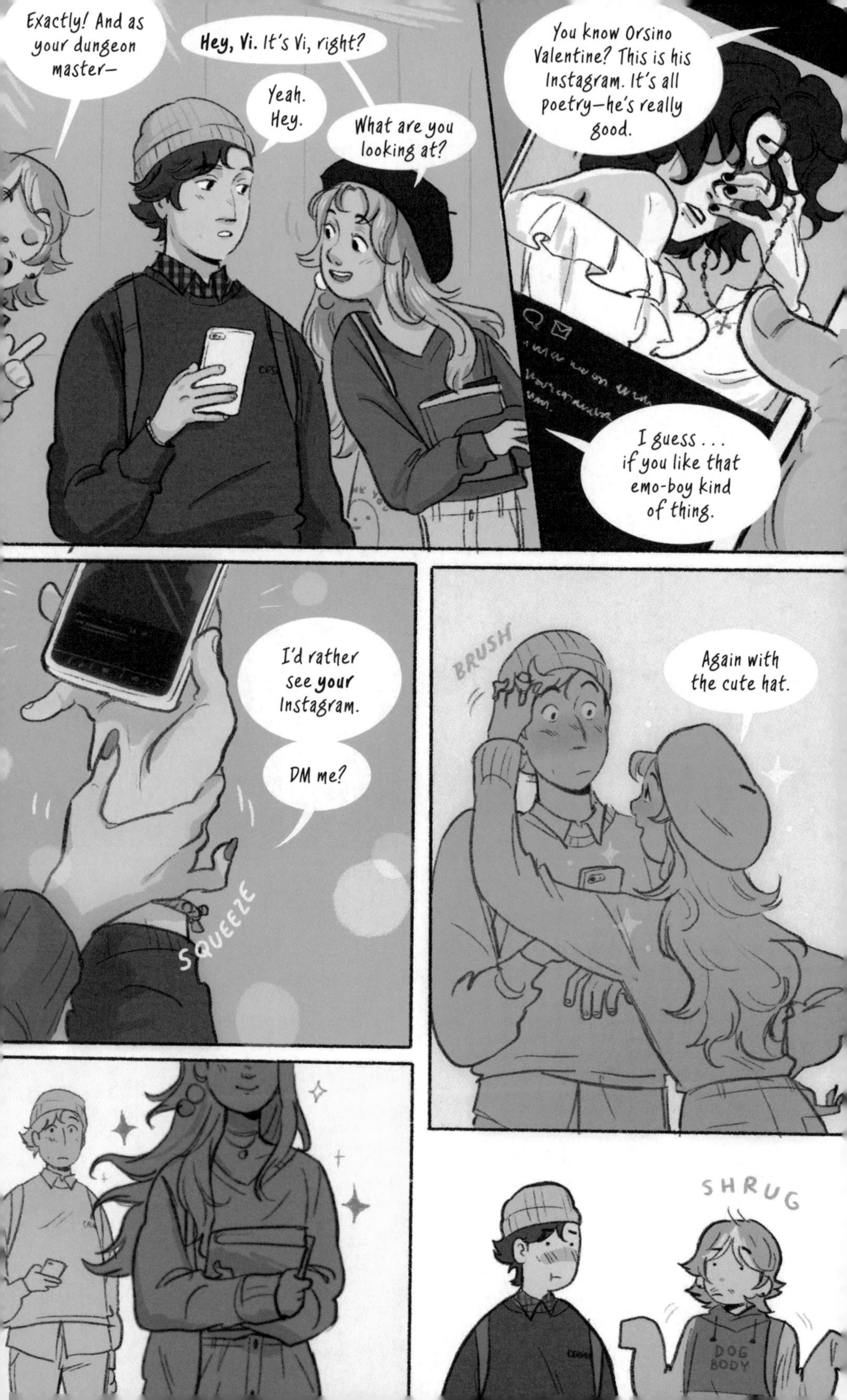

Exactly! And as your dungeon master—
Hey, Vi. It's Vi, right?
Yeah. Hey.
What are you looking at?
You know Orsino Valentine? This is his Instagram. It's all poetry—he's really good.
I guess . . . if you like that emo-boy kind of thing.
I'd rather see your Instagram.
DM me?
SQUEEZE
BRUSH
Again with the cute hat.
SHRUG
DOG BODY

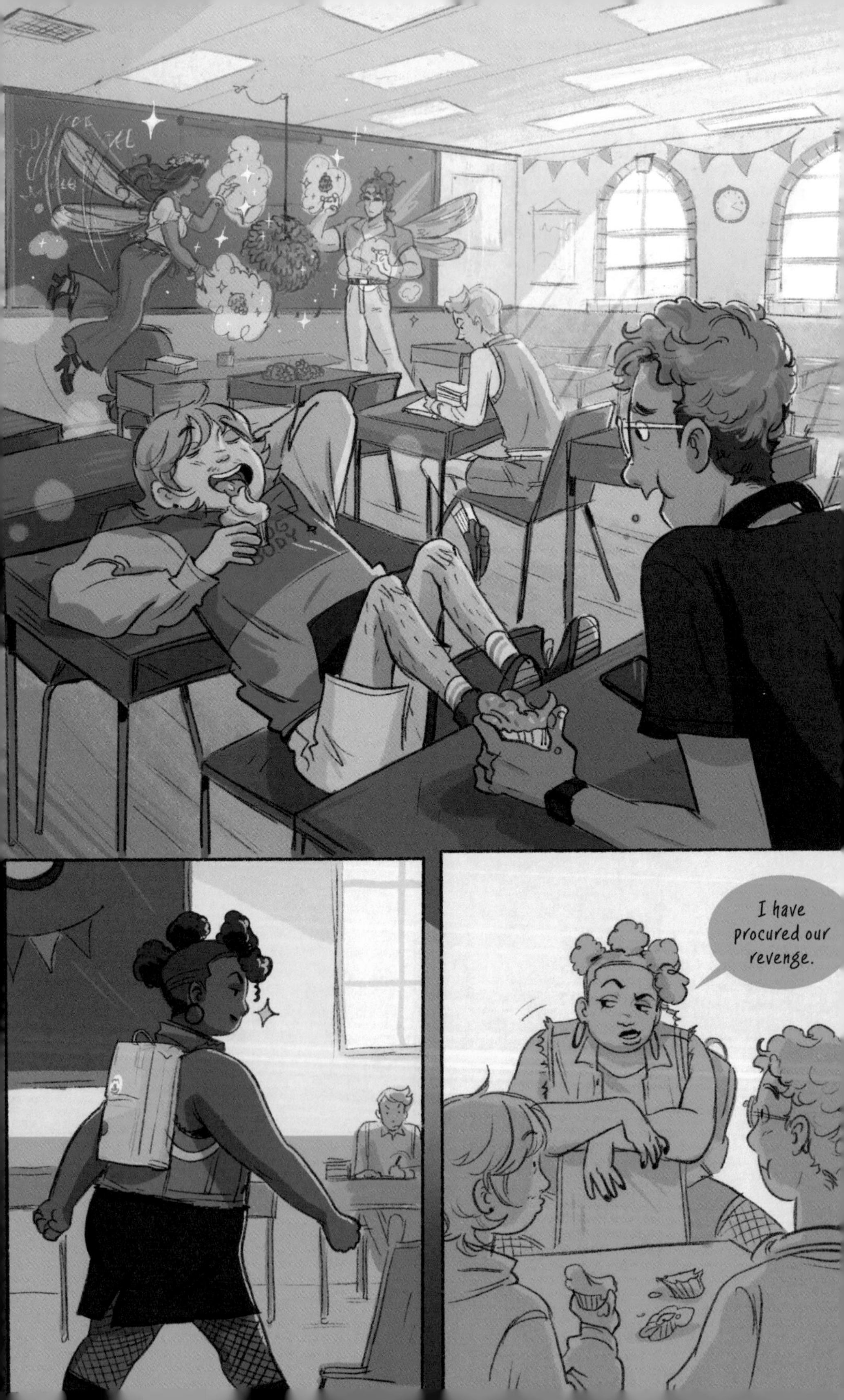
I have procured our revenge.

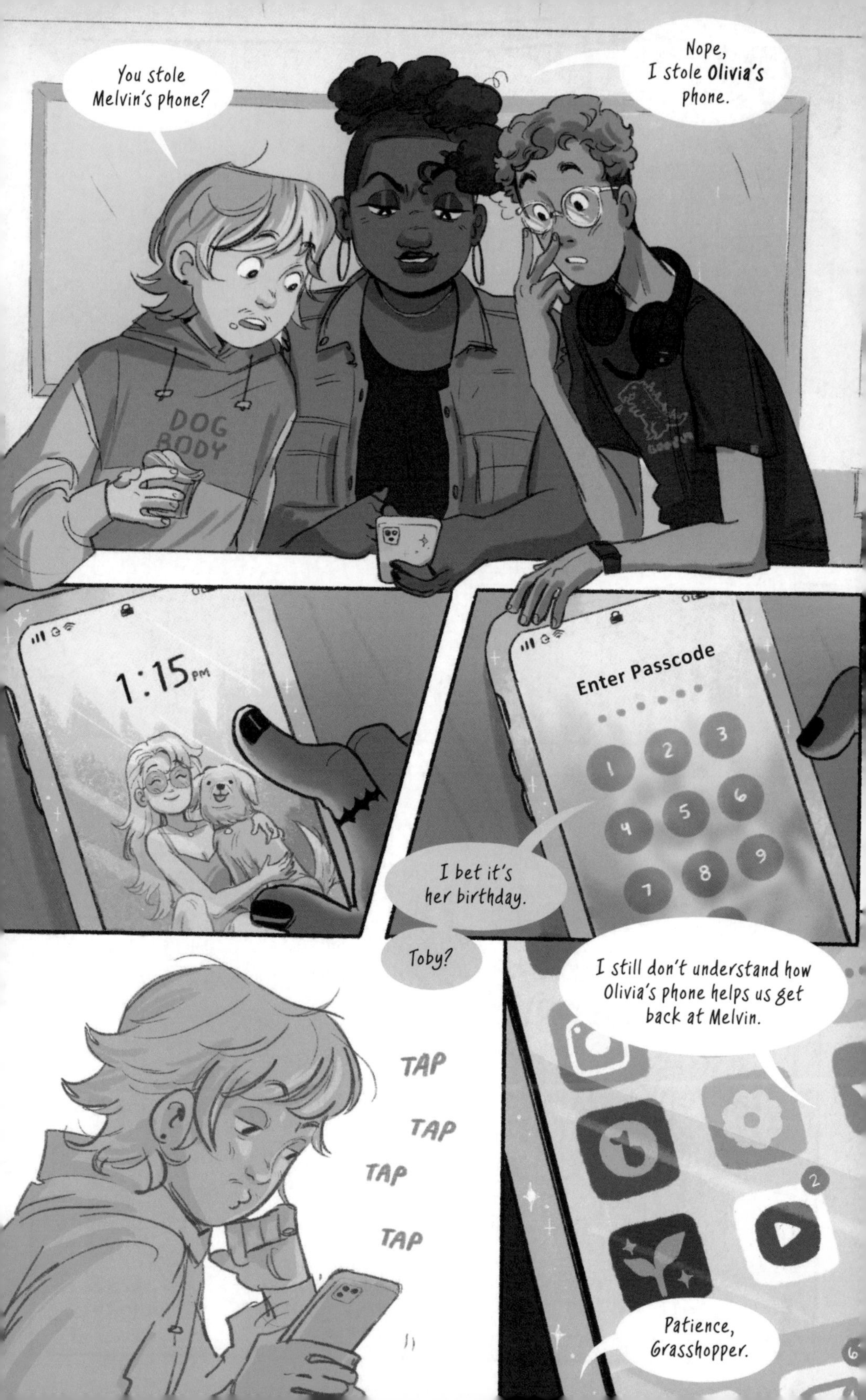
You stole Melvin's phone?
Nope, I stole Olivia's phone.
DOG BODY
1:15PM
Enter Passcode
I bet it's her birthday.
Toby?
TAP
TAP
TAP
TAP
I still don't understand how Olivia's phone helps us get back at Melvin.
Patience, Grasshopper.

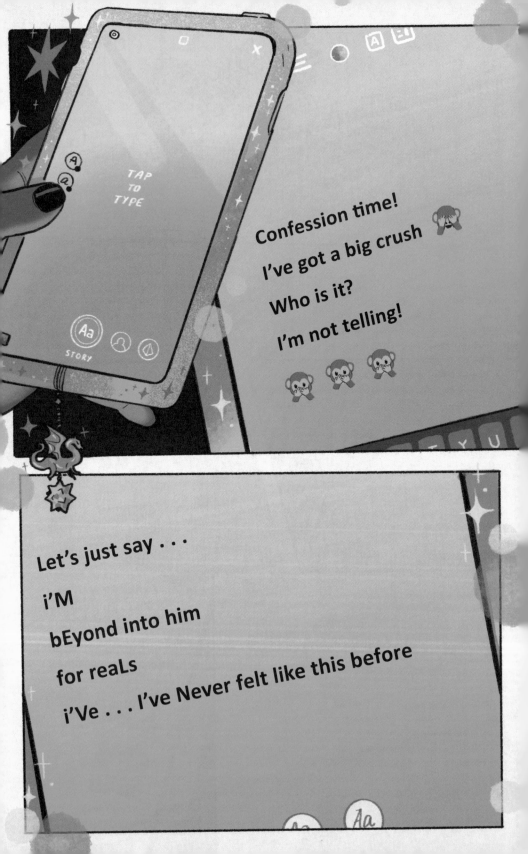

Confession time!
I've got a big crush 🙈
Who is it?
I'm not telling!
🙊 🙊 🙊

Let's just say . . .
i'M
bEyond into him
for reaLs
i'Ve . . . I've Never felt like this before

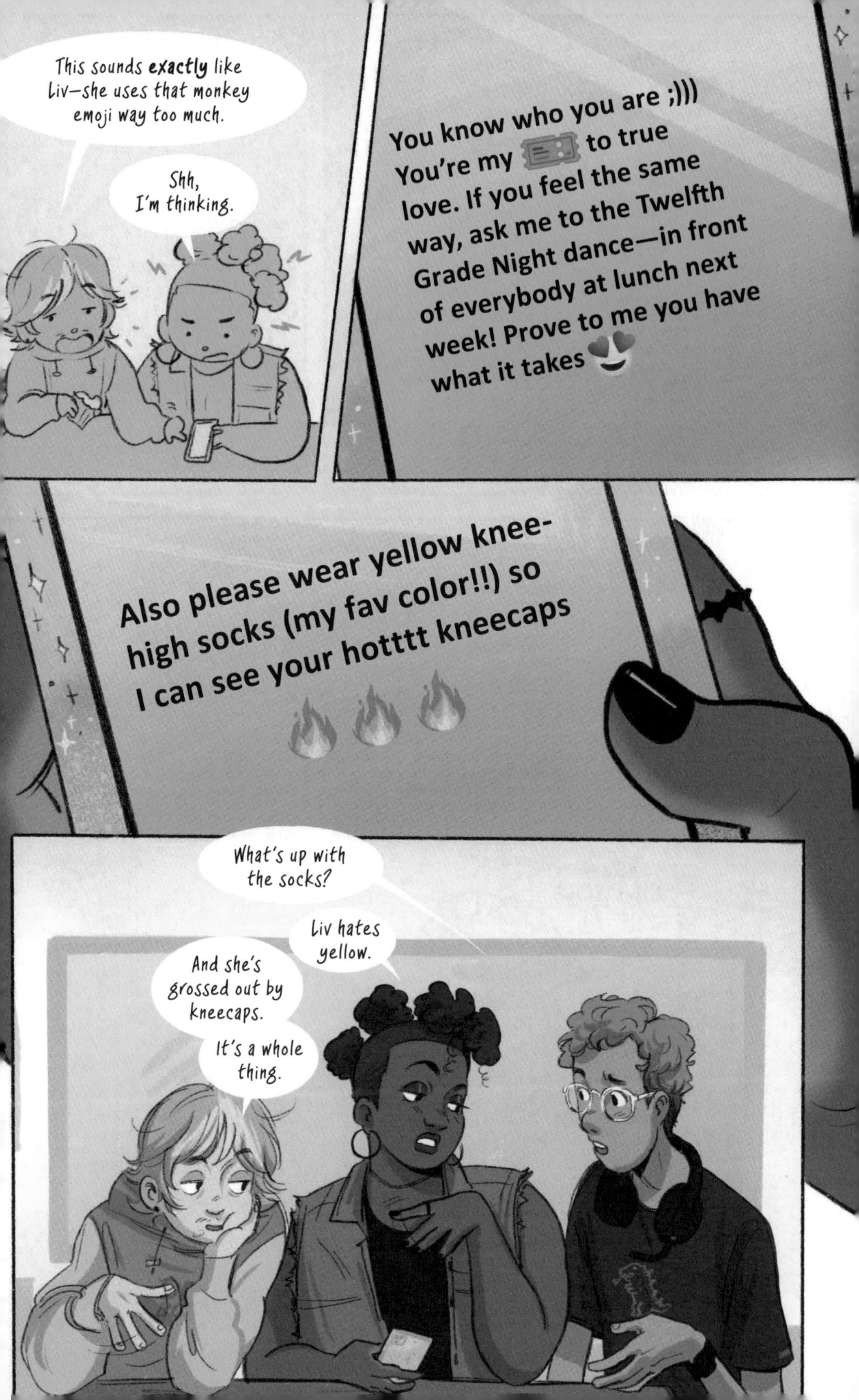
This sounds **exactly** like Liv—she uses that monkey emoji way too much.
Shh, I'm thinking.
You know who you are ;))) You're my to true love. If you feel the same way, ask me to the Twelfth Grade Night dance—in front of everybody at lunch next week! Prove to me you have what it takes
Also please wear yellow knee-high socks (my fav color!!) so I can see your hotttt kneecaps
What's up with the socks?
Liv hates yellow.
And she's grossed out by kneecaps.
It's a whole thing.

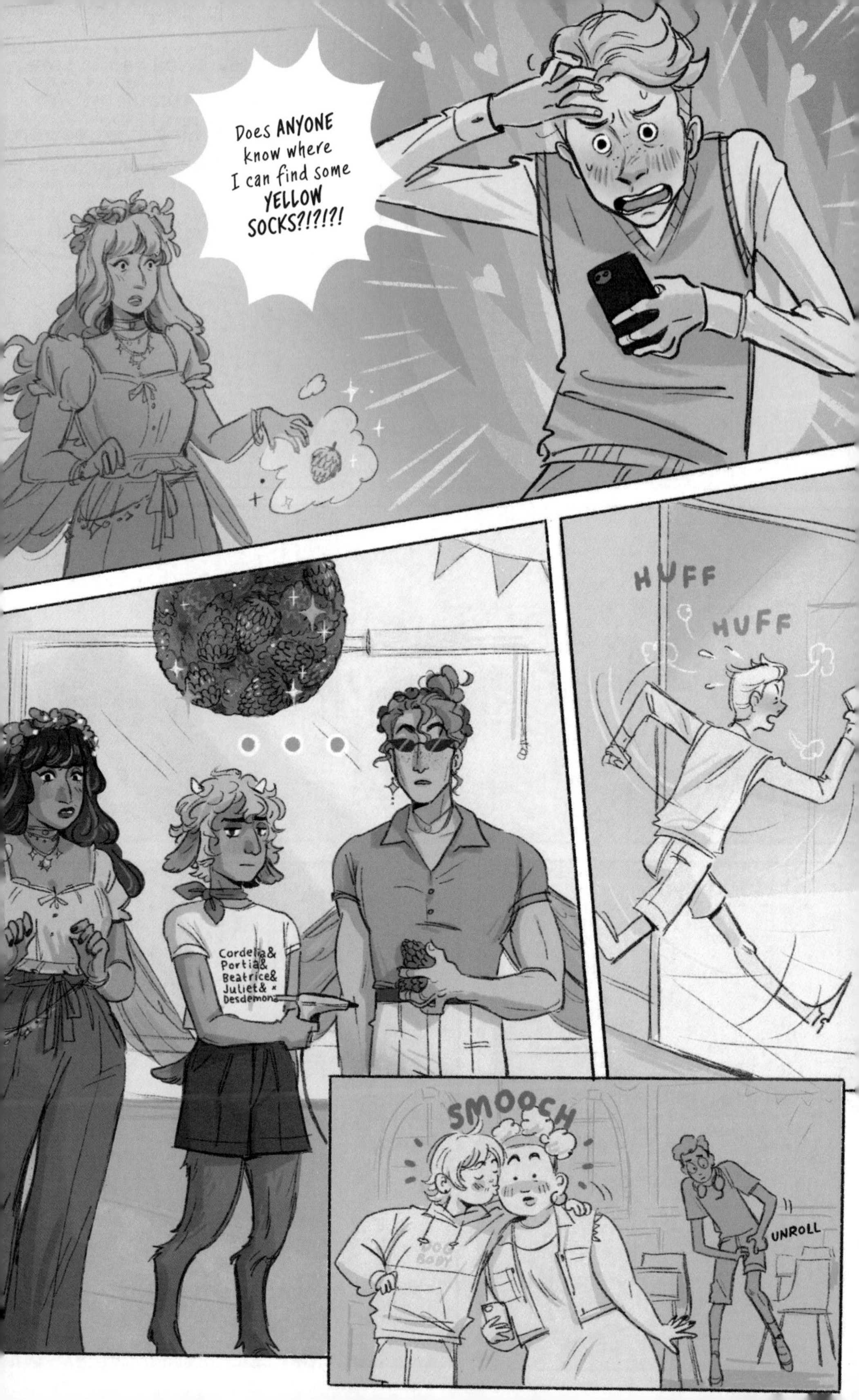
Does ANYONE know where I can find some YELLOW SOCKS?!?!?!
HUFF
HUFF
Cordelia&
Portia&
Beatrice&
Juliet&
Desdemona
SMOOCH
UNROLL

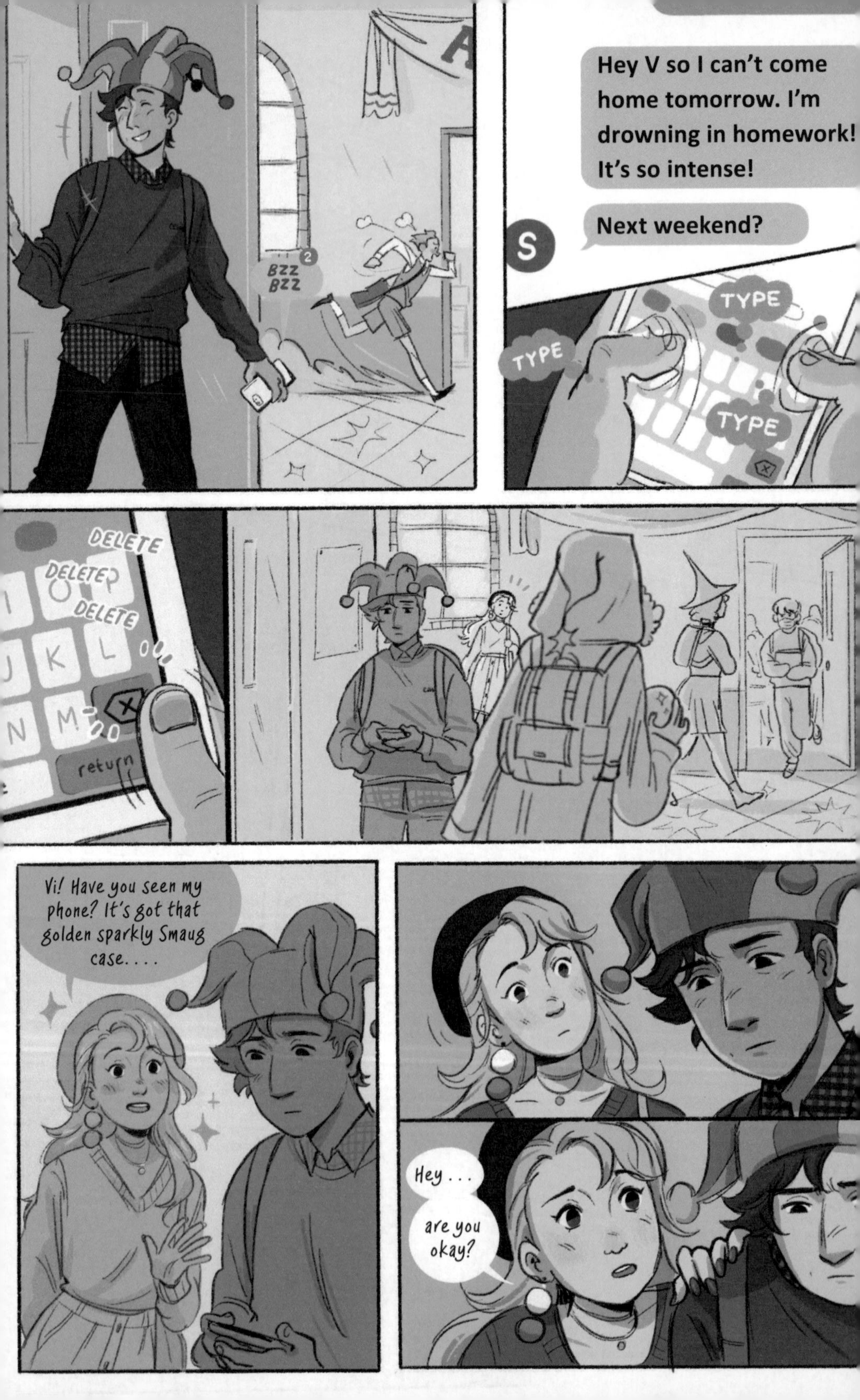
BZZ
BZZ
Hey V so I can't come home tomorrow. I'm drowning in homework! It's so intense!
Next weekend?
S
TYPE
TYPE
TYPE
DELETE
DELETE
DELETE
return
Vi! Have you seen my phone? It's got that golden sparkly Smaug case. . . .
Hey . . .
are you okay?

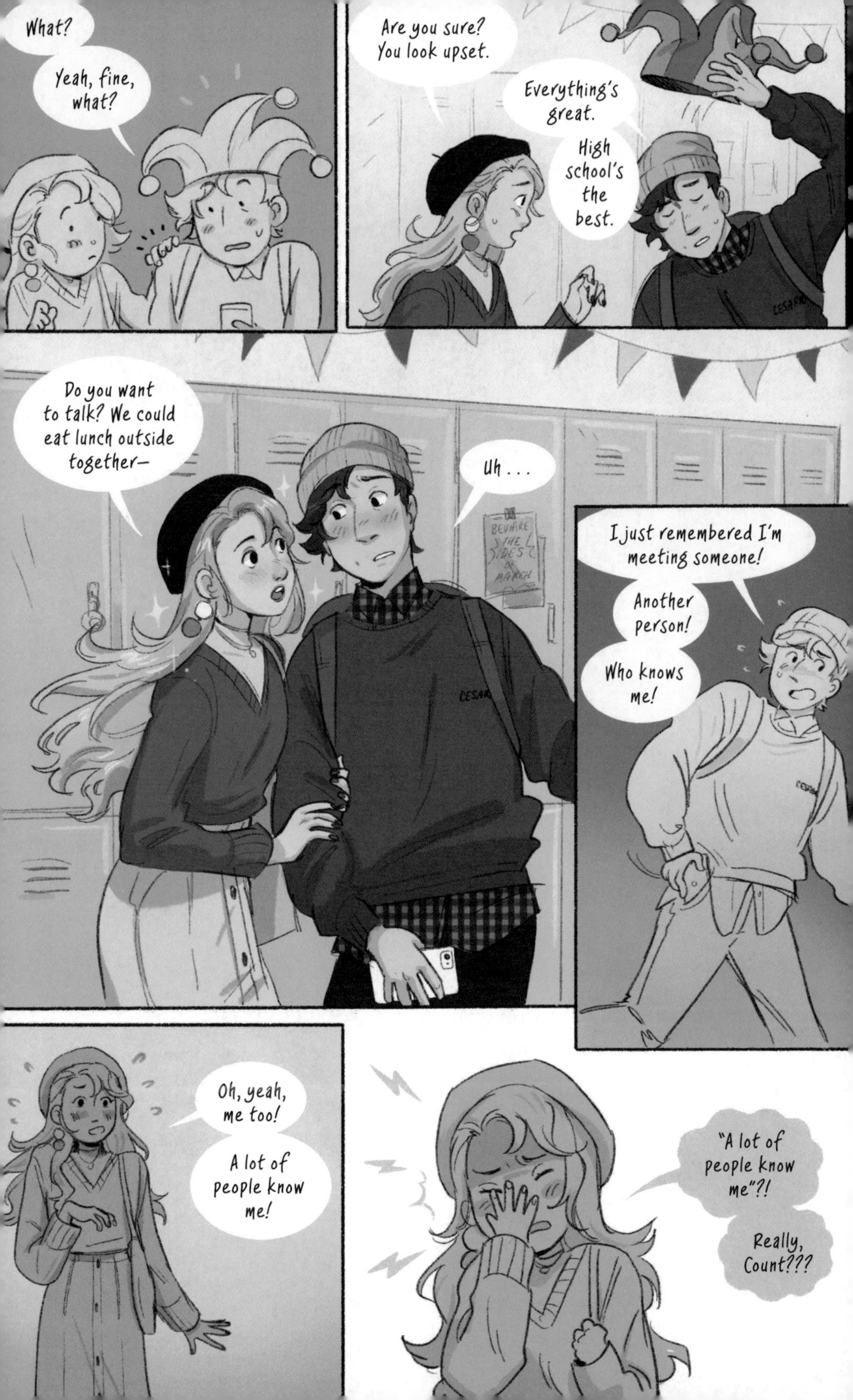

What?
Yeah, fine, what?
Are you sure? You look upset.
Everything's great.
High school's the best.
Do you want to talk? We could eat lunch outside together—
Uh . . .
BEWARE THE IDES OF MARCH
I just remembered I'm meeting someone!
Another person!
Who knows me!
Oh, yeah, me too!
A lot of people know me!
"A lot of people know me"?!
Really, Count???

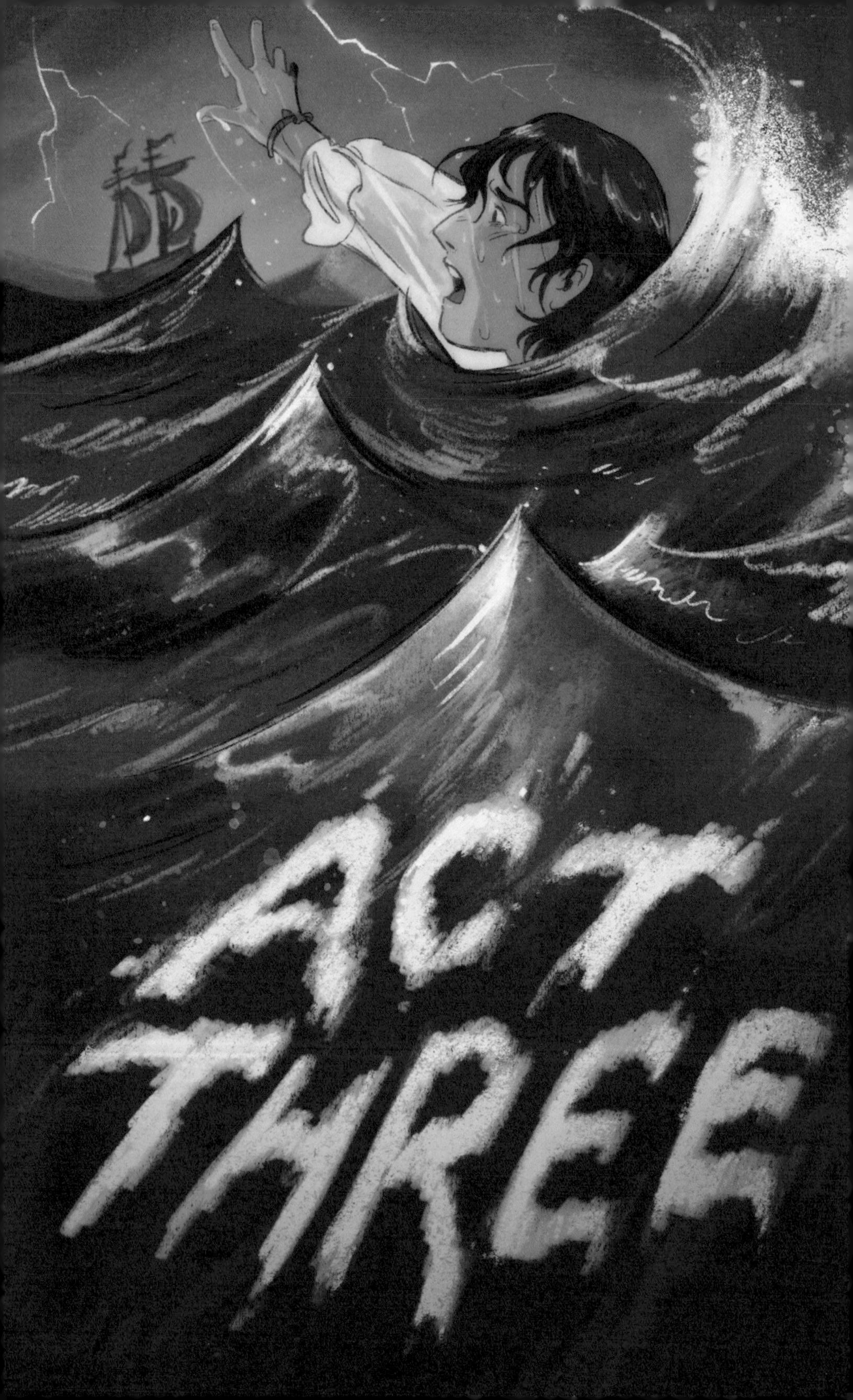
ACT
THREE

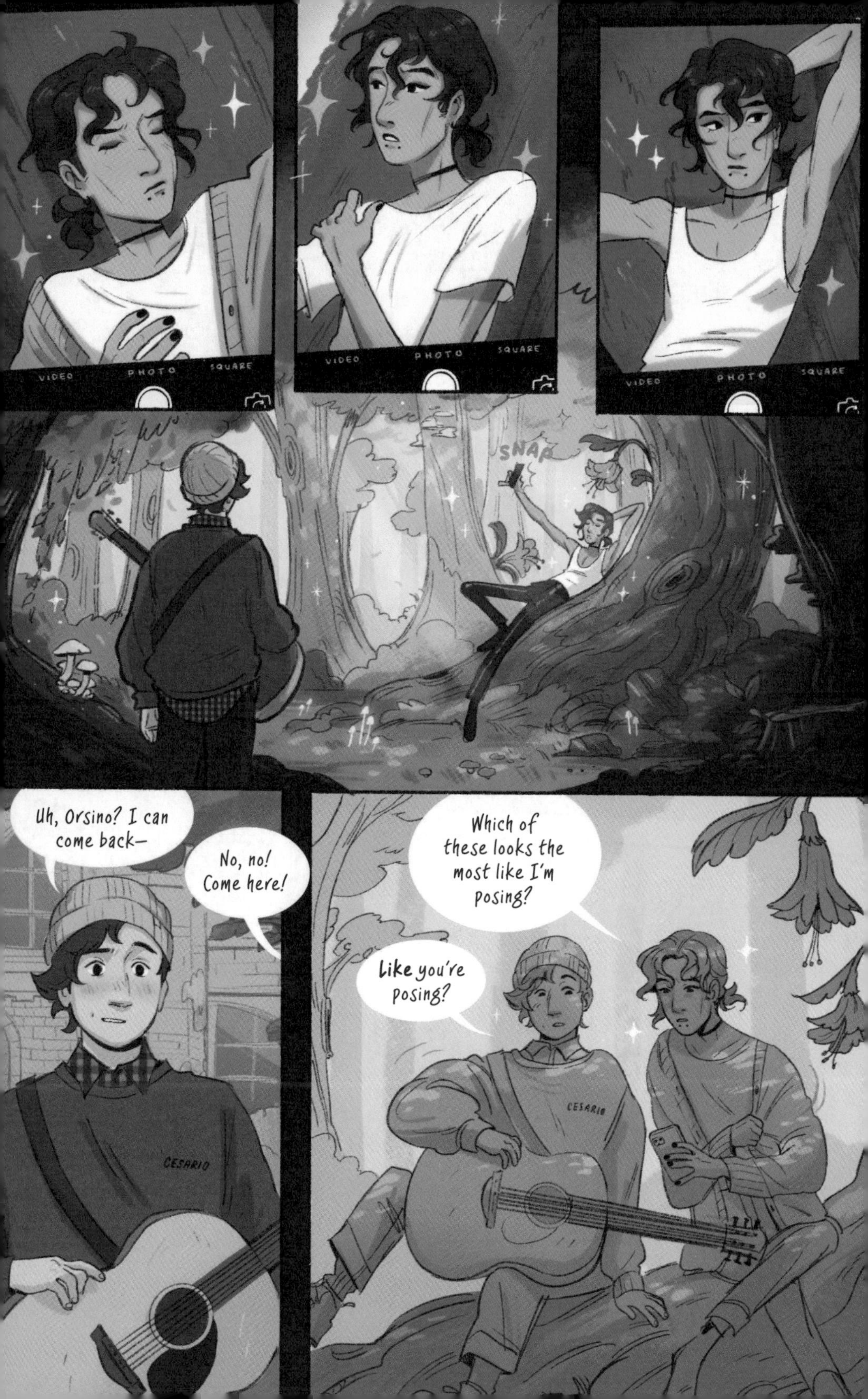
VIDEO PHOTO SQUARE
VIDEO PHOTO SQUARE
VIDEO PHOTO SQUARE
SNAP
Uh, Orsino? I can come back—
No, no! Come here!
CESARIO
Which of these looks the most like I'm posing?
Like you're posing?
CESARIO

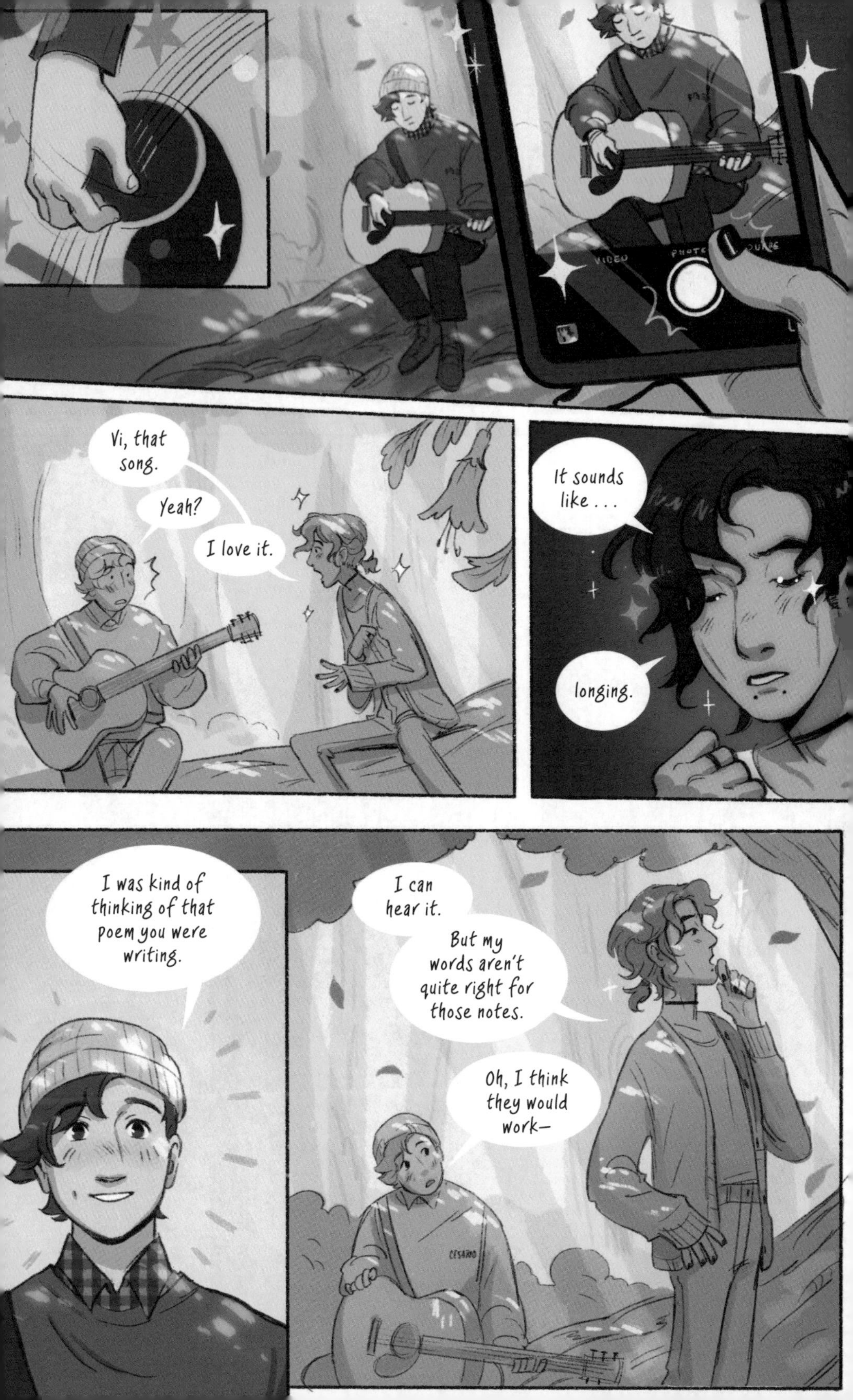
Vi, that song.
Yeah?
I love it.
It sounds like . . .
longing.
I was kind of thinking of that poem you were writing.
I can hear it.
But my words aren't quite right for those notes.
Oh, I think they would work—

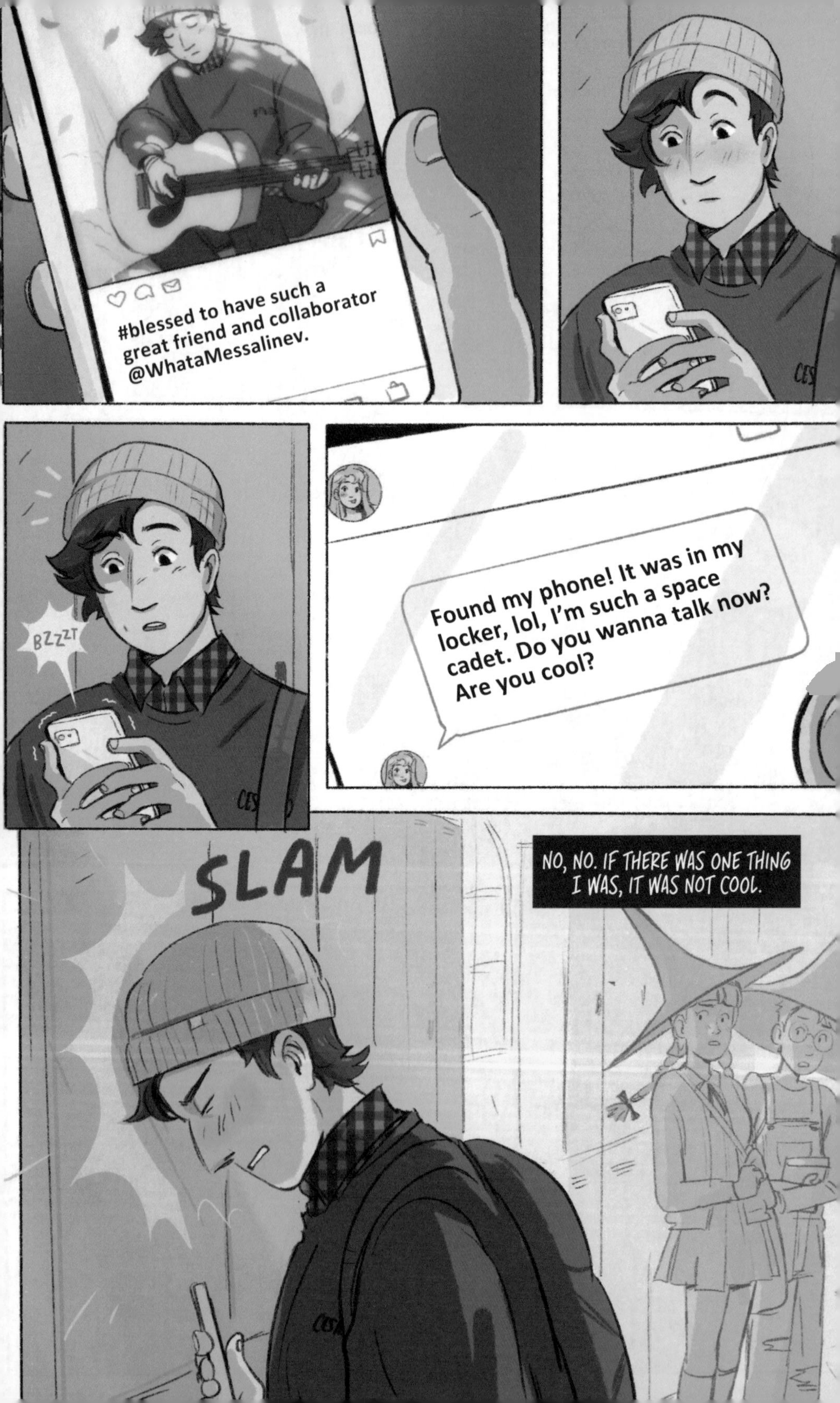
#blessed to have such a great friend and collaborator @WhataMessalinev.
BZZZT
Found my phone! It was in my locker, lol, I'm such a space cadet. Do you wanna talk now? Are you cool?
SLAM
NO, NO. IF THERE WAS ONE THING I WAS, IT WAS NOT COOL.

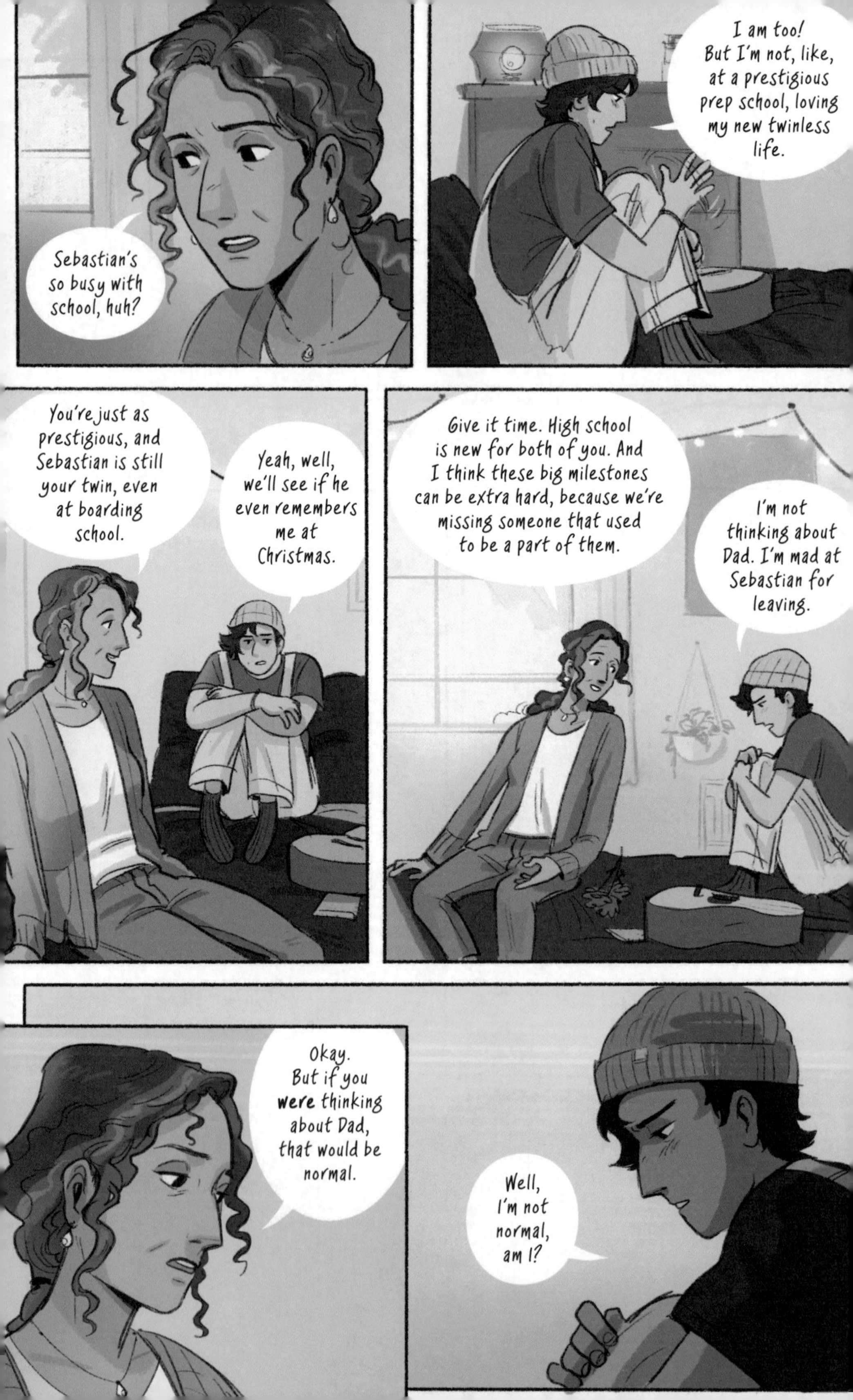
Sebastian's so busy with school, huh?
I am too! But I'm not, like, at a prestigious prep school, loving my new twinless life.
You're just as prestigious, and Sebastian is still your twin, even at boarding school.
Yeah, well, we'll see if he even remembers me at Christmas.
Give it time. High school is new for both of you. And I think these big milestones can be extra hard, because we're missing someone that used to be a part of them.
I'm not thinking about Dad. I'm mad at Sebastian for leaving.
Okay. But if you **were** thinking about Dad, that would be normal.
Well, I'm not normal, am I?

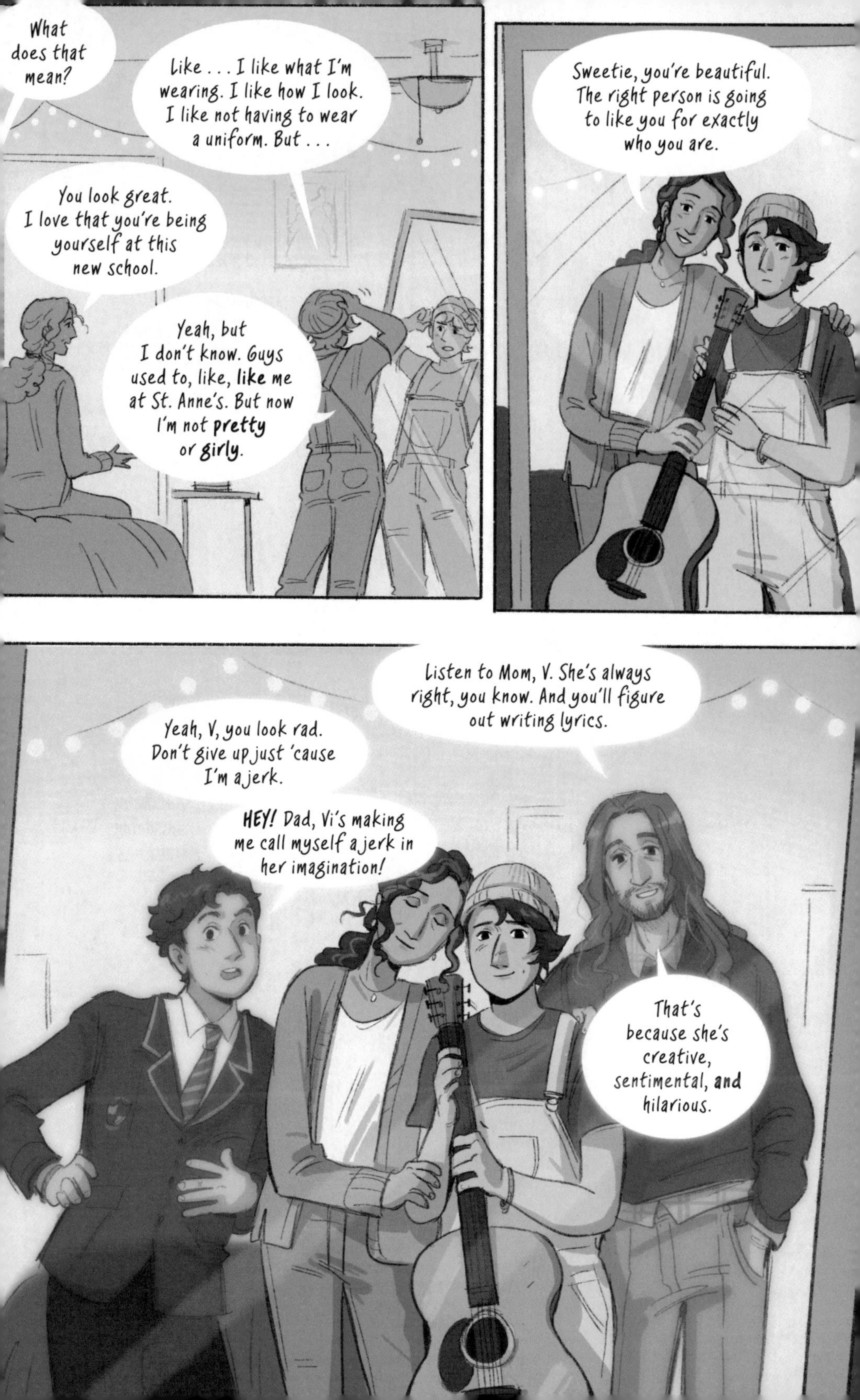
What does that mean?
Like . . . I like what I'm wearing. I like how I look. I like not having to wear a uniform. But . . .
You look great. I love that you're being yourself at this new school.
Yeah, but I don't know. Guys used to, like, **like** me at St. Anne's. But now I'm not **pretty** or **girly**.
Sweetie, you're beautiful. The right person is going to like you for exactly who you are.
Yeah, V, you look rad. Don't give up just 'cause I'm a jerk.
Listen to Mom, V. She's always right, you know. And you'll figure out writing lyrics.
HEY! Dad, Vi's making me call myself a jerk in her imagination!
That's because she's creative, sentimental, **and** hilarious.

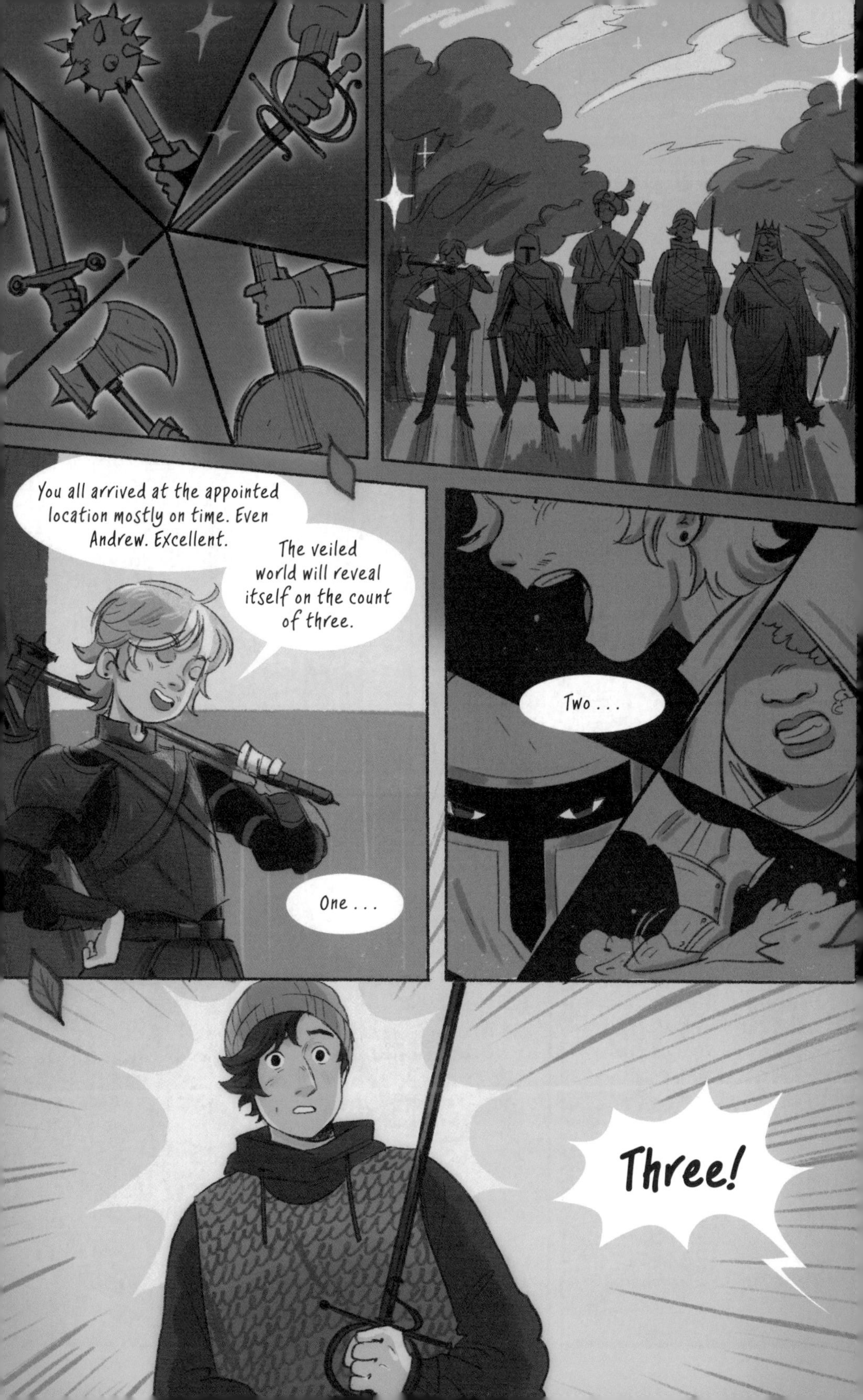
You all arrived at the appointed location mostly on time. Even Andrew. Excellent.
The veiled world will reveal itself on the count of three.
One . . .
Two . . .
Three!

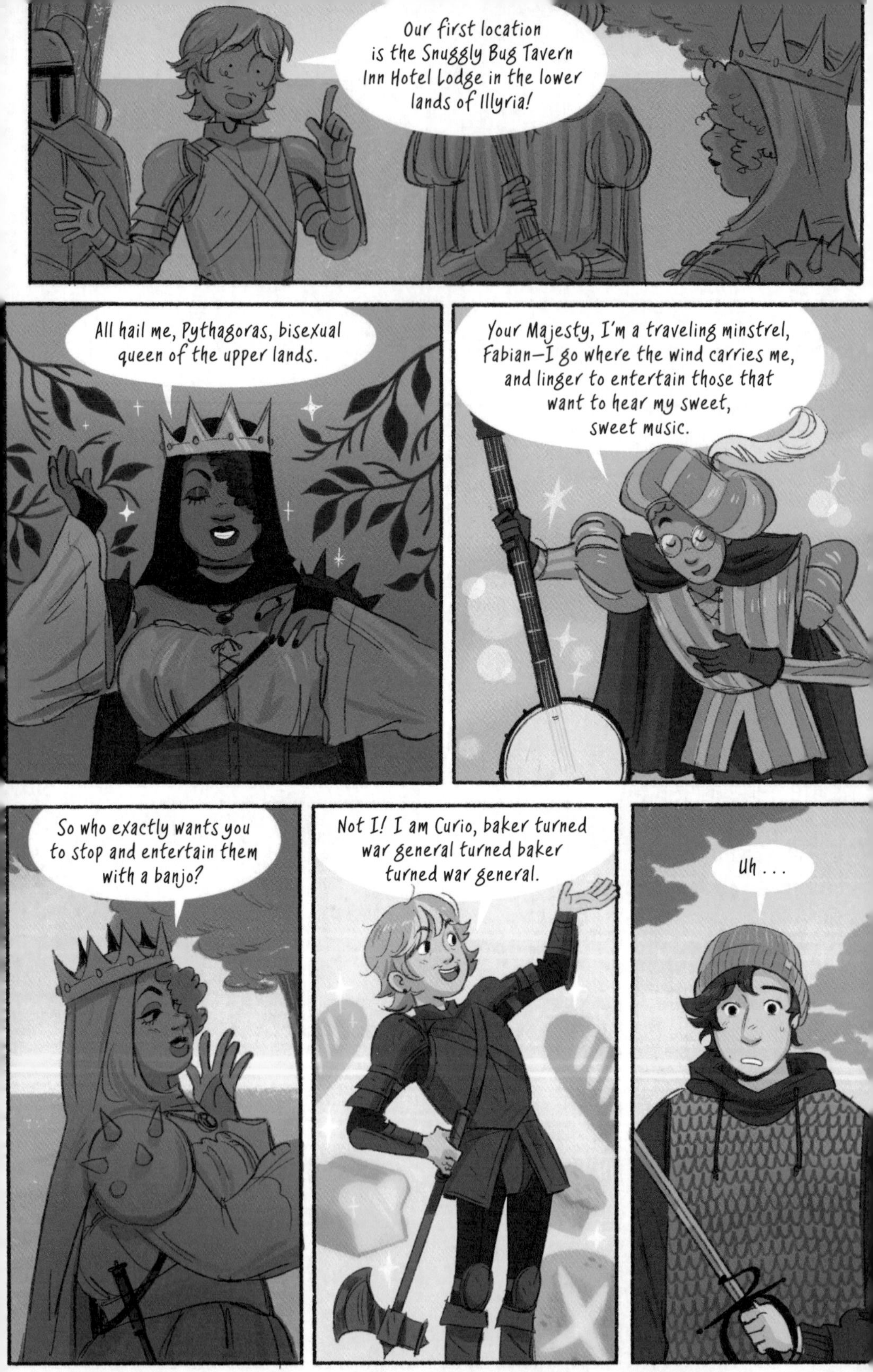
Our first location is the Snuggly Bug Tavern Inn Hotel Lodge in the lower lands of Illyria!
All hail me, Pythagoras, bisexual queen of the upper lands.
Your Majesty, I'm a traveling minstrel, Fabian—I go where the wind carries me, and linger to entertain those that want to hear my sweet, sweet music.
So who exactly wants you to stop and entertain them with a banjo?
Not I! I am Curio, baker turned war general turned baker turned war general.
Uh . . .

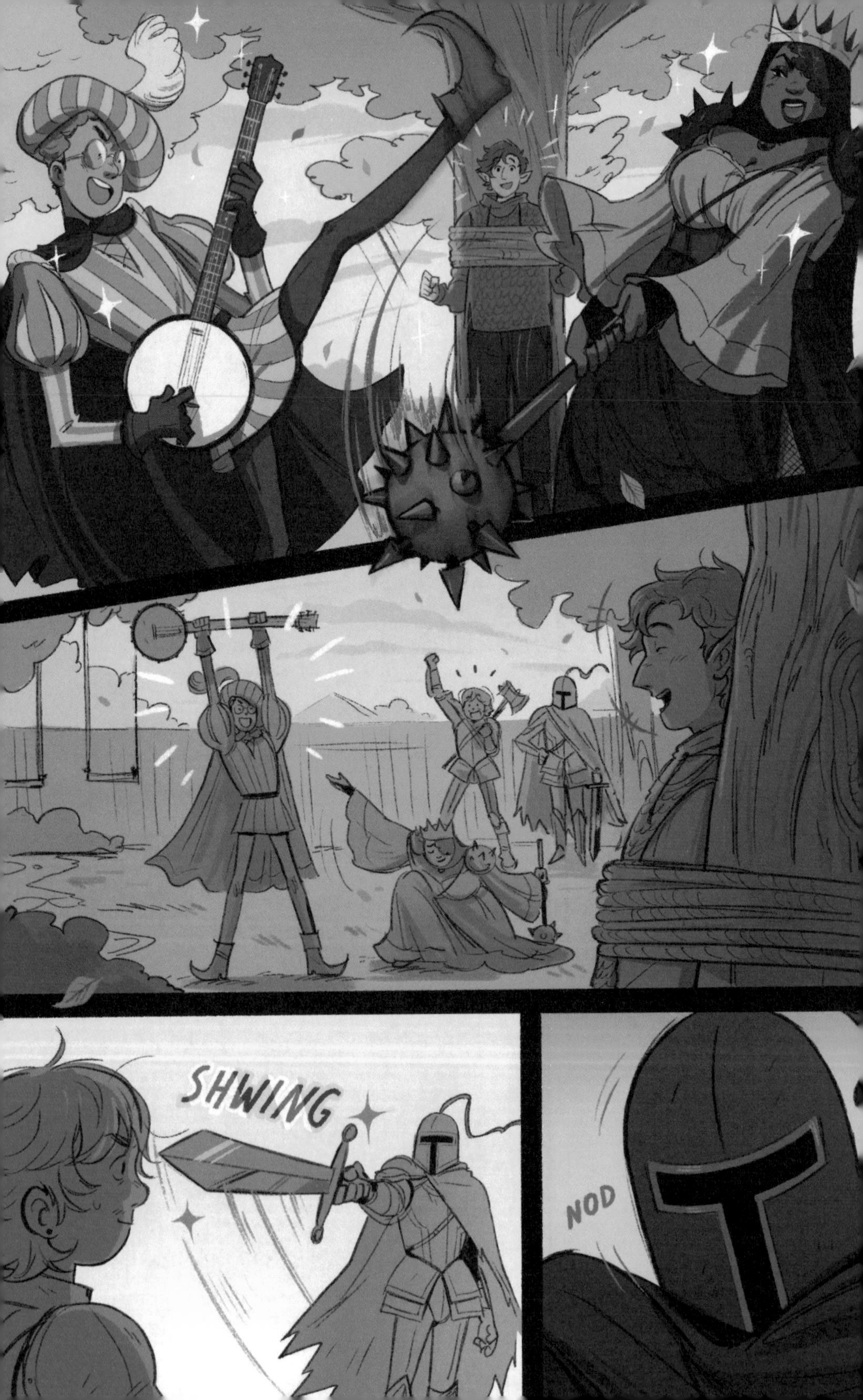
SHWING
NOD

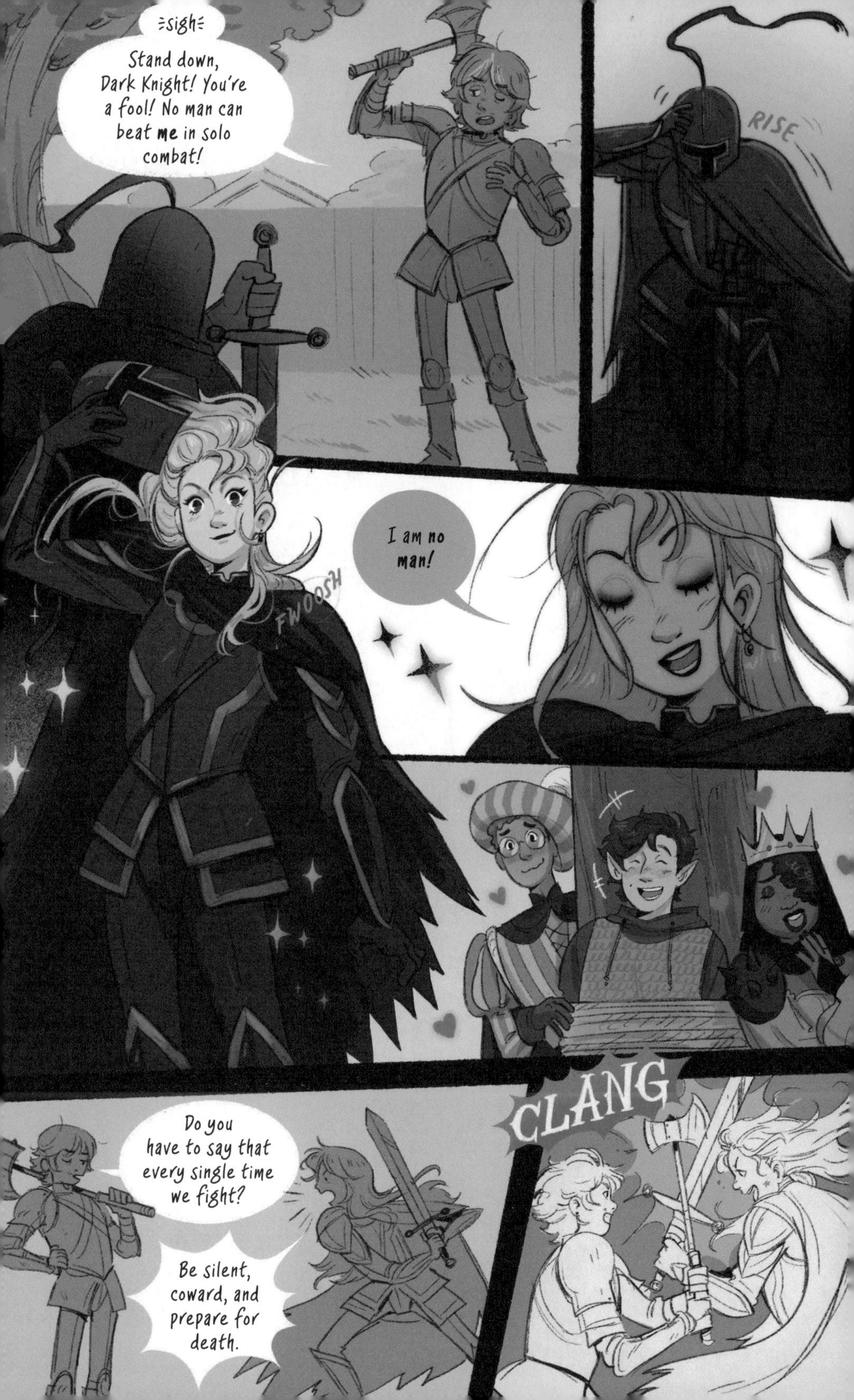

sigh
Stand down, Dark Knight! You're a fool! No man can beat me in solo combat!
RISE
I am no man!
FWOOSH
Do you have to say that every single time we fight?
Be silent, coward, and prepare for death.
CLANG

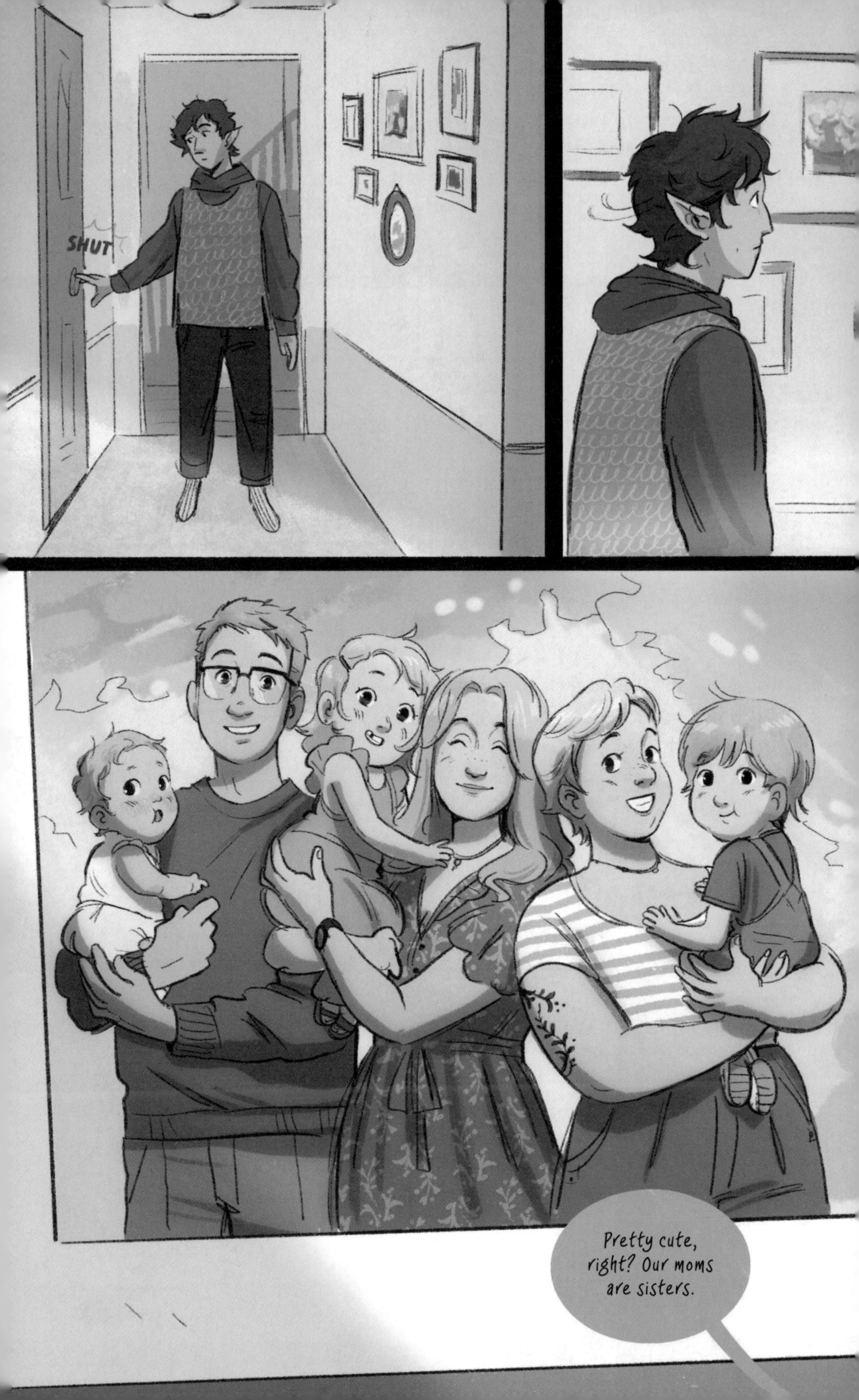
SHUT
Pretty cute, right? Our moms are sisters.

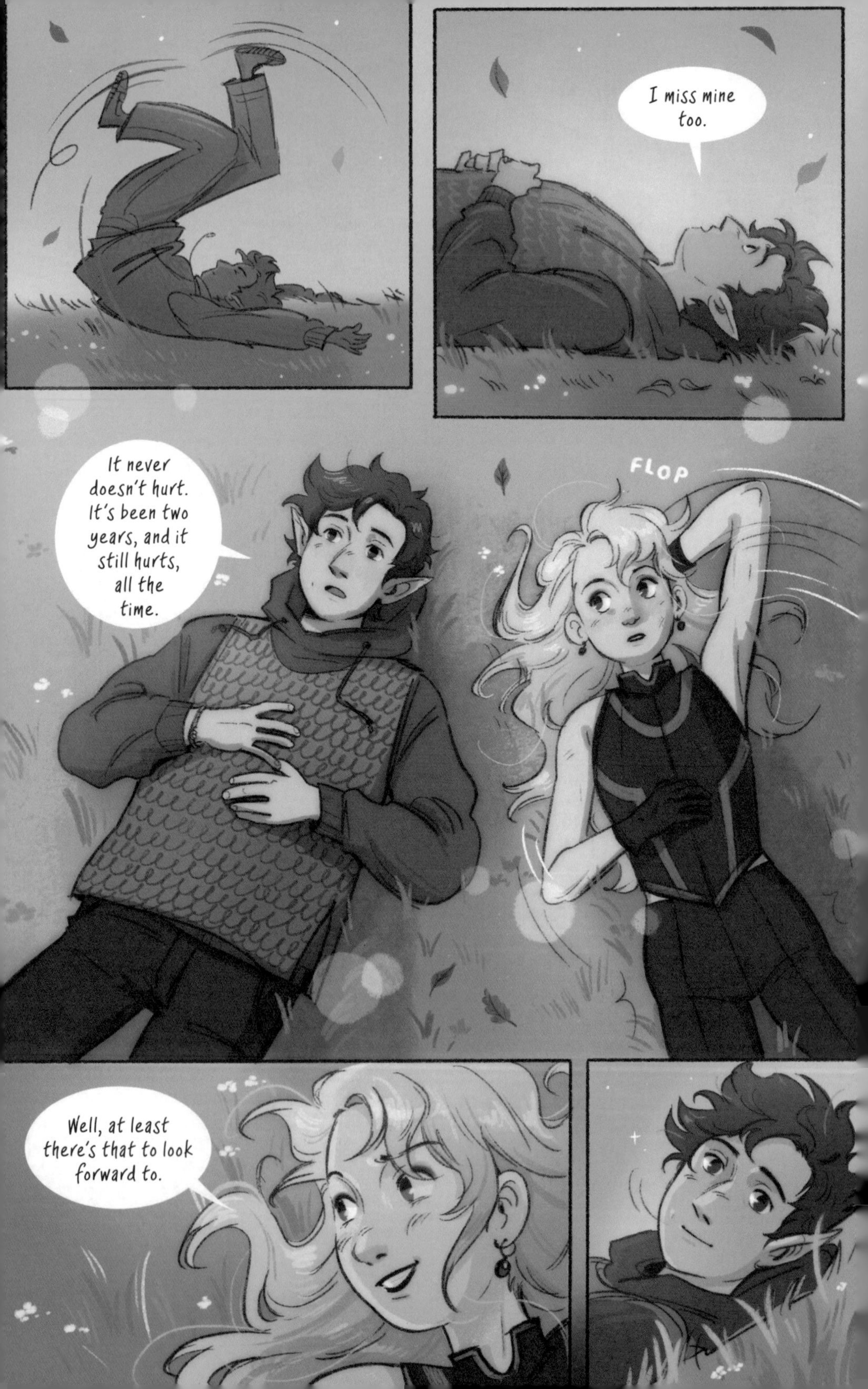
I miss mine too.
It never doesn't hurt. It's been two years, and it still hurts, all the time.
FLOP
Well, at least there's that to look forward to.

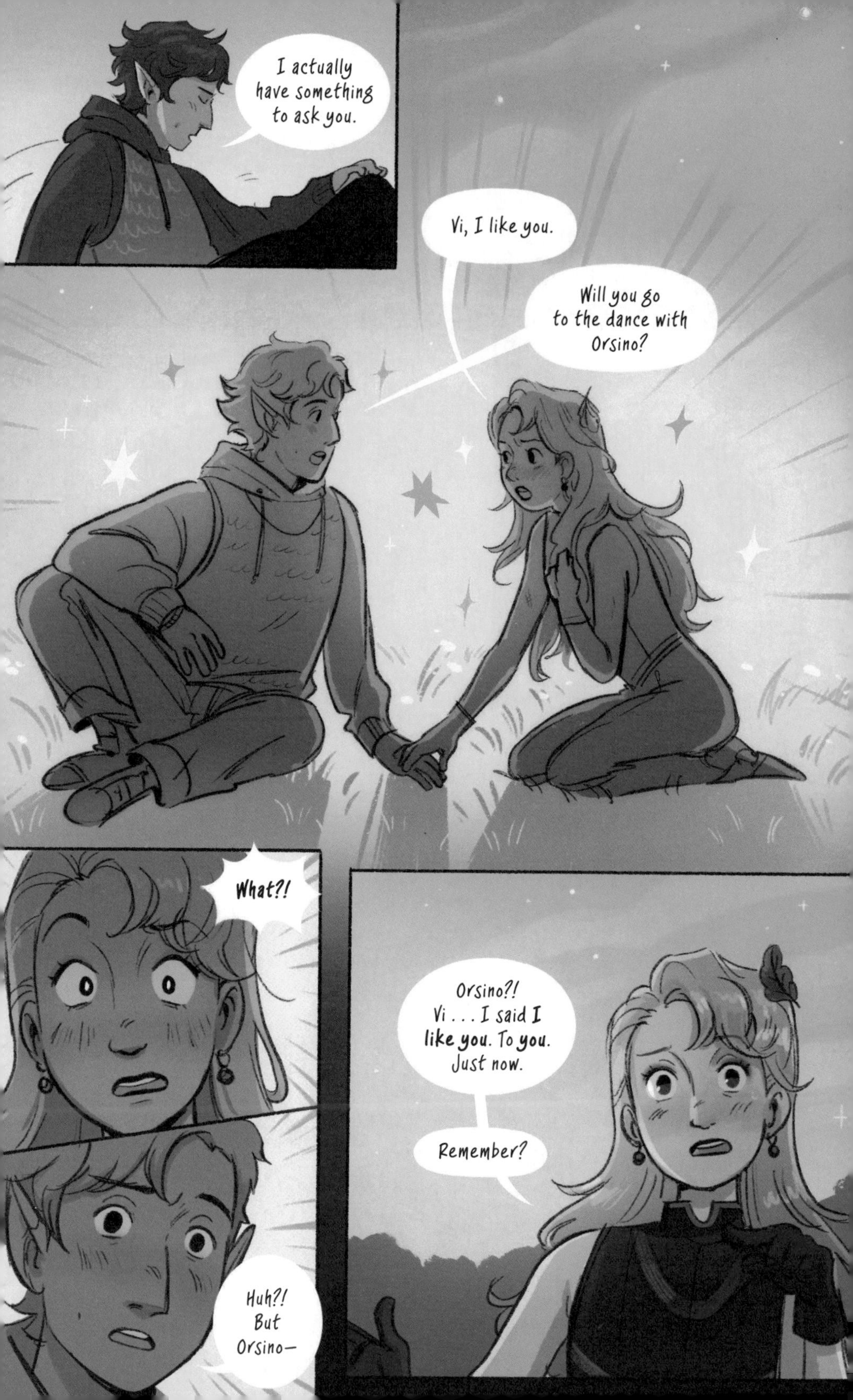
I actually have something to ask you.
Vi, I like you.
Will you go to the dance with Orsino?
What?!
Huh?! But Orsino—
Orsino?! Vi . . . I said **I like you**. To **you**. Just now.
Remember?

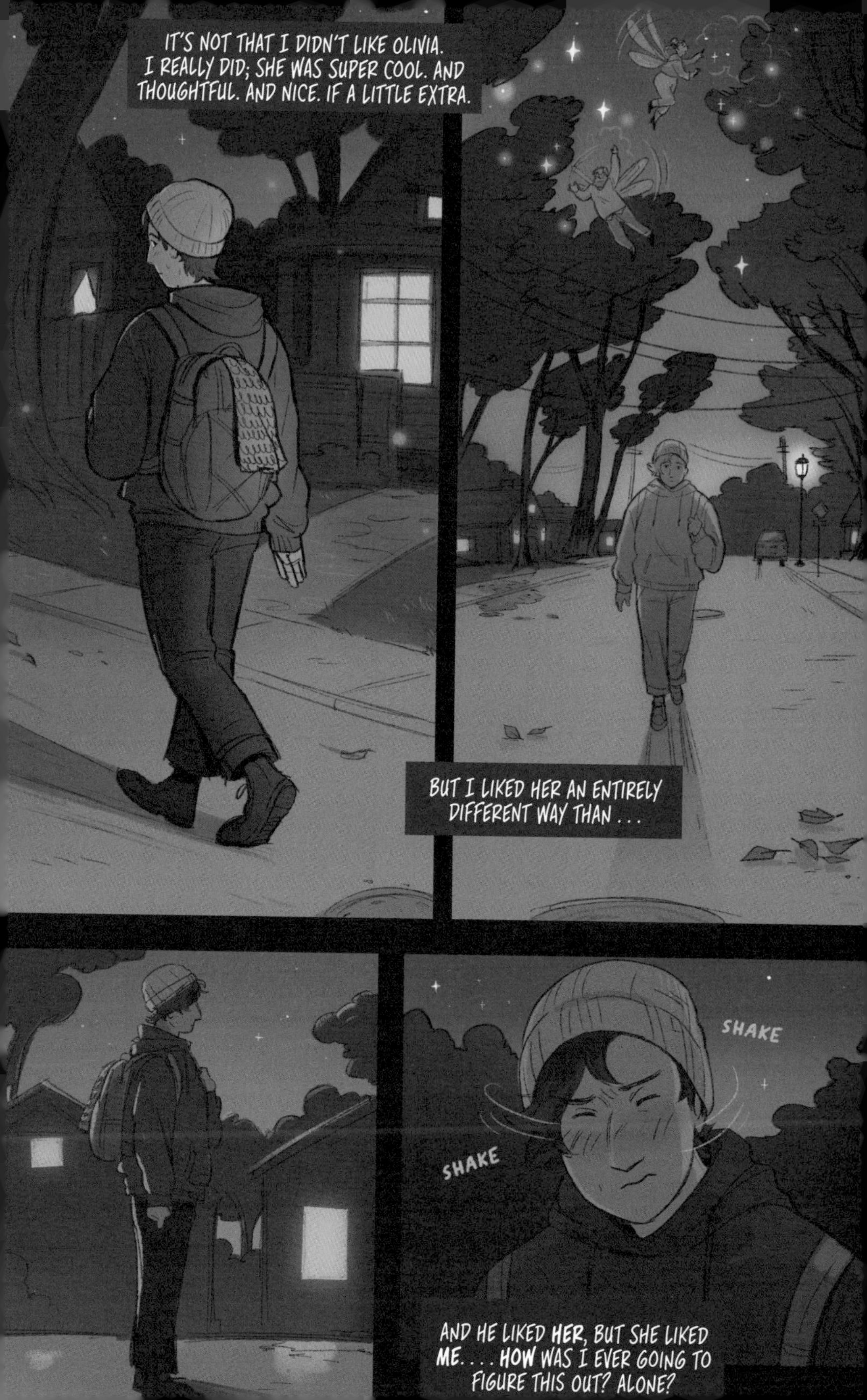
IT'S NOT THAT I DIDN'T LIKE OLIVIA. I REALLY DID; SHE WAS SUPER COOL. AND THOUGHTFUL. AND NICE. IF A LITTLE EXTRA.
BUT I LIKED HER AN ENTIRELY DIFFERENT WAY THAN . . .
SHAKE
SHAKE
AND HE LIKED **HER**, BUT SHE LIKED **ME**. . . . **HOW** WAS I EVER GOING TO FIGURE THIS OUT? ALONE?

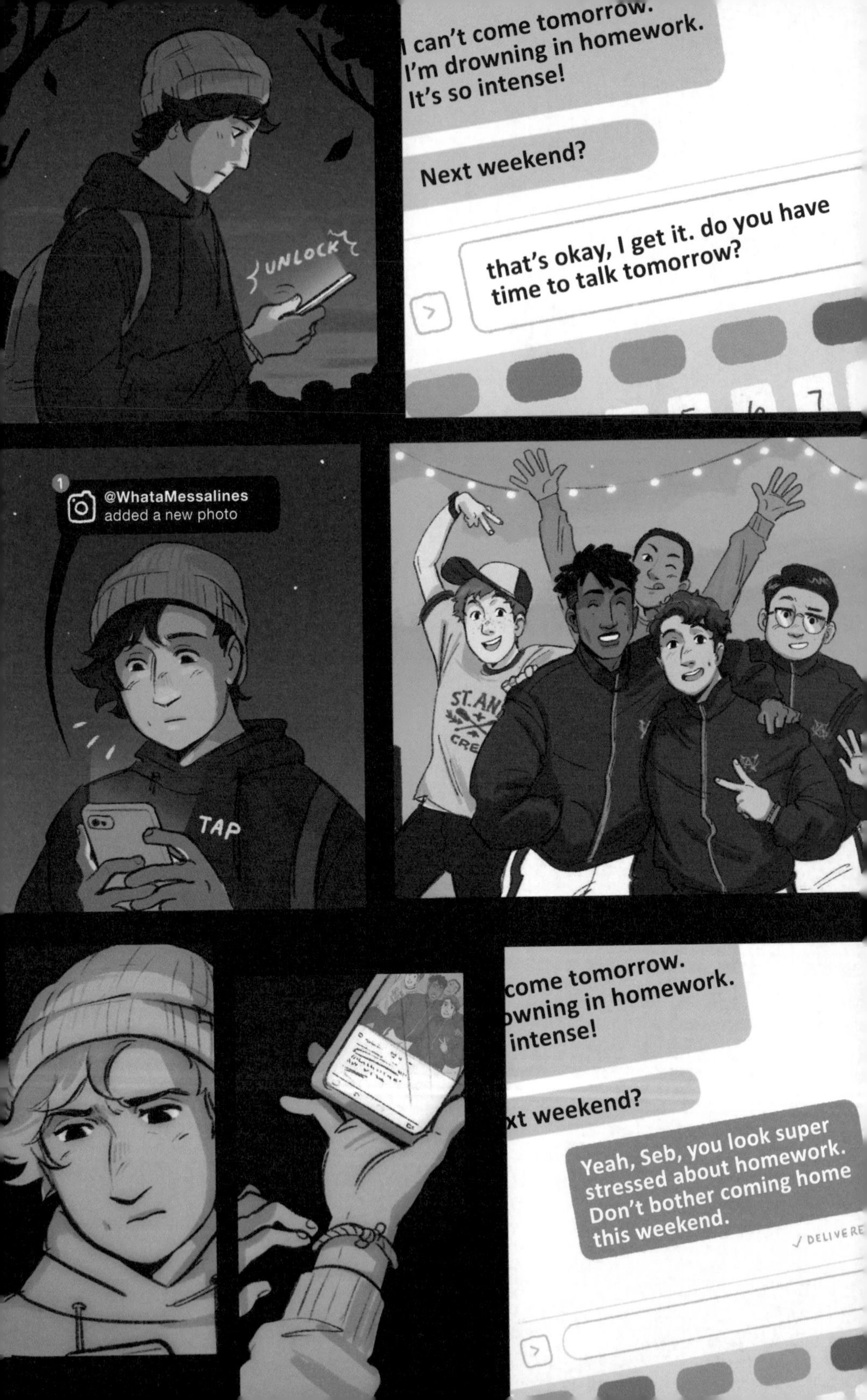

UNLOCK
I can't come tomorrow.
I'm drowning in homework.
It's so intense!
Next weekend?
that's okay, I get it. do you have time to talk tomorrow?
@WhataMessalines
added a new photo
TAP
ST. AN
CRE
come tomorrow.
wning in homework.
intense!
xt weekend?
Yeah, Seb, you look super stressed about homework. Don't bother coming home this weekend.
DELIVERE

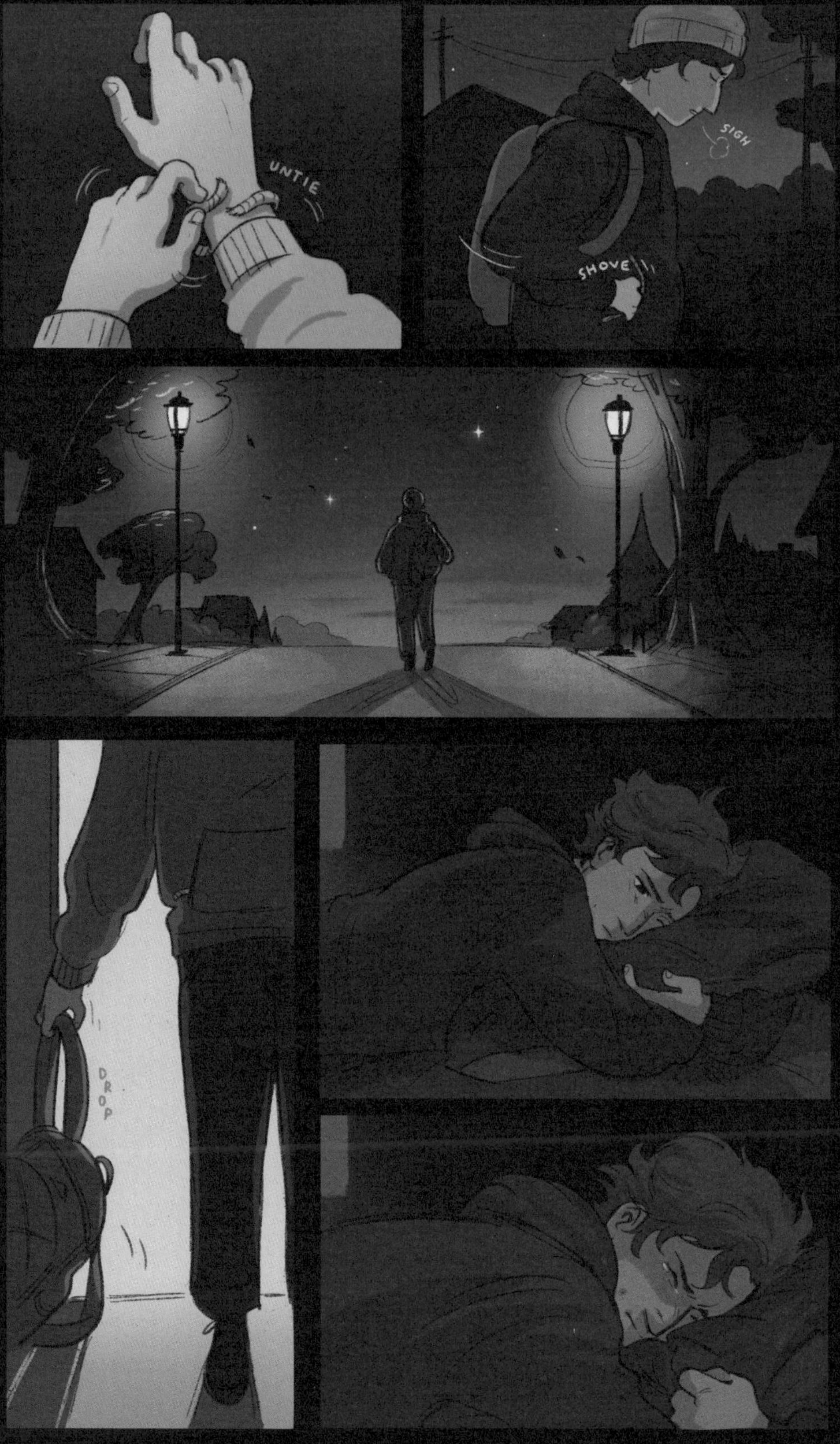
UNTIE
SIGH
SHOVE
DROP

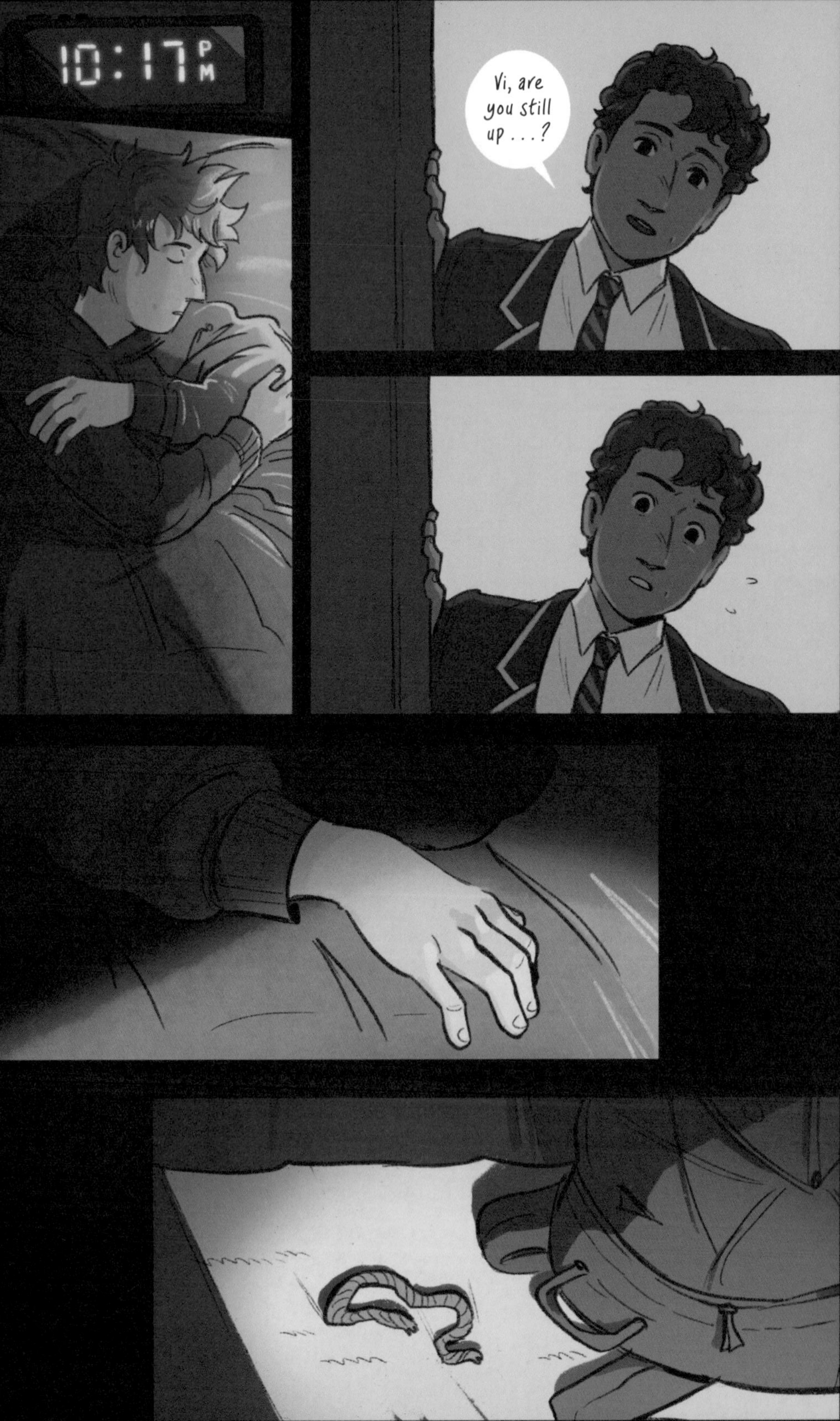
10:17 PM
Vi, are you still up . . . ?

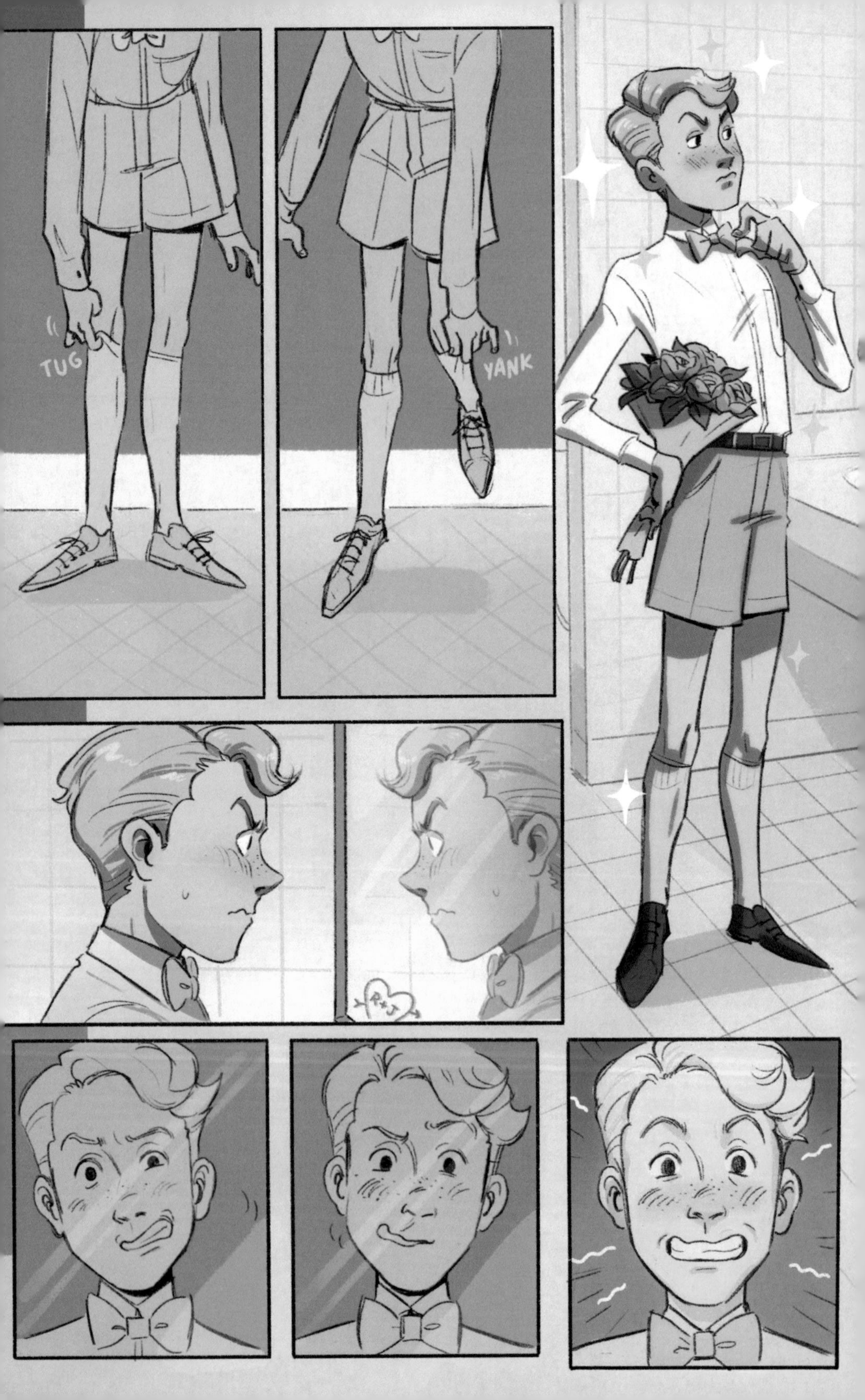
TUG
YANK
R+J

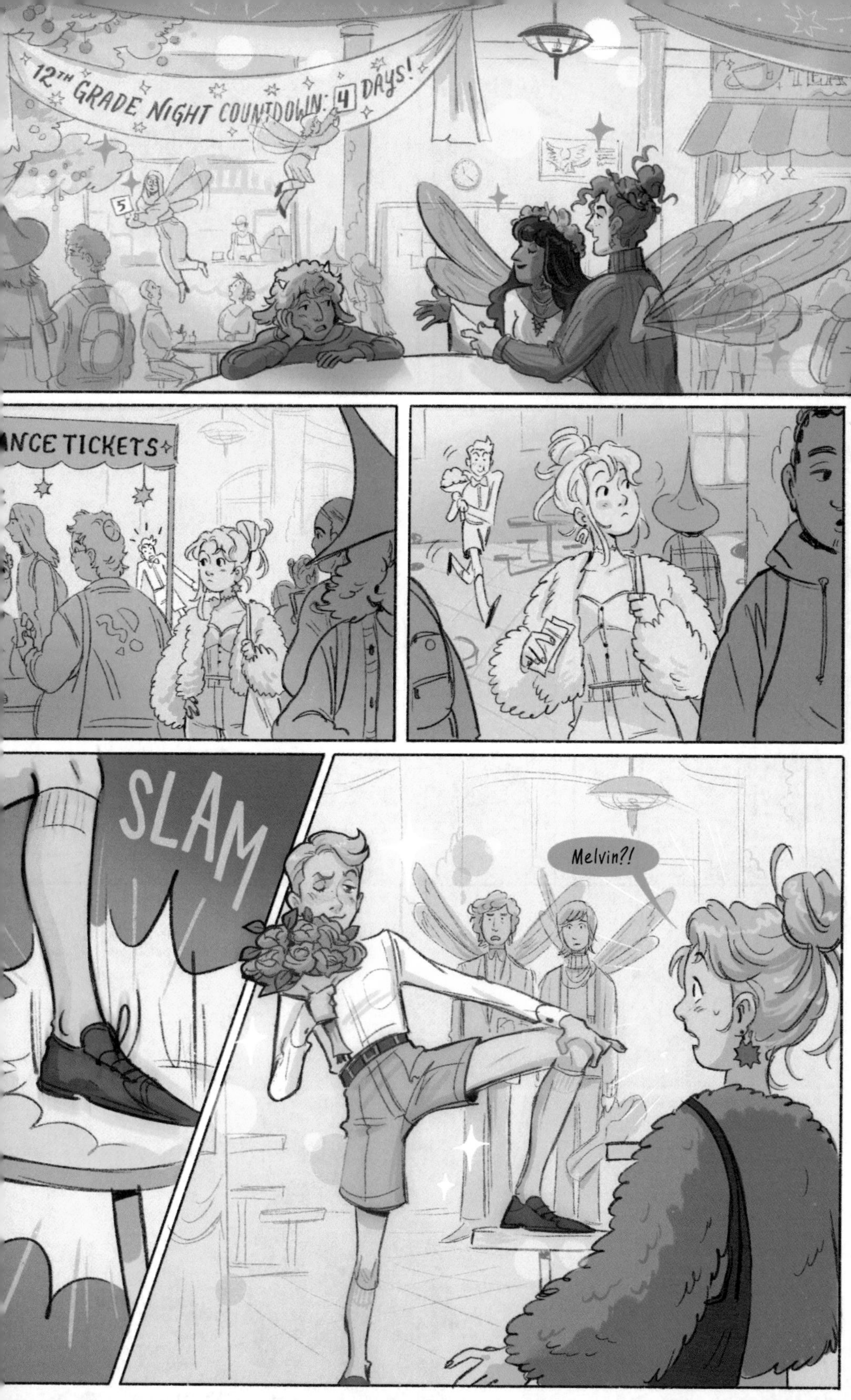
12TH GRADE NIGHT COUNTDOWN: 4 DAYS!
5
ANCE TICKETS
SLAM
Melvin?!

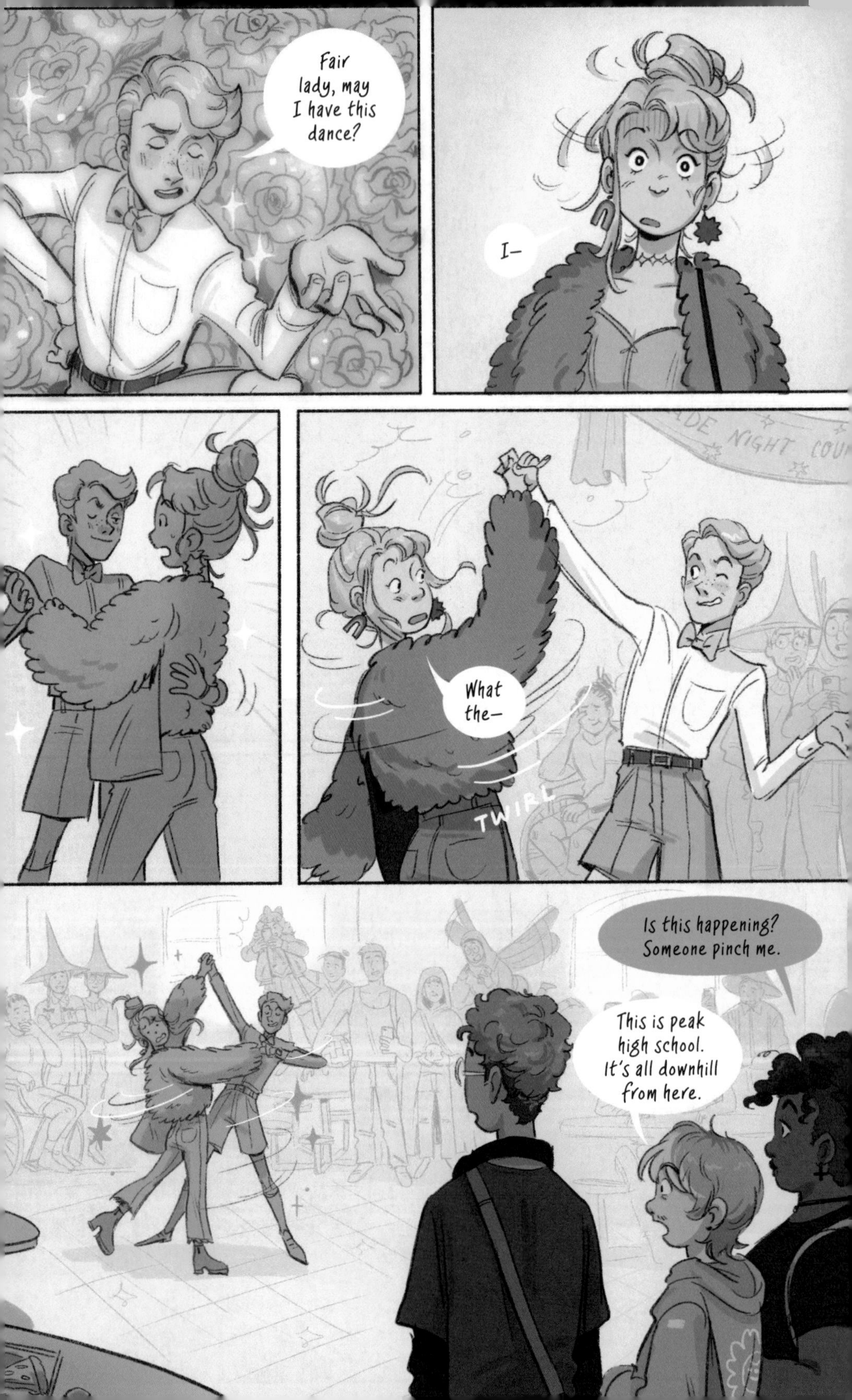
Fair lady, may I have this dance?
I–
What the–
TWIRL
Is this happening? Someone pinch me.
This is peak high school. It's all downhill from here.

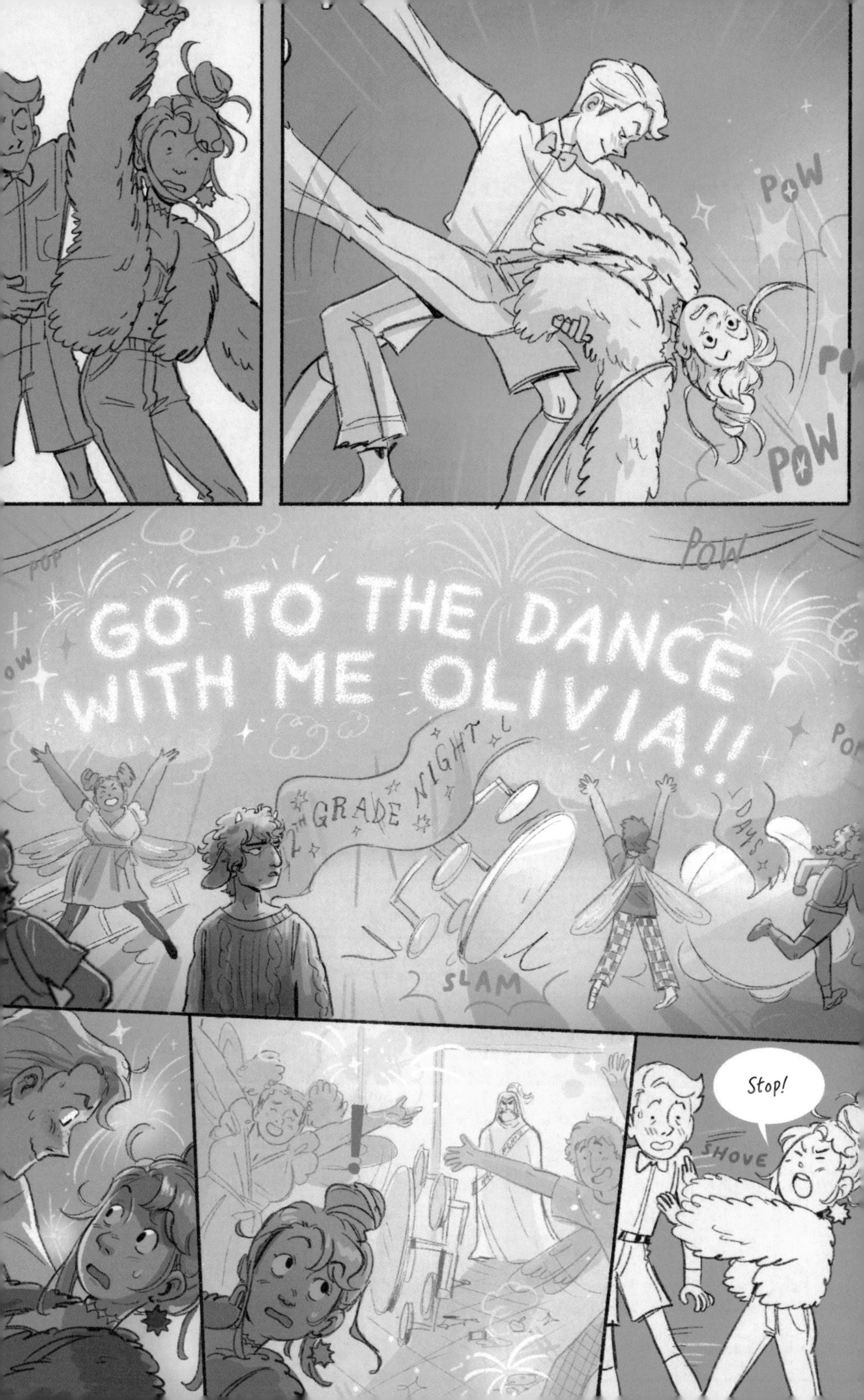
POW
POW
POP
POW
GO TO THE DANCE WITH ME OLIVIA!!
7th GRADE NIGHT
SLAM
!
SHOVE
Stop!

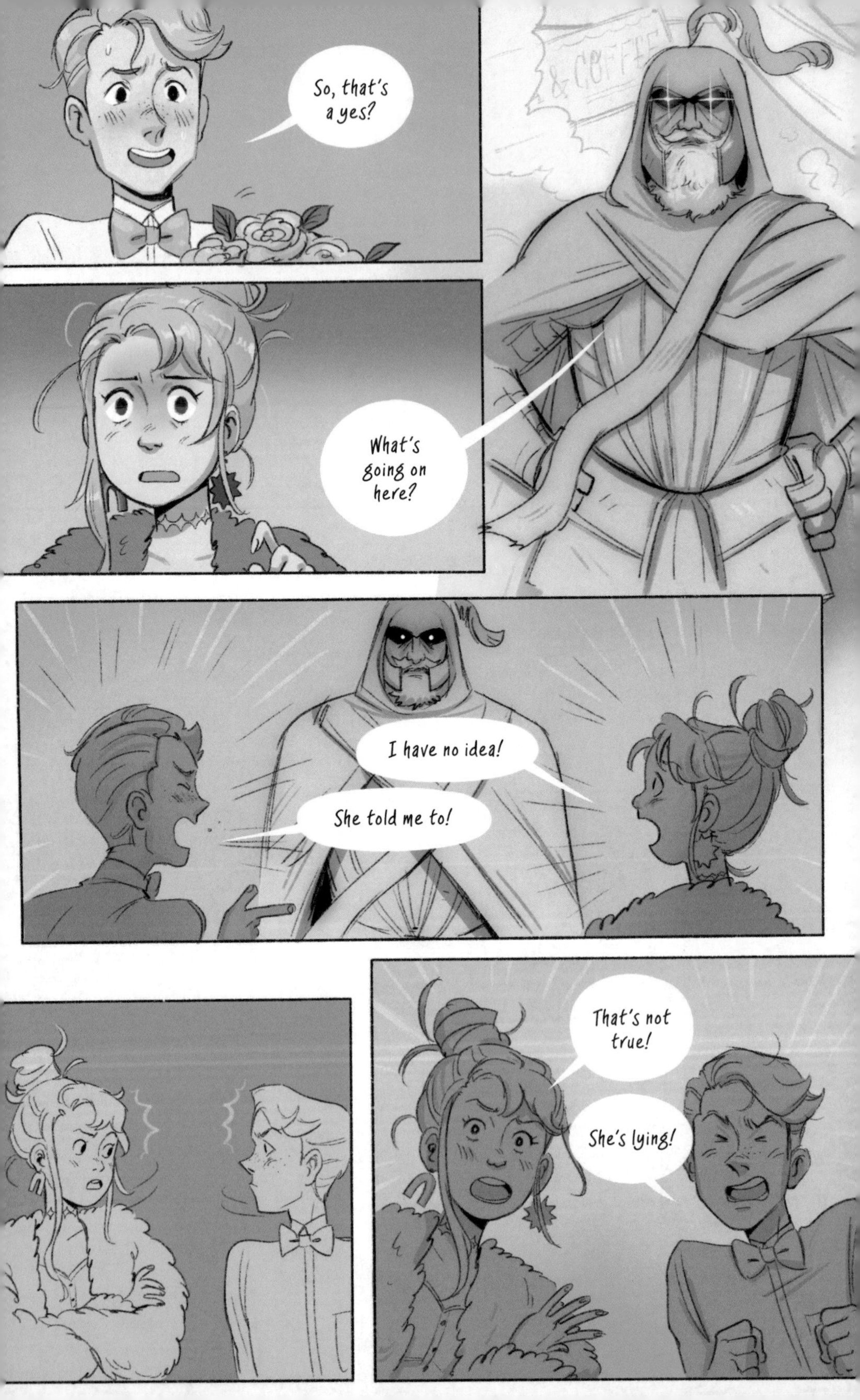

& COFFEE
So, that's a yes?
What's going on here?
I have no idea!
She told me to!
That's not true!
She's lying!

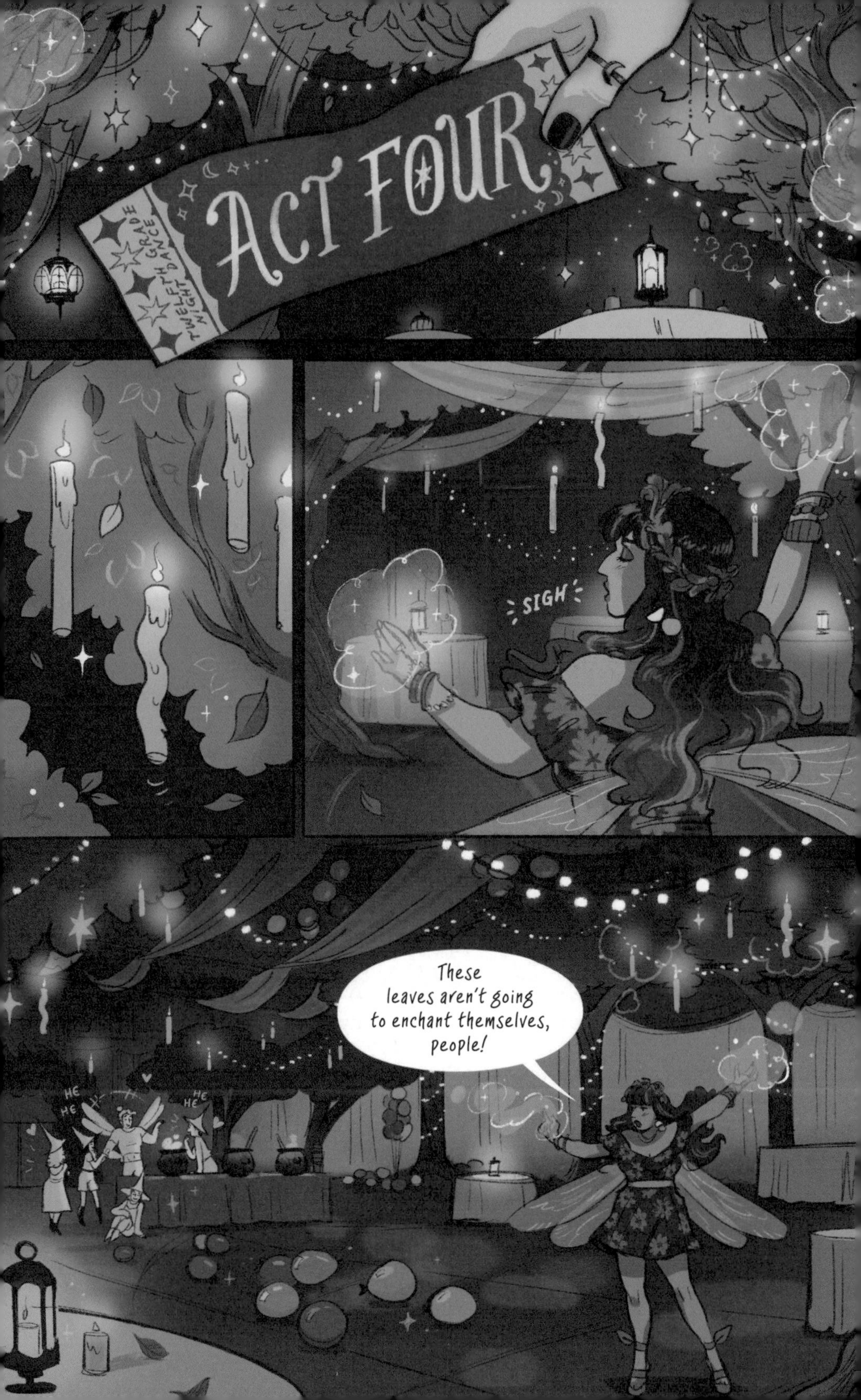
ACT FOUR
TWELFTH GRADE NIGHT DANCE
SIGH
These leaves aren't going to enchant themselves, people!
HE HE
HE HE

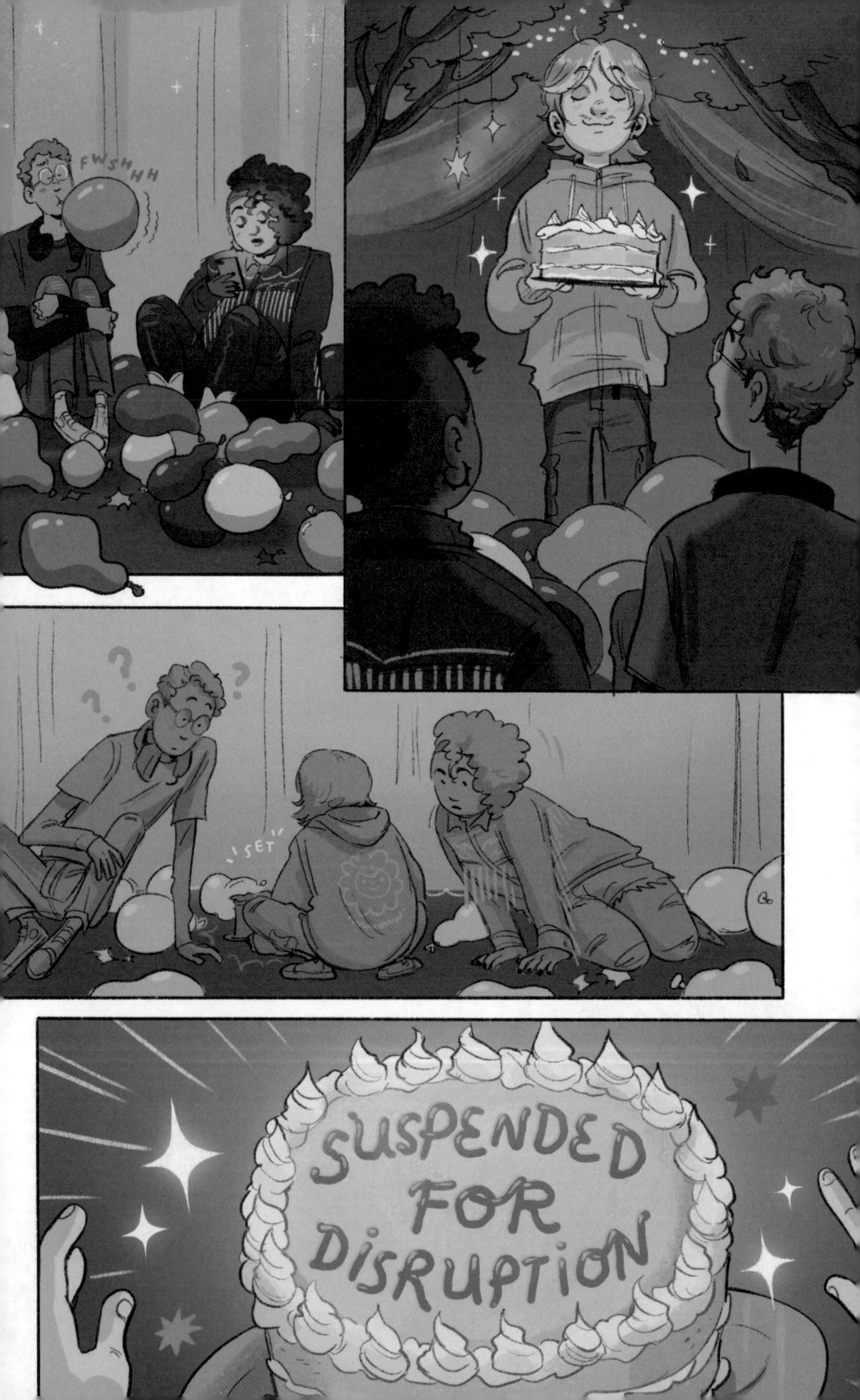
FWSHHH
SET
SUSPENDED FOR DISRUPTION

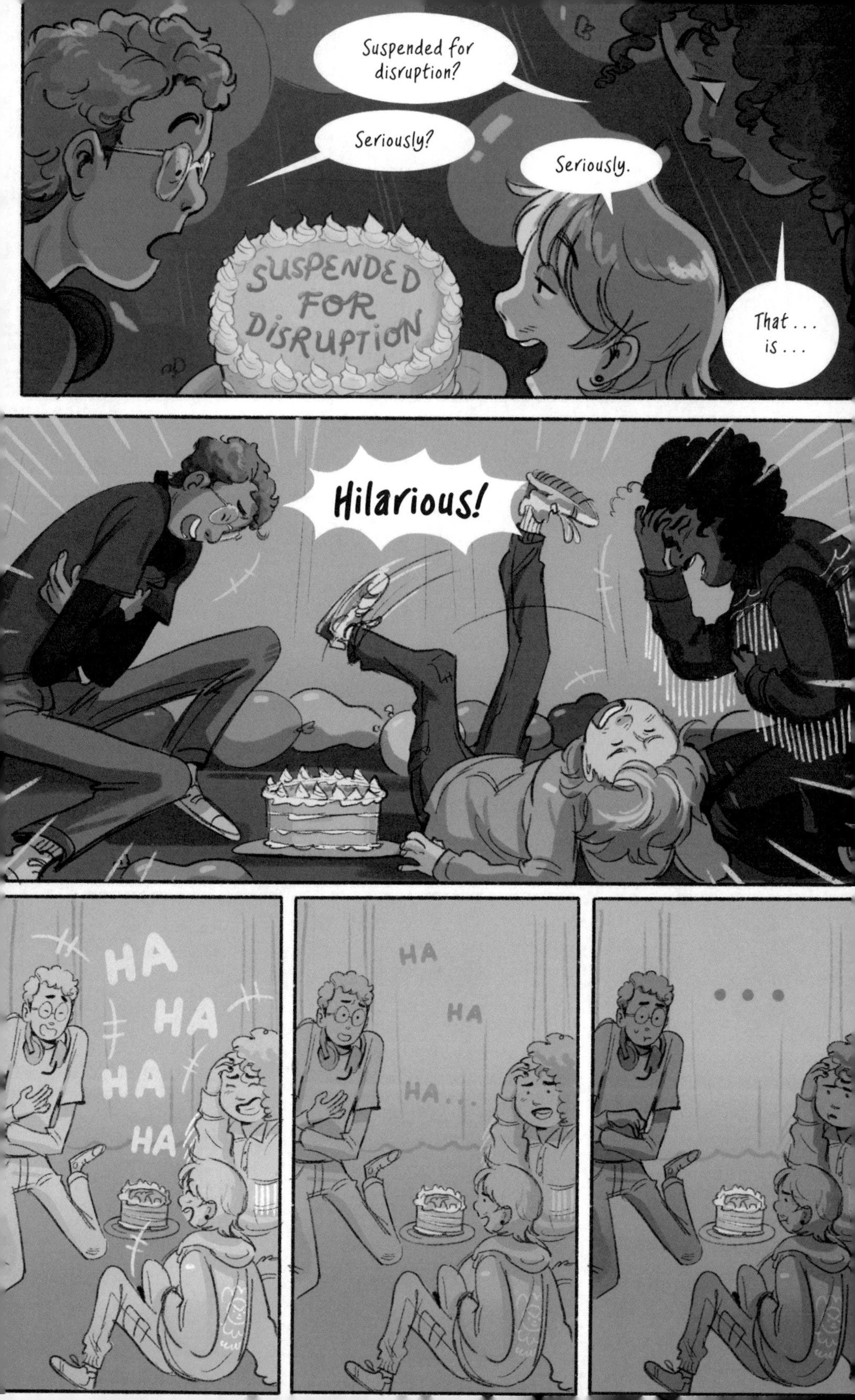
Suspended for disruption?
Seriously?
Seriously.
SUSPENDED FOR DISRUPTION
That . . . is . . .
Hilarious!
HA HA HA HA
HA HA HA . . .
. . .

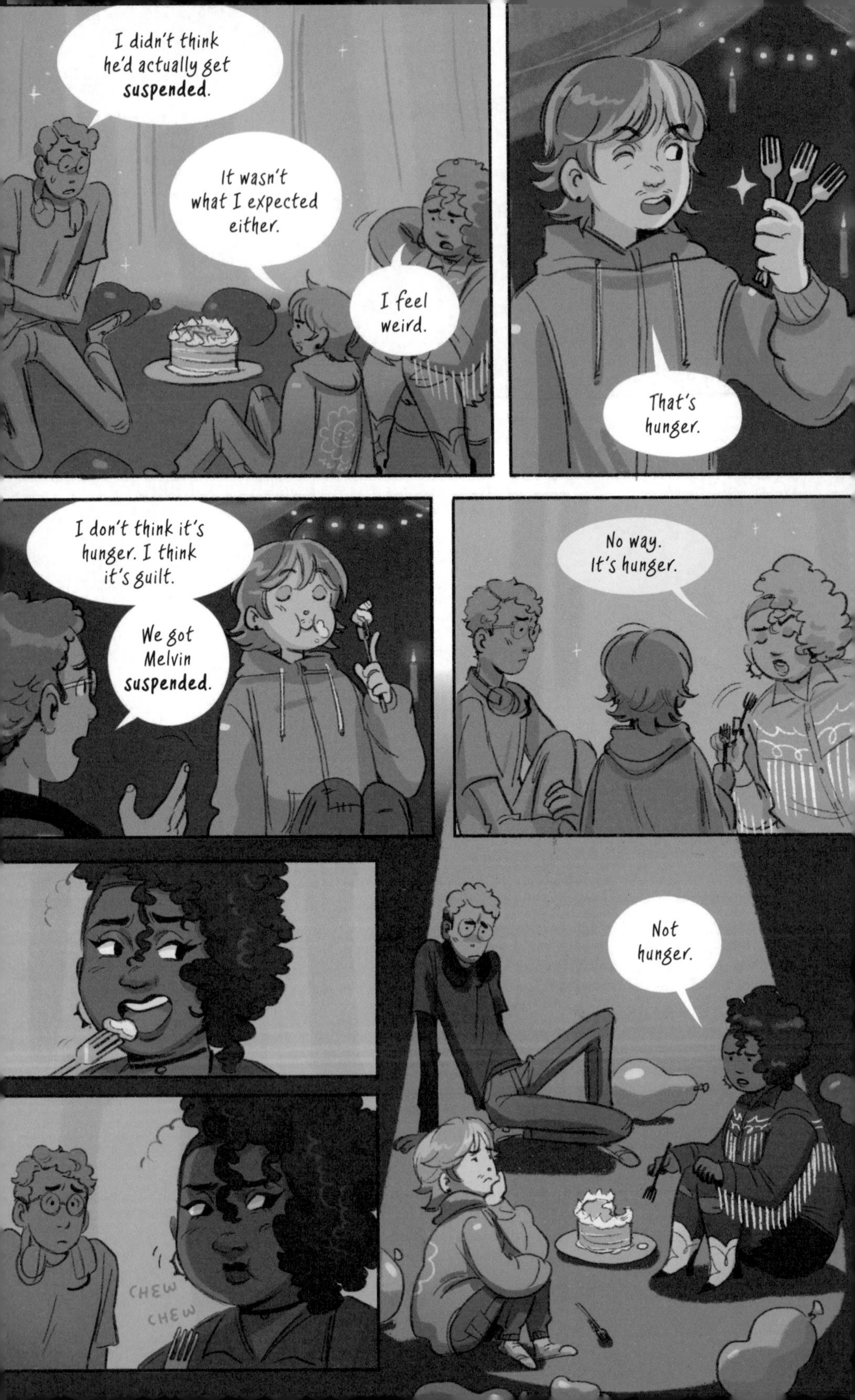
I didn't think he'd actually get **suspended**.
It wasn't what I expected either.
I feel weird.
That's hunger.
I don't think it's hunger. I think it's guilt.
We got Melvin **suspended**.
No way. It's hunger.
CHEW CHEW
Not hunger.

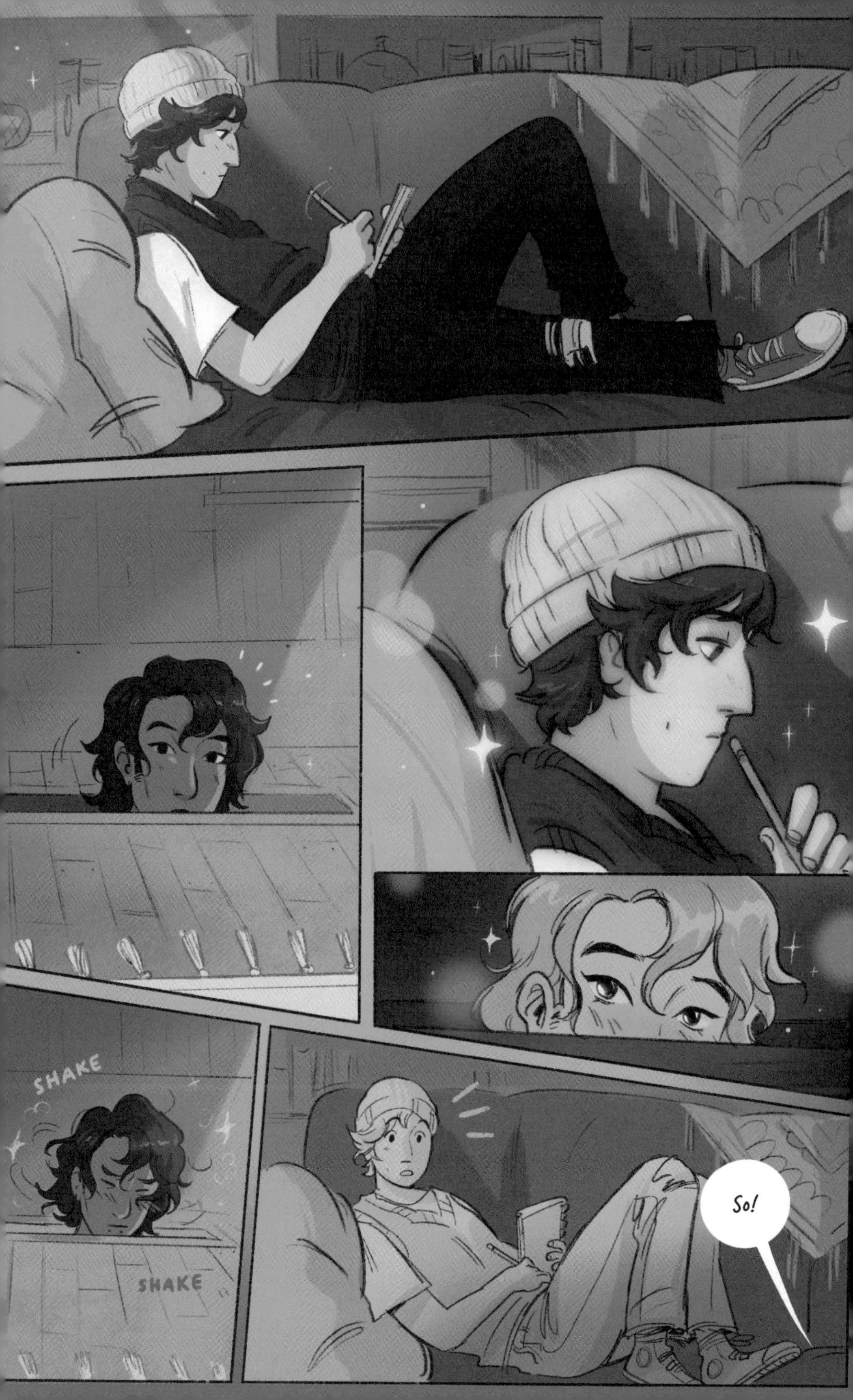
SHAKE
SHAKE
So!

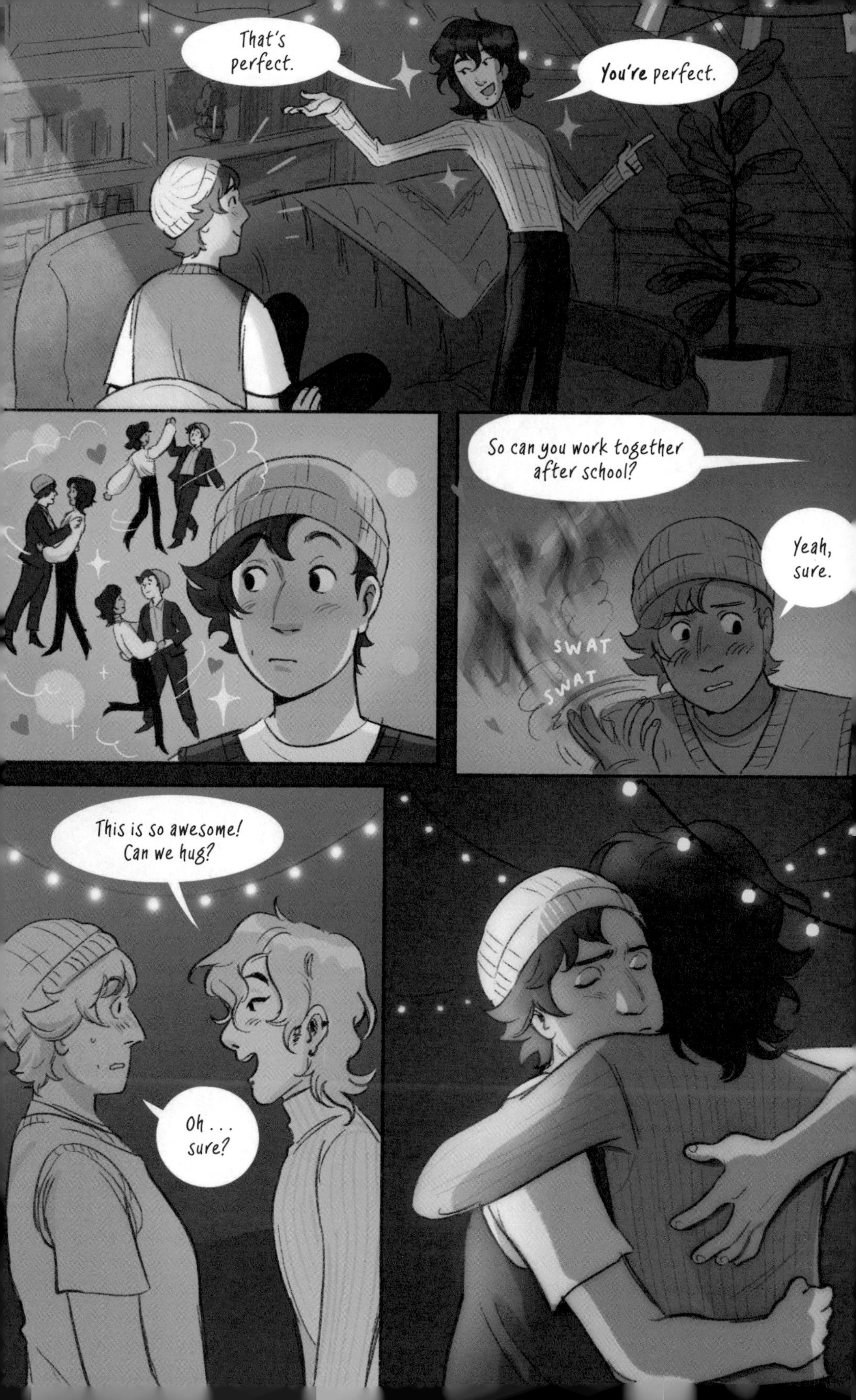
That's perfect.
You're perfect.
So can you work together after school?
SWAT
SWAT
Yeah, sure.
This is so awesome! Can we hug?
Oh . . . sure?

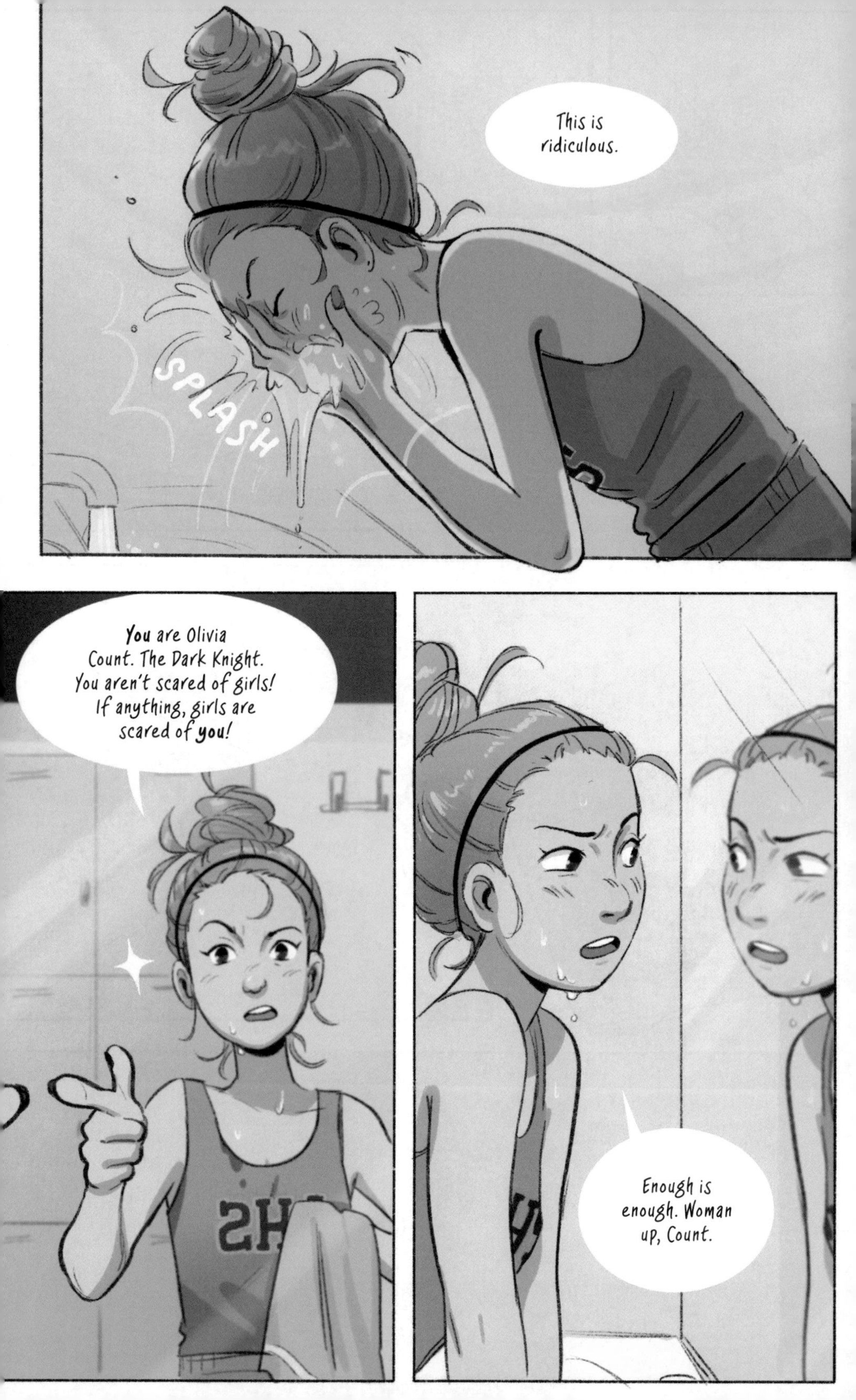
This is ridiculous.
SPLASH
You are Olivia Count. The Dark Knight. You aren't scared of girls! If anything, girls are scared of you!
SHS
Enough is enough. Woman up, Count.

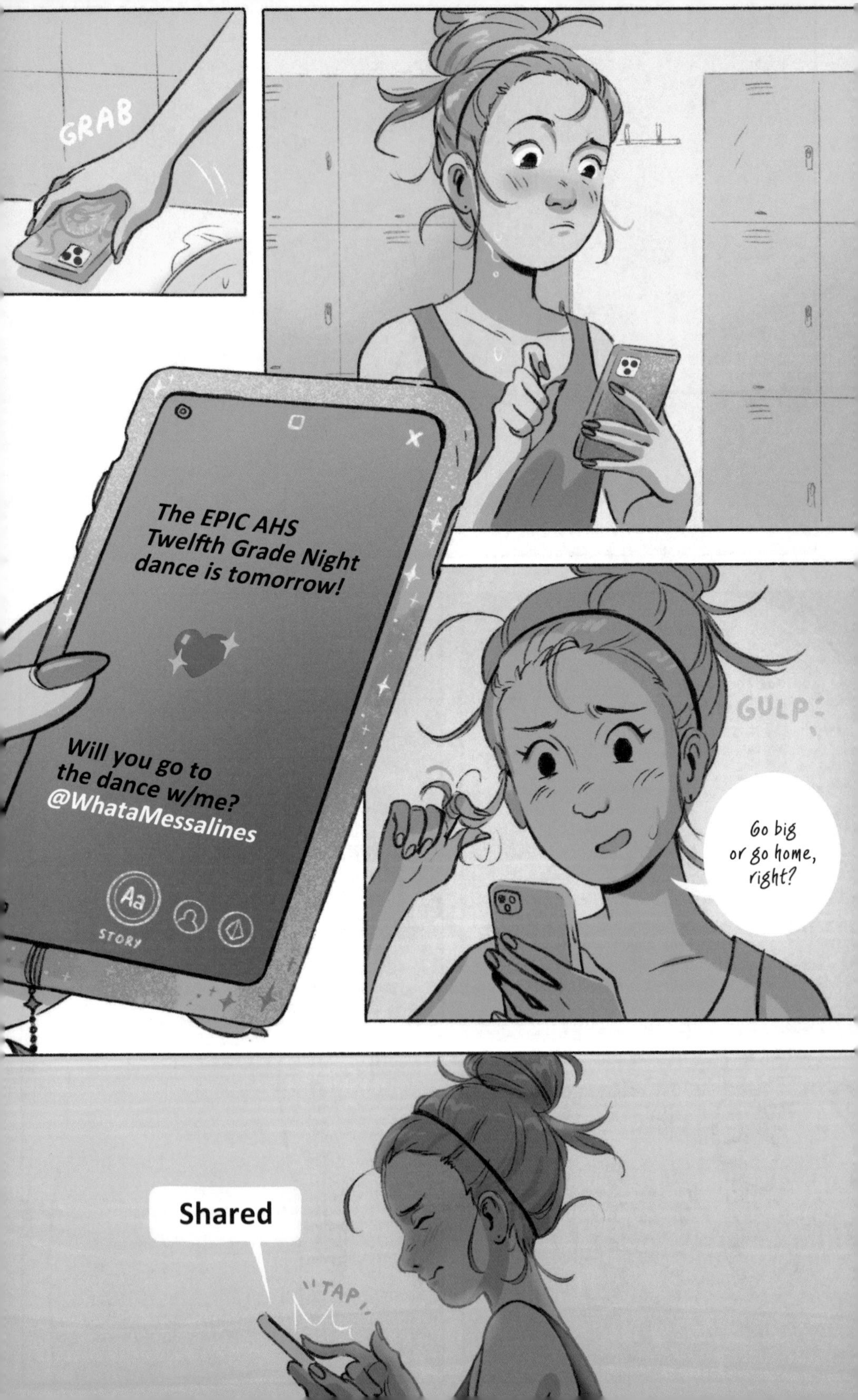
GRAB
The EPIC AHS Twelfth Grade Night dance is tomorrow!
Will you go to the dance w/me? @WhataMessalines
Aa
STORY
GULP
Go big or go home, right?
Shared
TAP

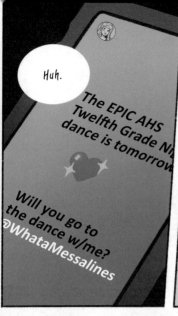

Huh.

The EPIC AHS Twelfth Grade Night dance is tomorrow

Will you go to the dance w/me? @WhataMessalines

@CountTakesQueen

Olivia Count

she/her

FOLLOW

MESSA

Wow.

Why yes, ridiculously hot stranger, I will go to the AHS Twelfth Grade Night dance with you.

Our first high school dance . . . There are some things we should do together.

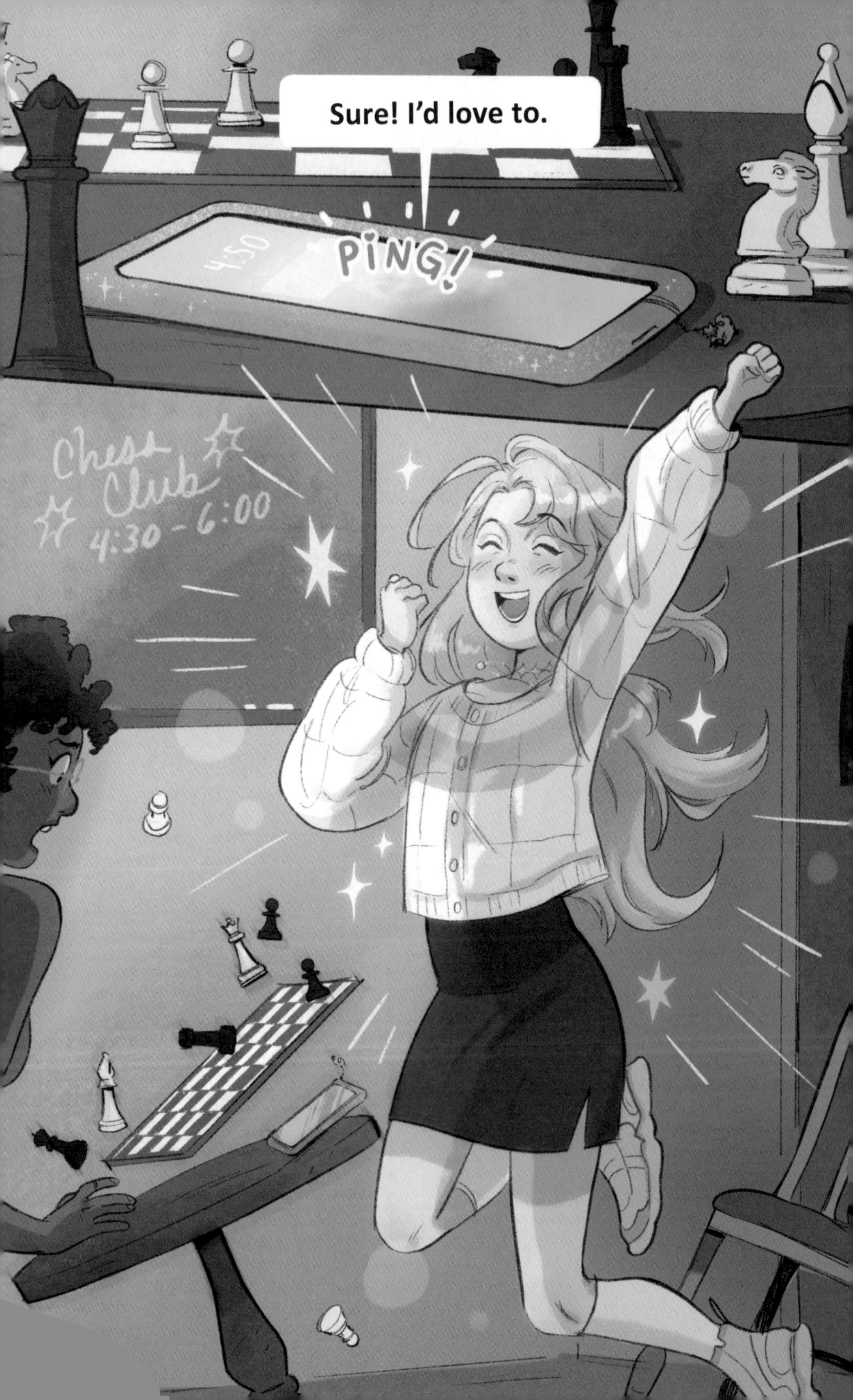
Sure! I'd love to.
4:50
PING!
Chess Club
4:30-6:00

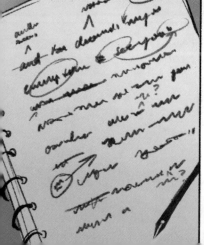

We've been working so long my phone died. I have no idea what time it is!

Me neither, but I never know at this school.

I haven't written something like this—something that I love—in so long. This just perfectly captures how I feel . . .

about Olivia.

She has to love it, right? Like, this is objectively really good.

What?

Yeah. It's pretty good.

Yeah. I'm sure she'll like it.

Yeah.

NUDGE

I'm so glad we met, Vi, and that we're writing partners. Maybe this is cheesy to say, but it feels like we get each other. Like you know how I feel.

Right, well, it's just writing.

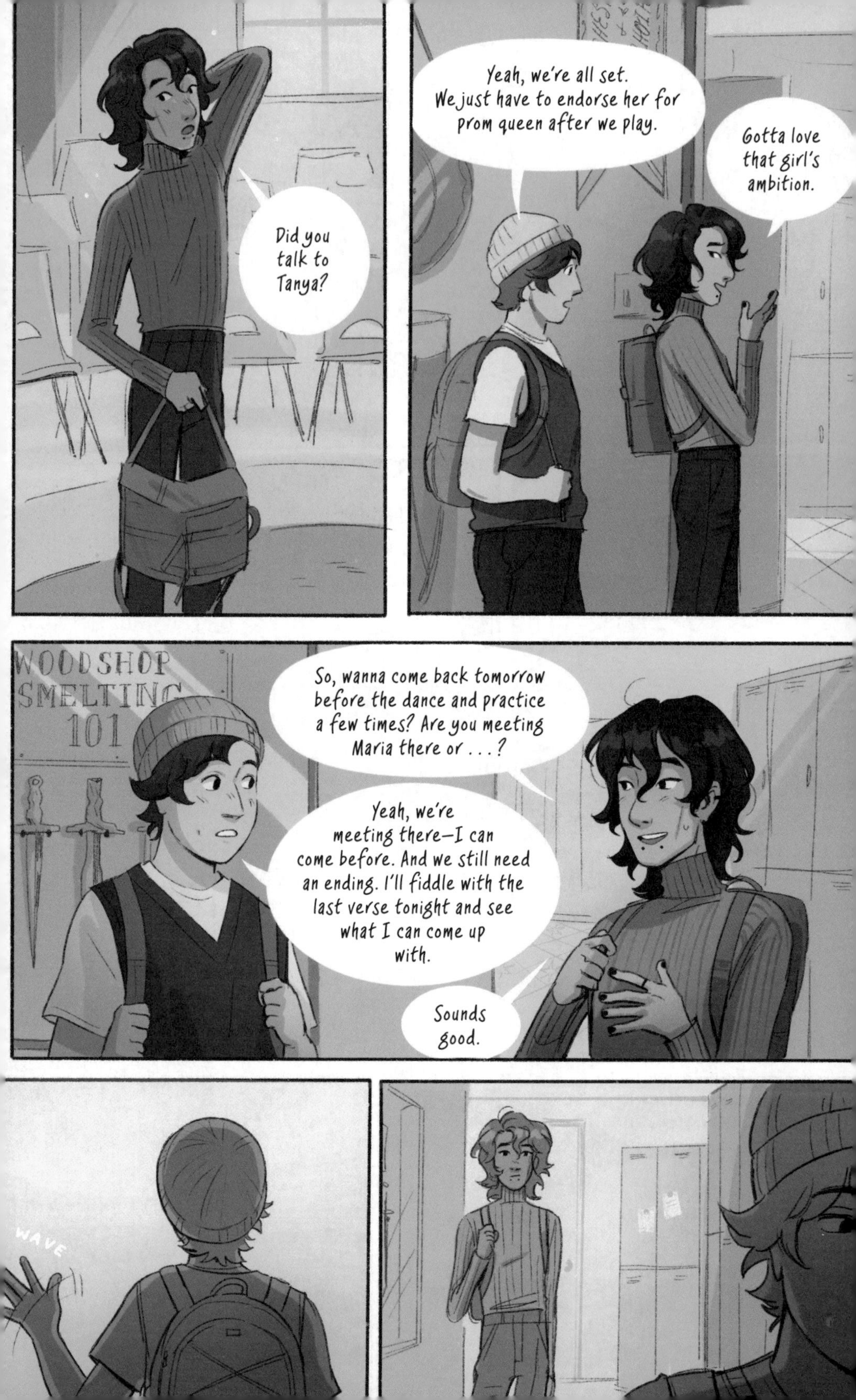
Did you talk to Tanya?
Yeah, we're all set. We just have to endorse her for prom queen after we play.
Gotta love that girl's ambition.
WOODSHOP SMELTING 101
So, wanna come back tomorrow before the dance and practice a few times? Are you meeting Maria there or . . . ?
Yeah, we're meeting there—I can come before. And we still need an ending. I'll fiddle with the last verse tonight and see what I can come up with.
Sounds good.
WAVE

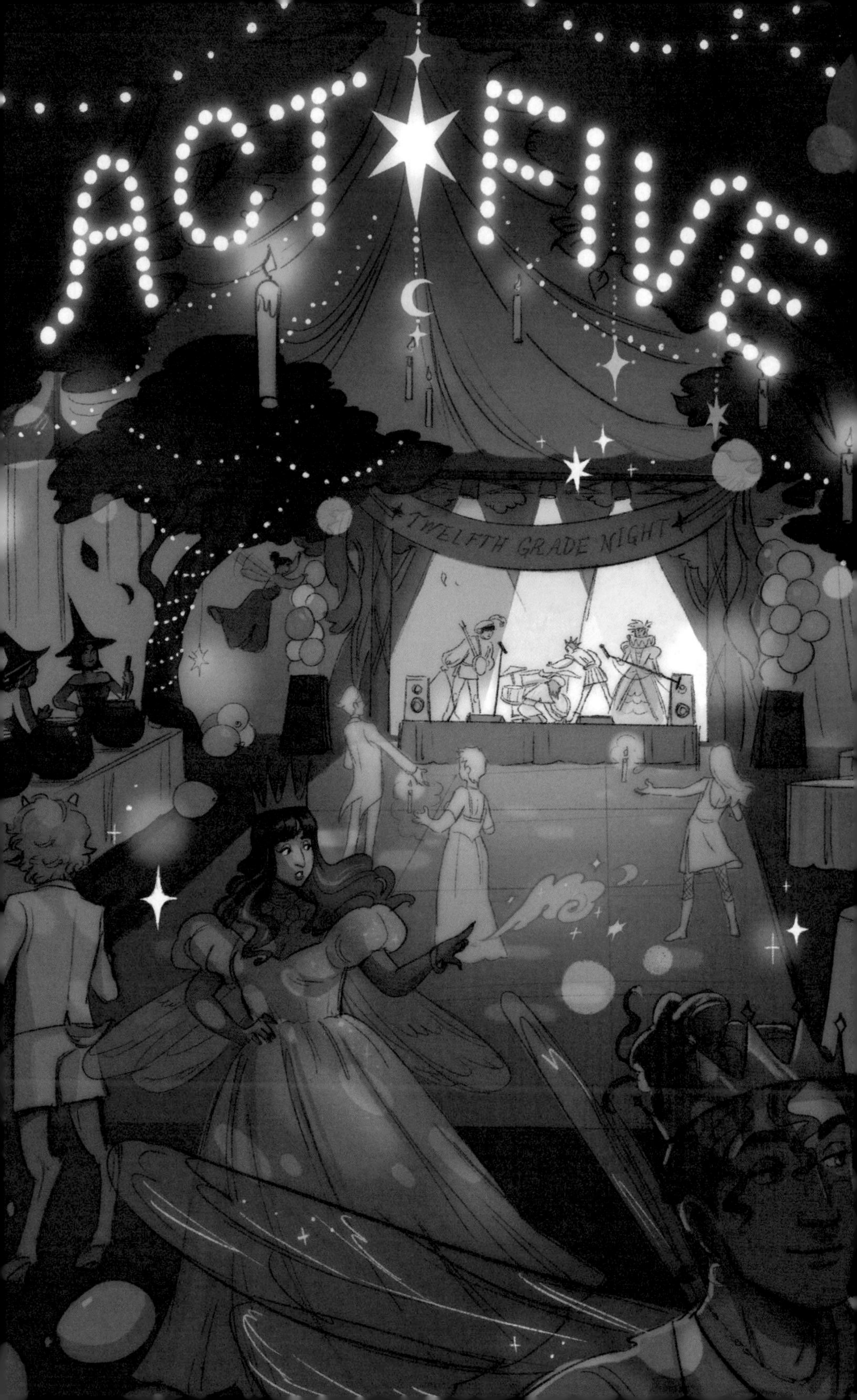
ACT FIVE
TWELFTH GRADE NIGHT

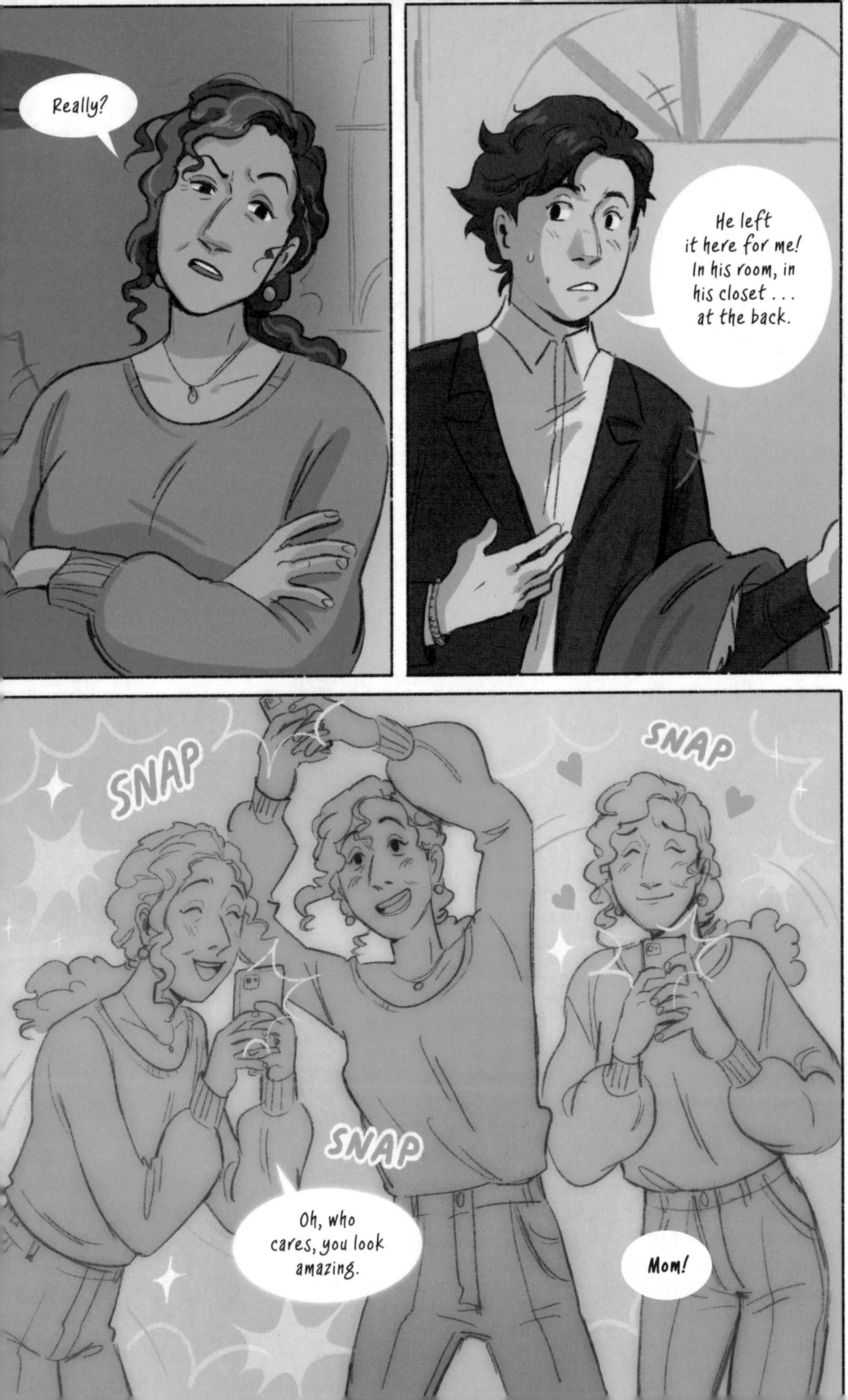
Really?
He left it here for me! In his room, in his closet . . . at the back.
SNAP
SNAP
SNAP
Oh, who cares, you look amazing.
Mom!

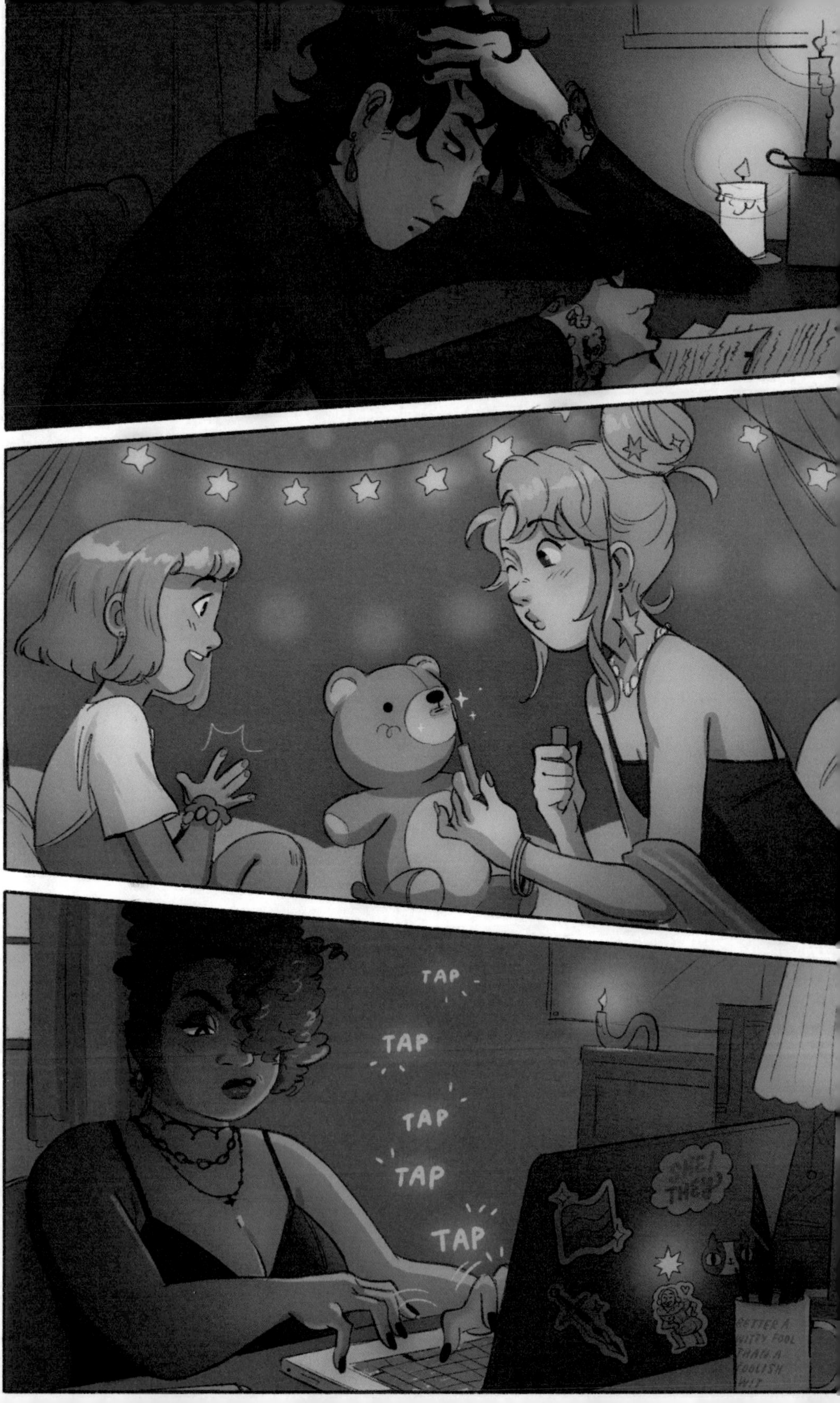
TAP
TAP
TAP
TAP
TAP
SHE/ THEY
BETTER A WITTY FOOL THAN A FOOLISH WIT

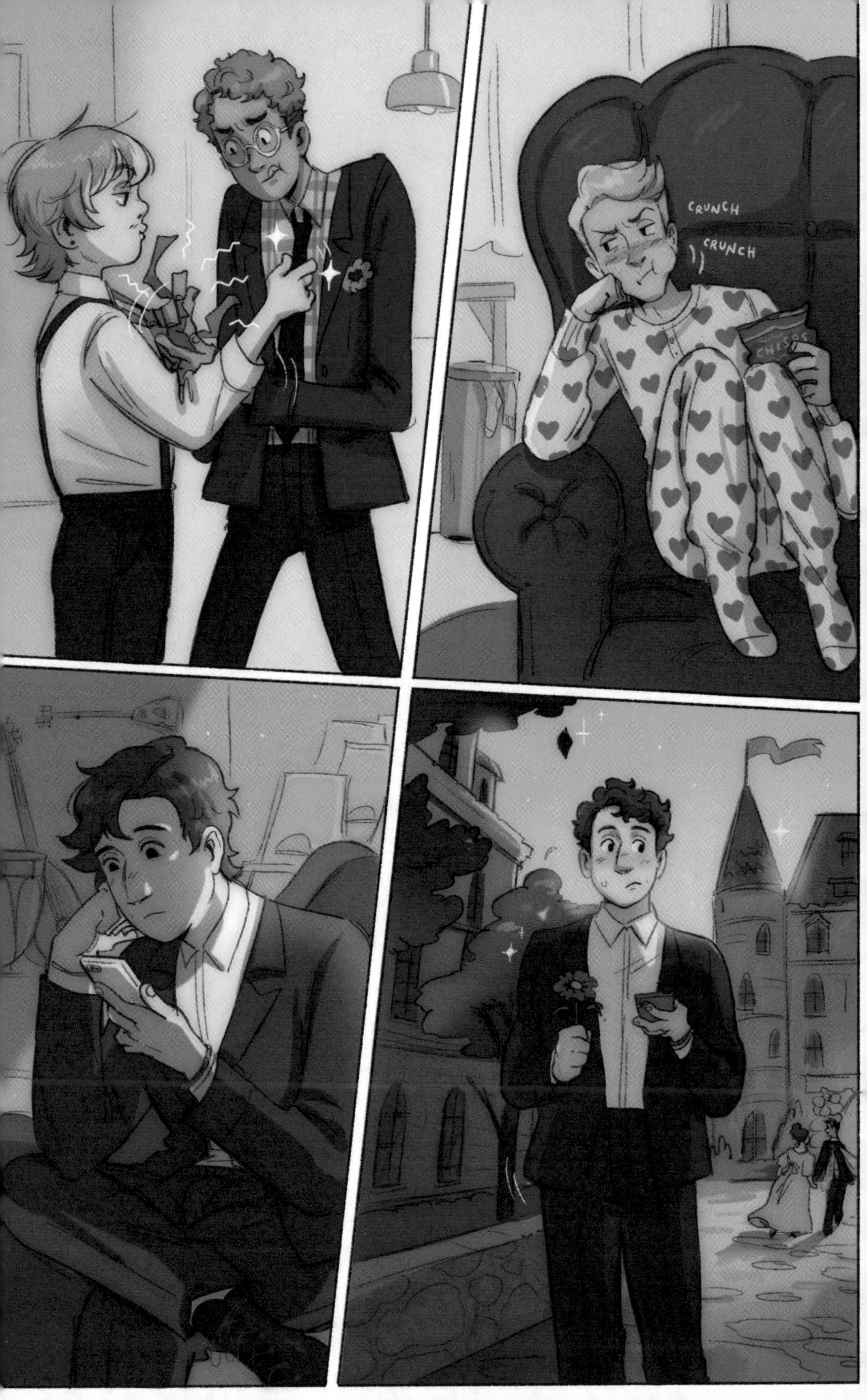
CRUNCH
CRUNCH
CHIPS

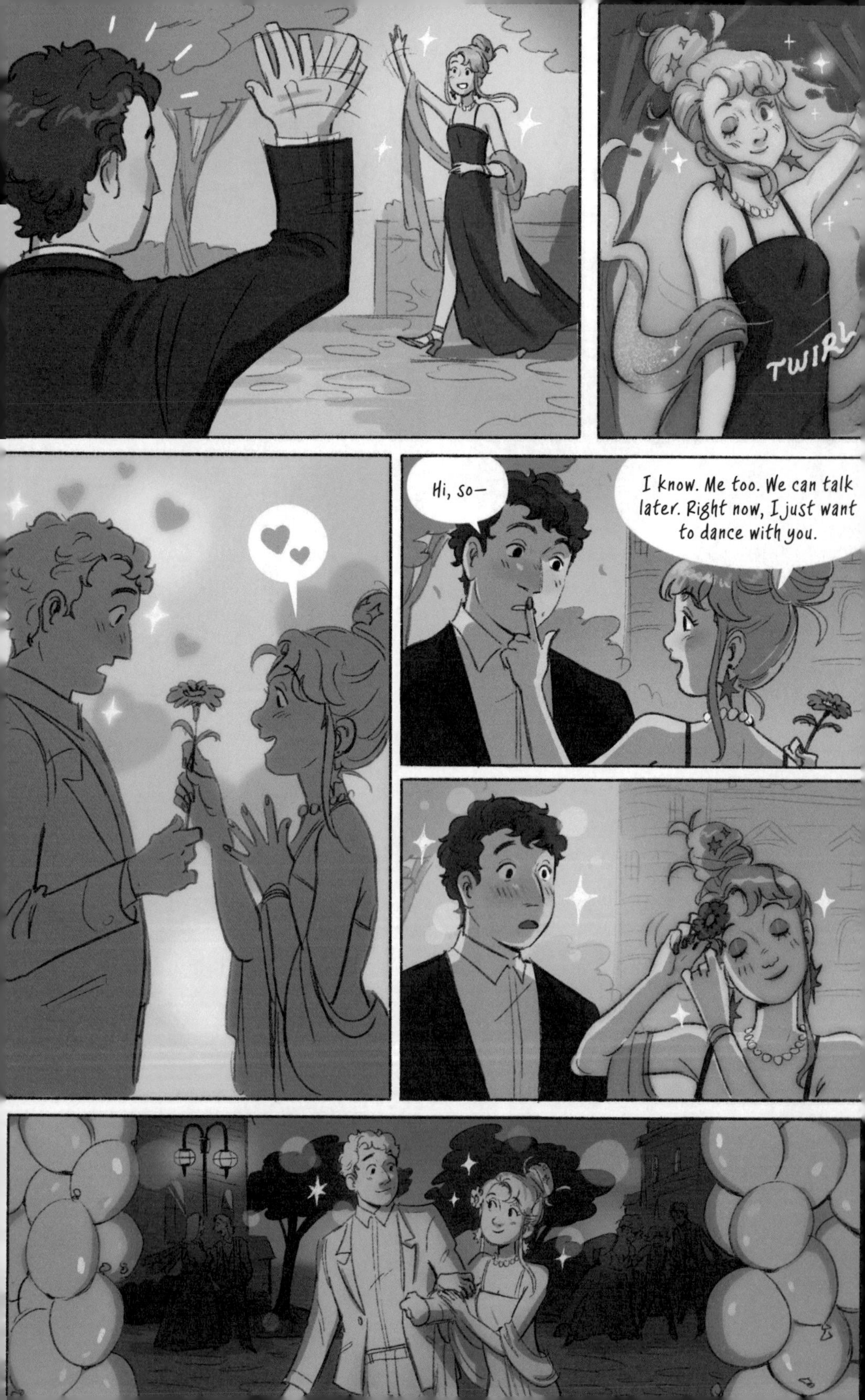
TWIRL
Hi, so—
I know. Me too. We can talk later. Right now, I just want to dance with you.

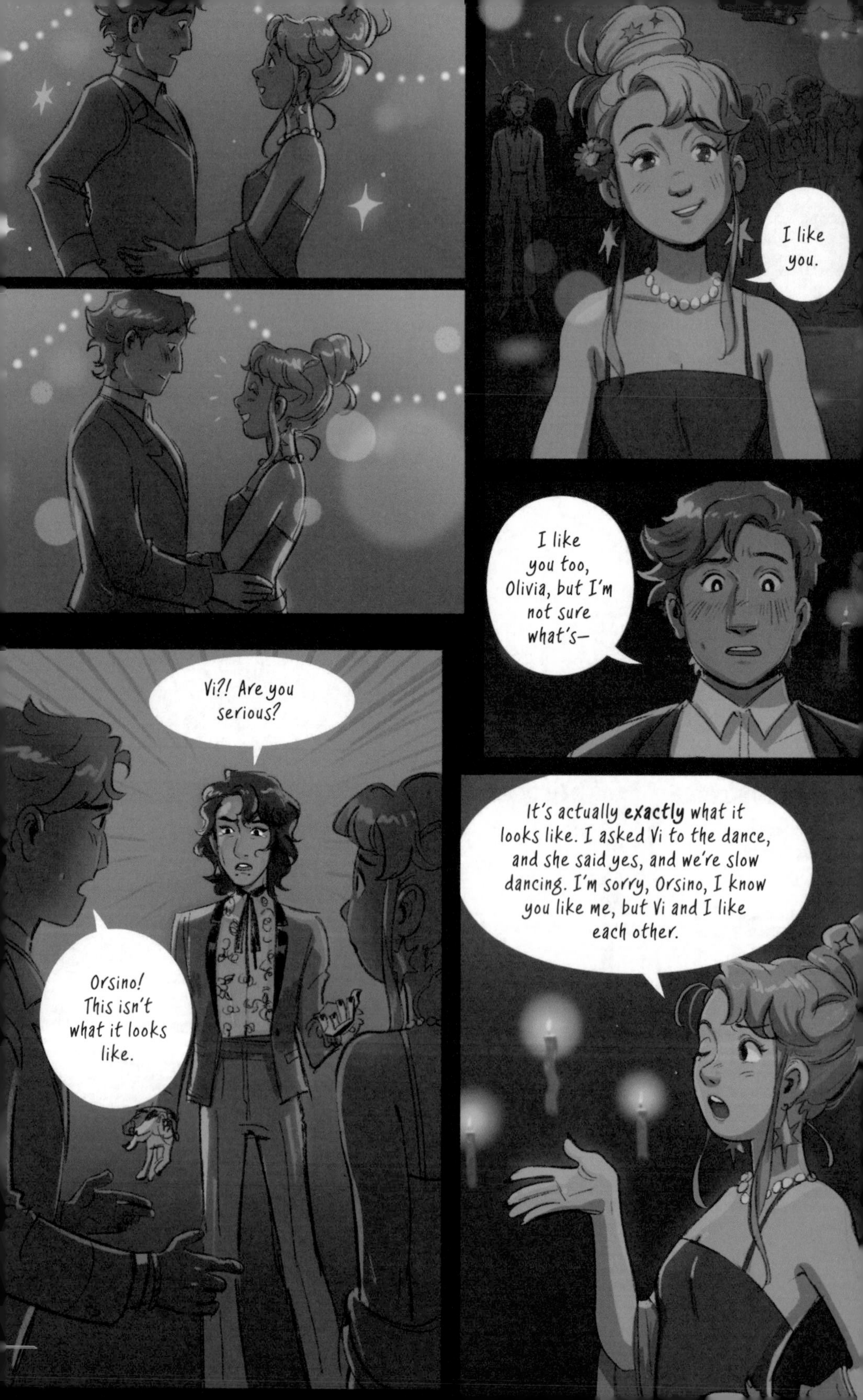
I like you.
I like you too, Olivia, but I'm not sure what's—
Orsino! This isn't what it looks like.
Vi?! Are you serious?
It's actually **exactly** what it looks like. I asked Vi to the dance, and she said yes, and we're slow dancing. I'm sorry, Orsino, I know you like me, but Vi and I like each other.

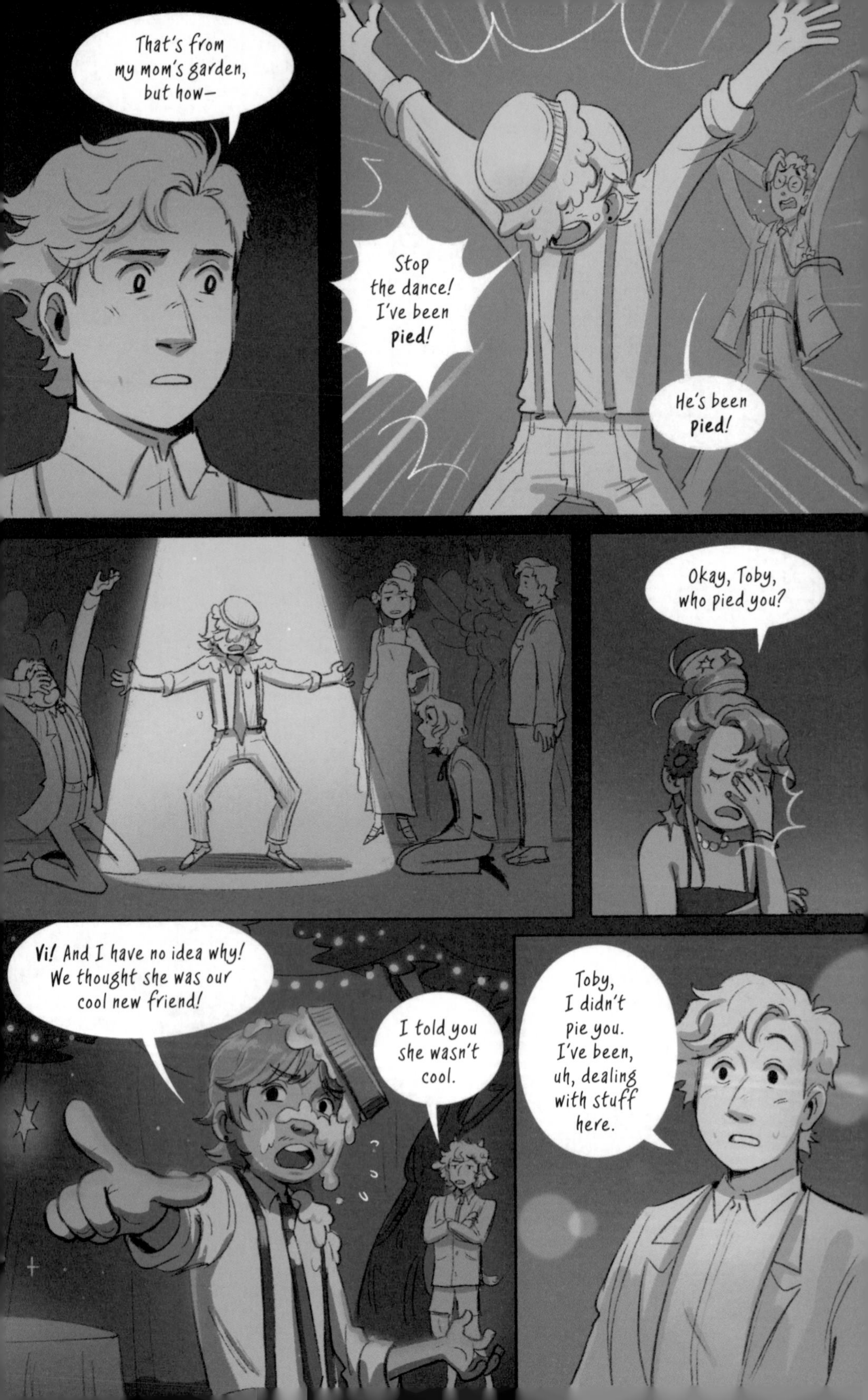
That's from my mom's garden, but how—
Stop the dance! I've been **pied**!
He's been **pied**!
Okay, Toby, who pied you?
Vi! And I have no idea why! We thought she was our cool new friend!
I told you she wasn't cool.
Toby, I didn't pie you. I've been, uh, dealing with stuff here.

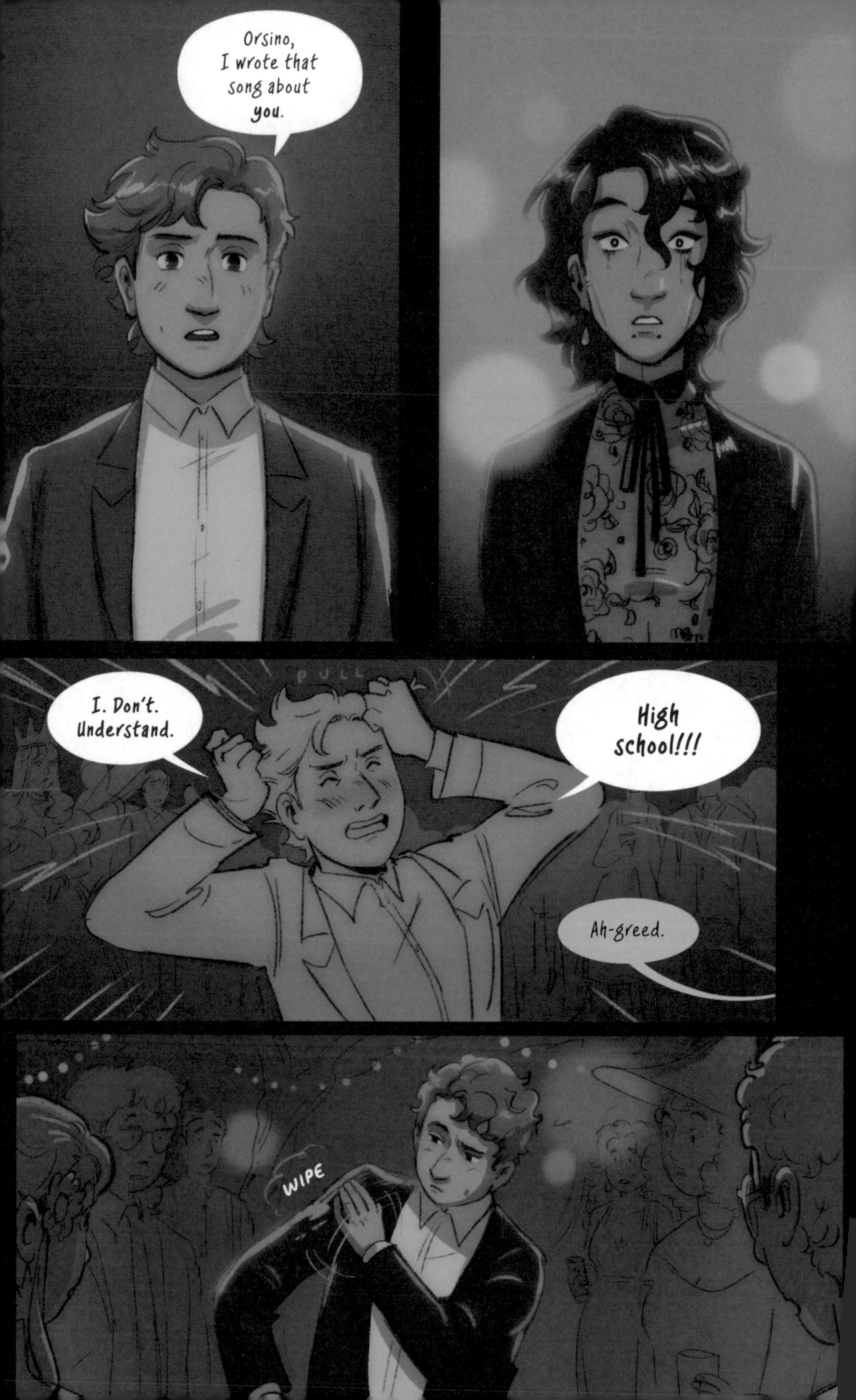
Orsino, I wrote that song about you.
I. Don't. Understand.
PULL
High school!!!
Ah-greed.
WIPE

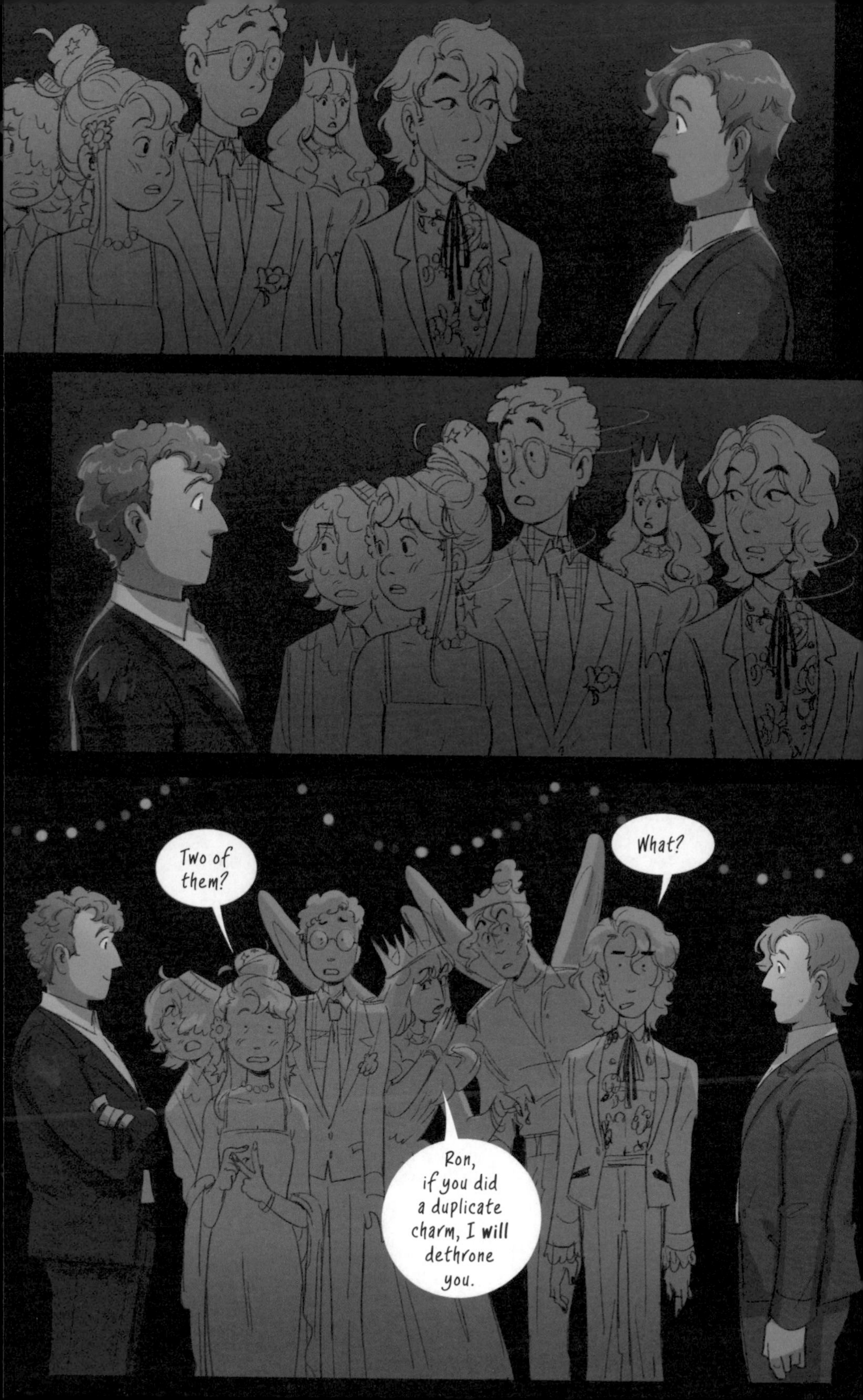
Two of them?
What?
Ron, if you did a duplicate charm, I will dethrone you.

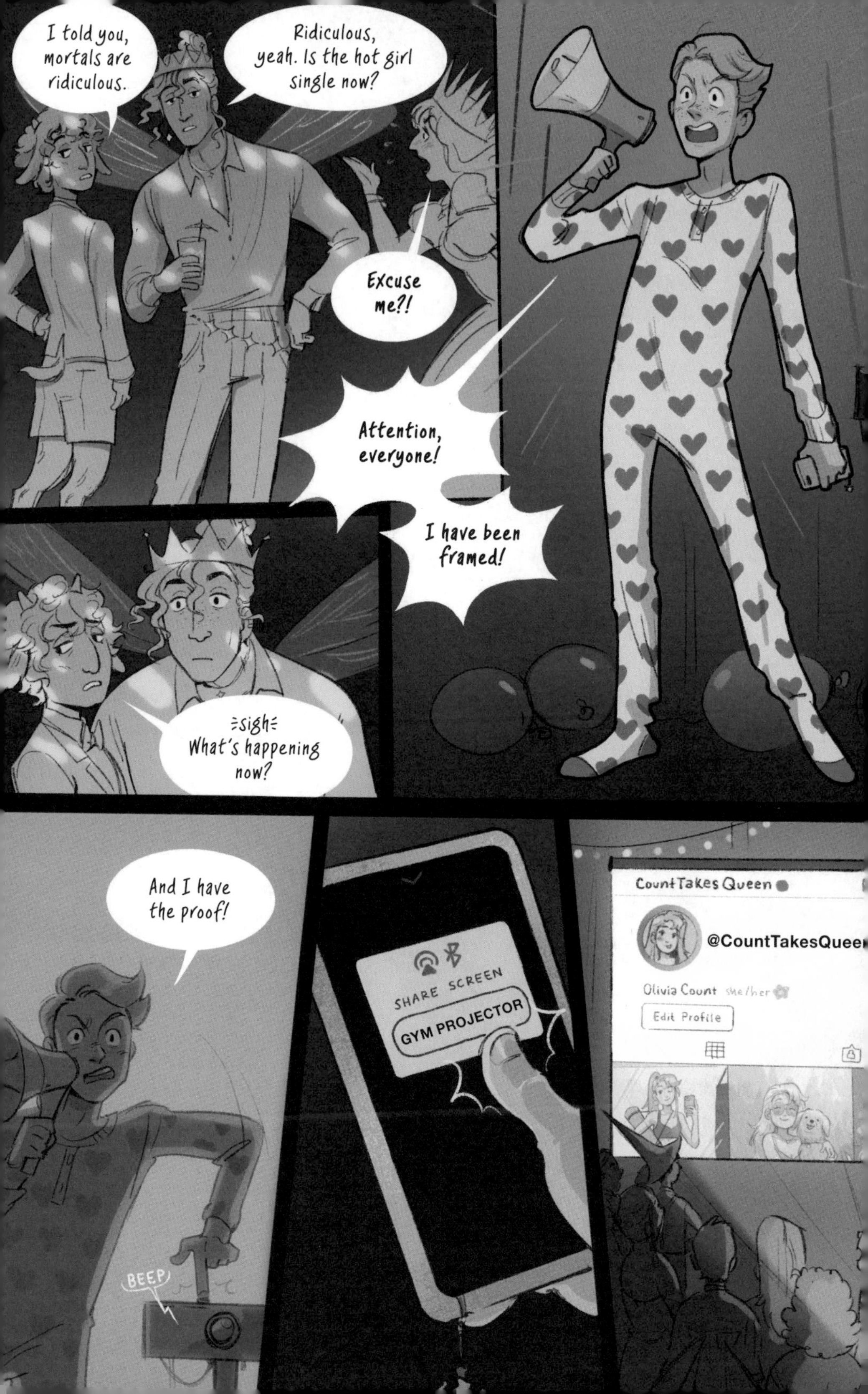
I told you, mortals are ridiculous.
Ridiculous, yeah. Is the hot girl single now?
Excuse me?!
Attention, everyone!
I have been framed!
≈sigh≈ What's happening now?
And I have the proof!
BEEP
SHARE SCREEN
GYM PROJECTOR
CountTakes Queen
@CountTakesQueen
Olivia Count she/her
Edit Profile

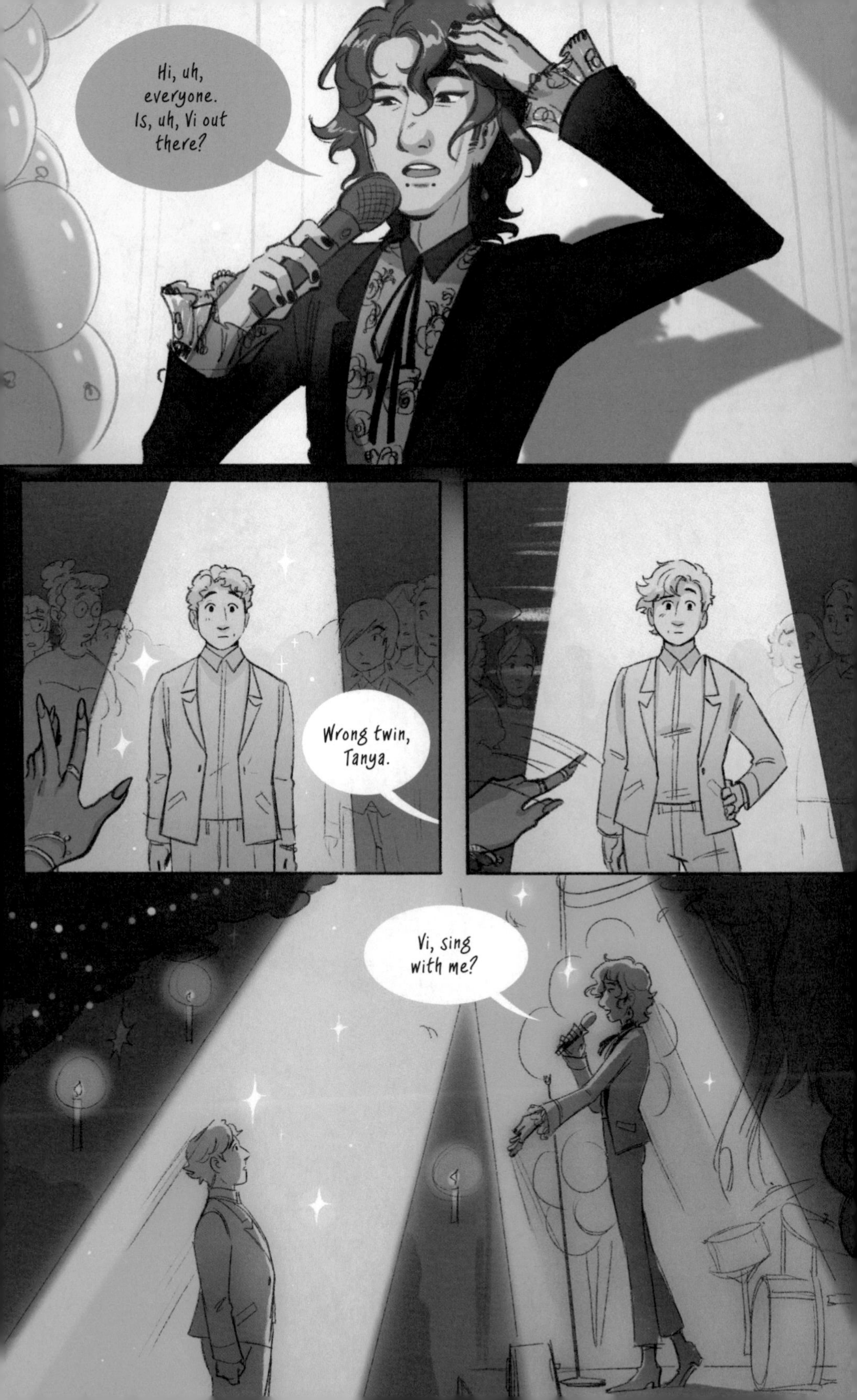
Hi, uh, everyone. Is, uh, Vi out there?
Wrong twin, Tanya.
Vi, sing with me?

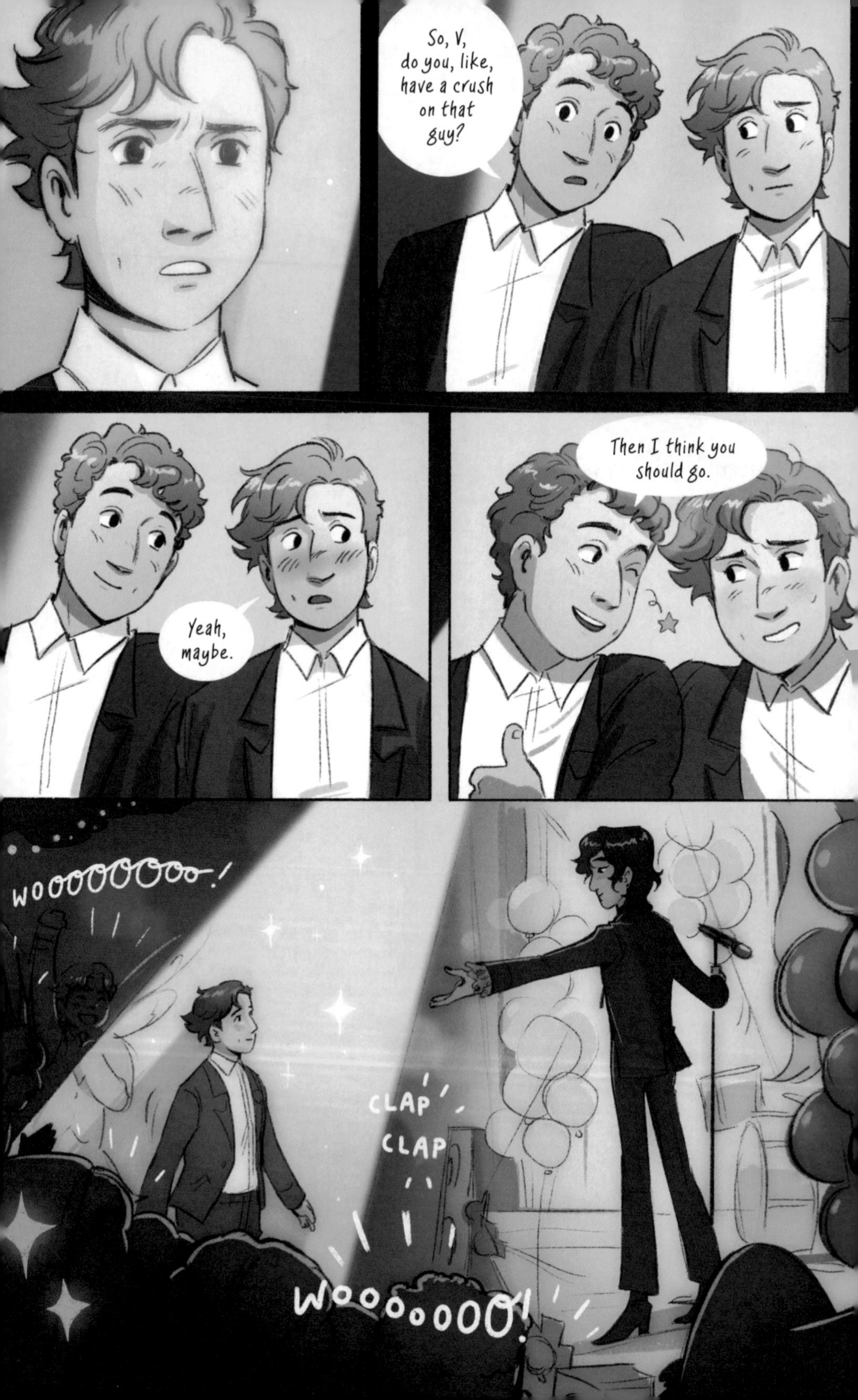
So, V, do you, like, have a crush on that guy?
Yeah, maybe.
Then I think you should go.
WOOOOOOOo!
CLAP
CLAP
WOOoooOO!

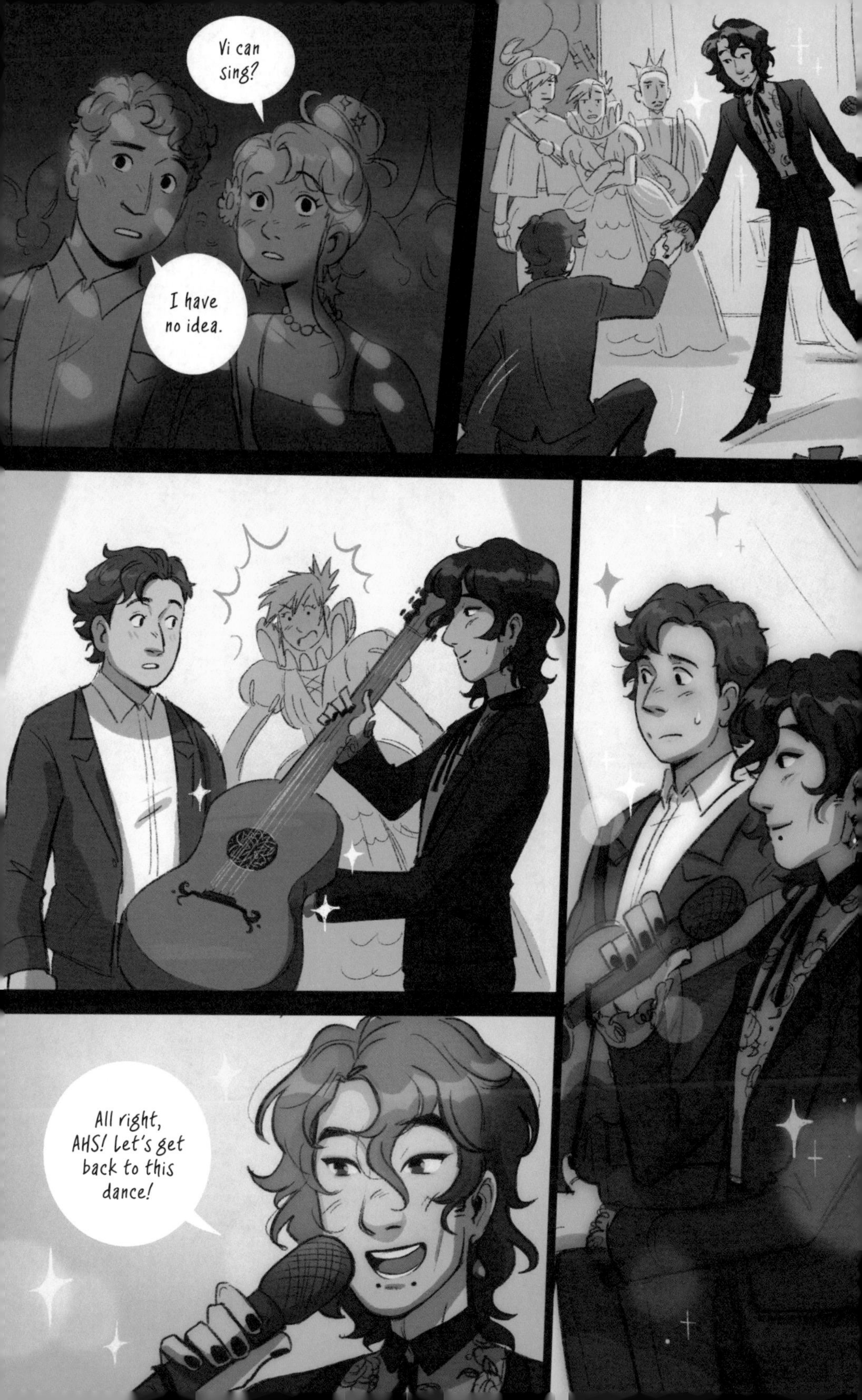
Vi can sing?
I have no idea.
All right, AHS! Let's get back to this dance!

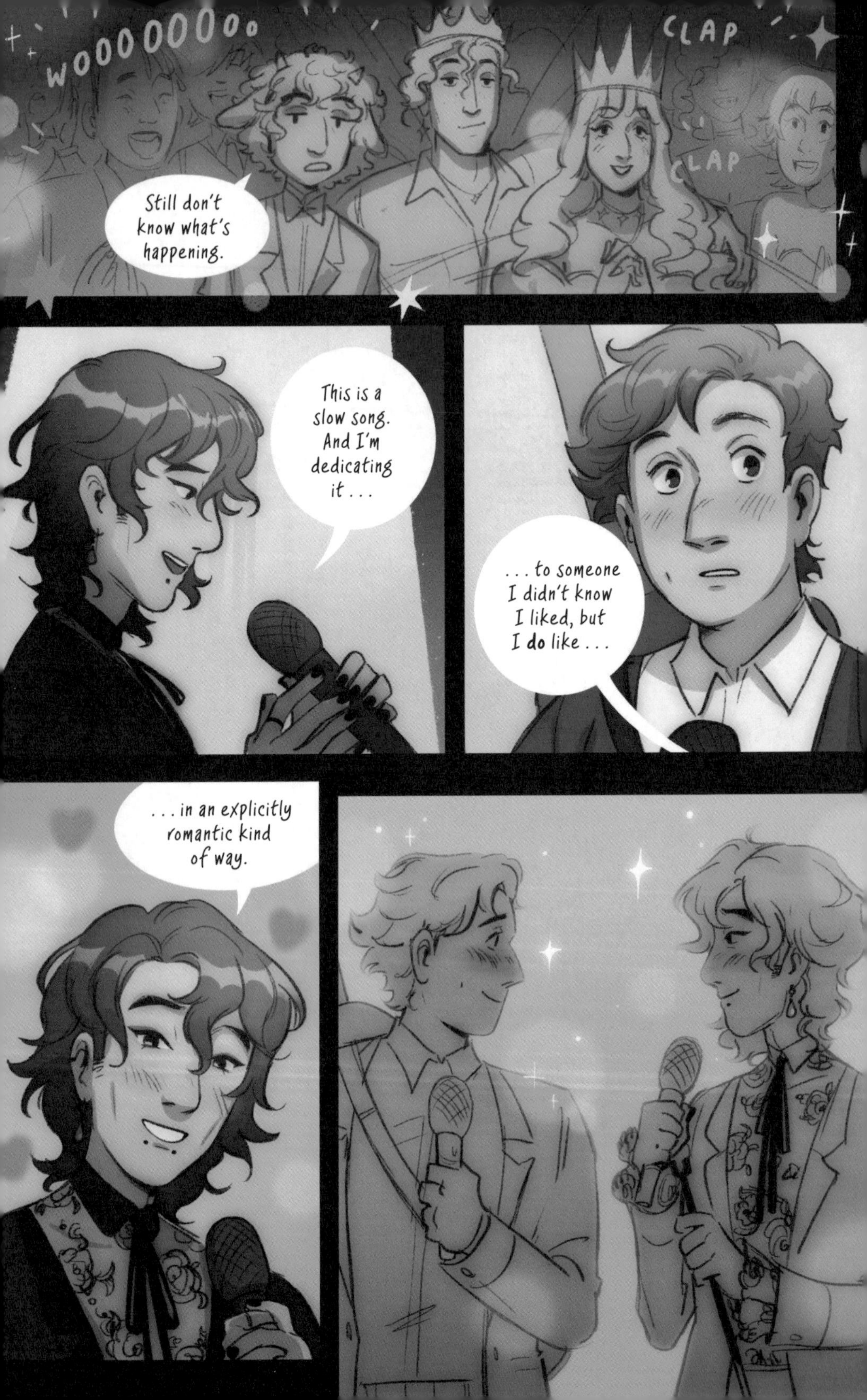
WOOOOOOOo
CLAP
CLAP
Still don't know what's happening.
This is a slow song. And I'm dedicating it . . .
. . . to someone I didn't know I liked, but I do like . . .
. . . in an explicitly romantic kind of way.

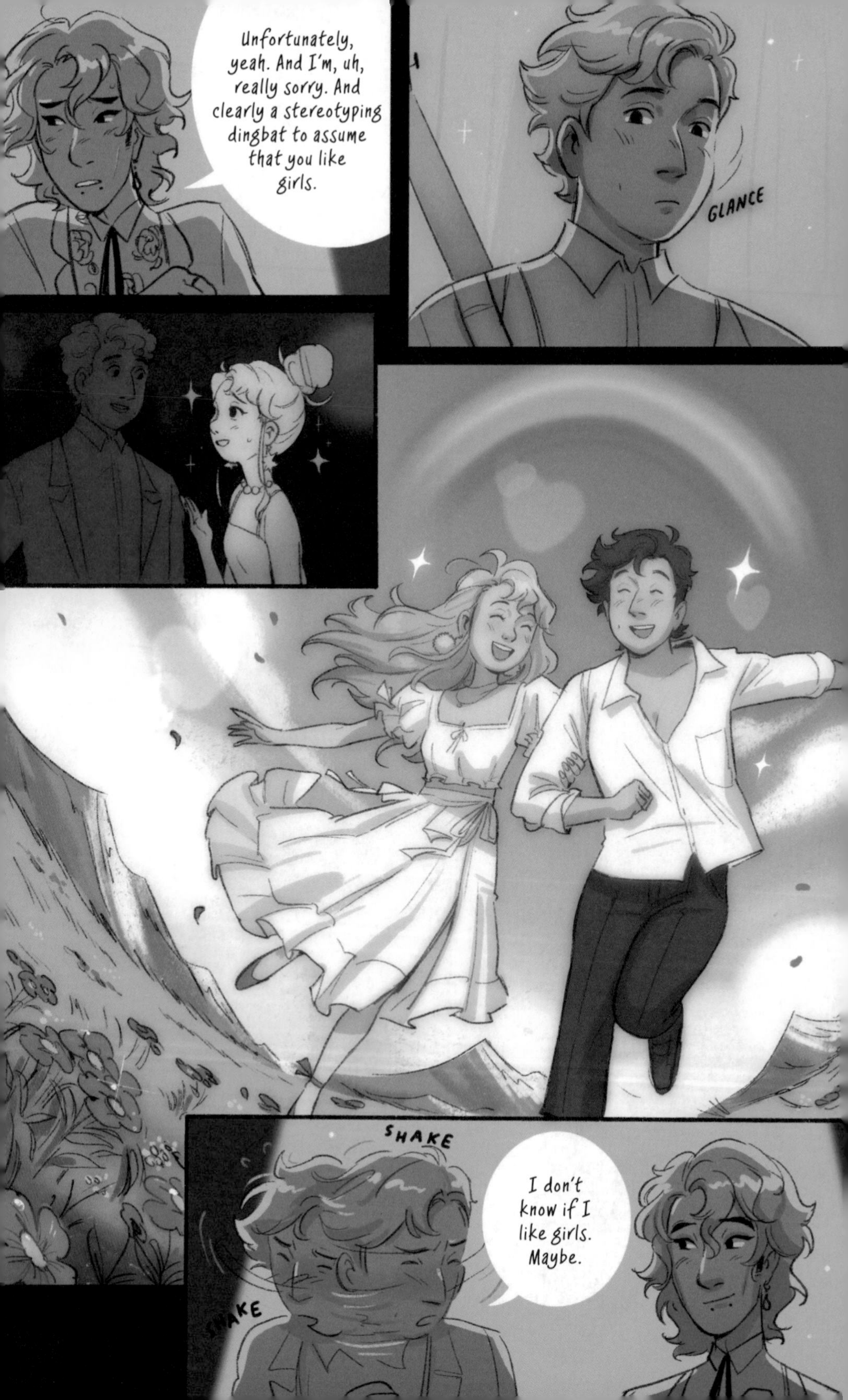
Unfortunately, yeah. And I'm, uh, really sorry. And clearly a stereotyping dingbat to assume that you like girls.
GLANCE
SHAKE
SHAKE
I don't know if I like girls. Maybe.

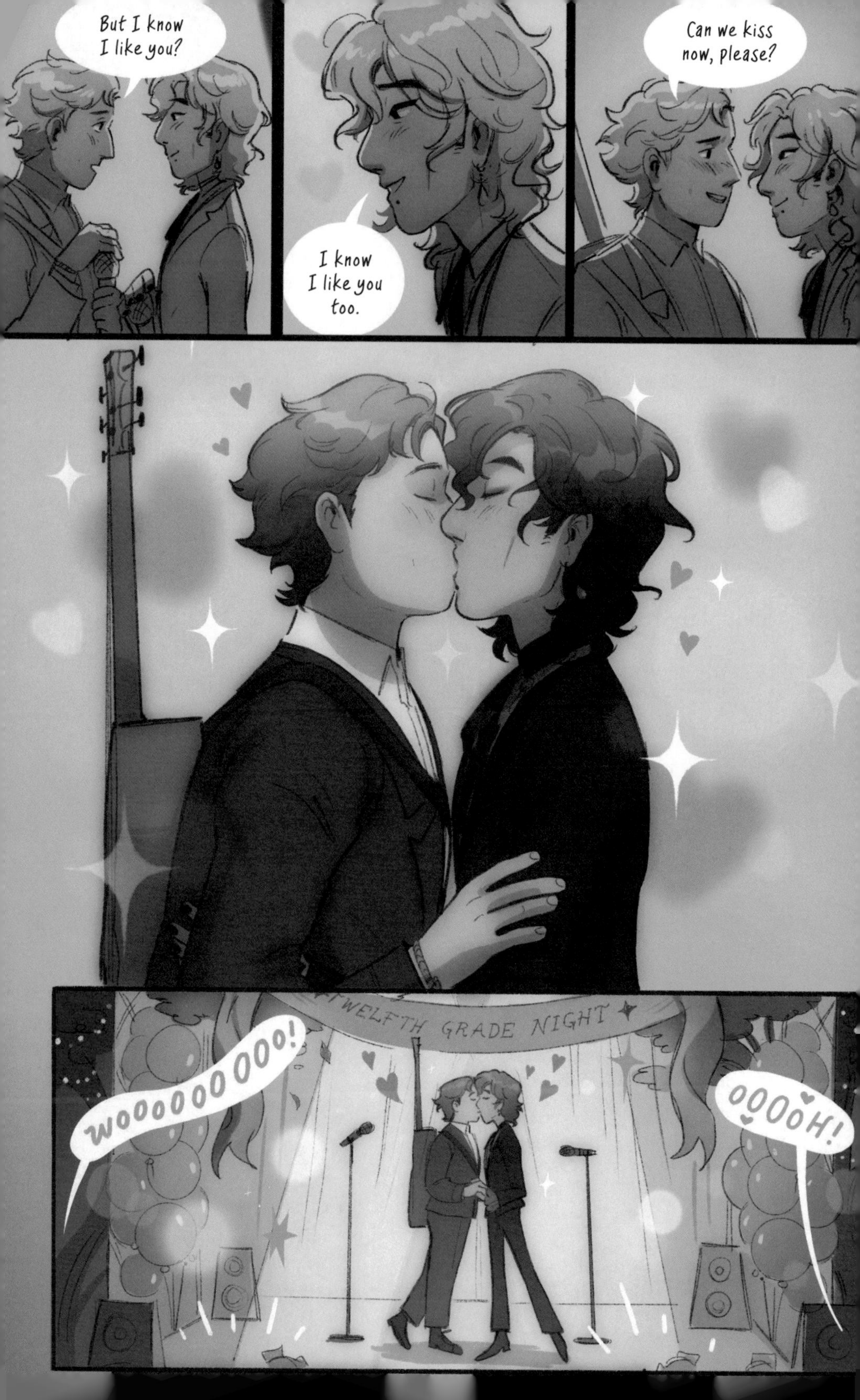
But I know I like you?
I know I like you too.
Can we kiss now, please?
TWELFTH GRADE NIGHT
WOOOOOOOOO!
OOOOH!

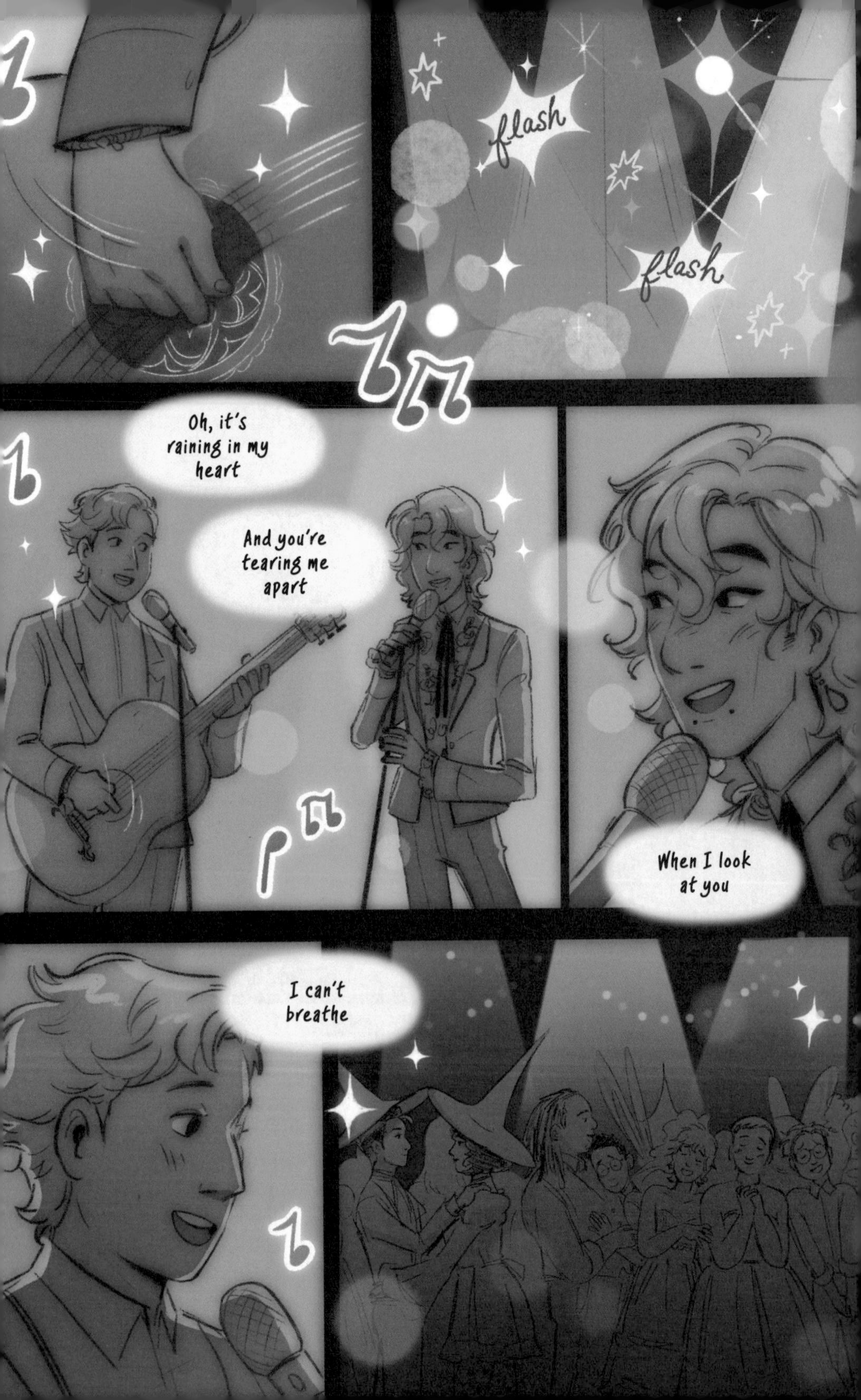
flash
flash
Oh, it's raining in my heart
And you're tearing me apart
When I look at you
I can't breathe

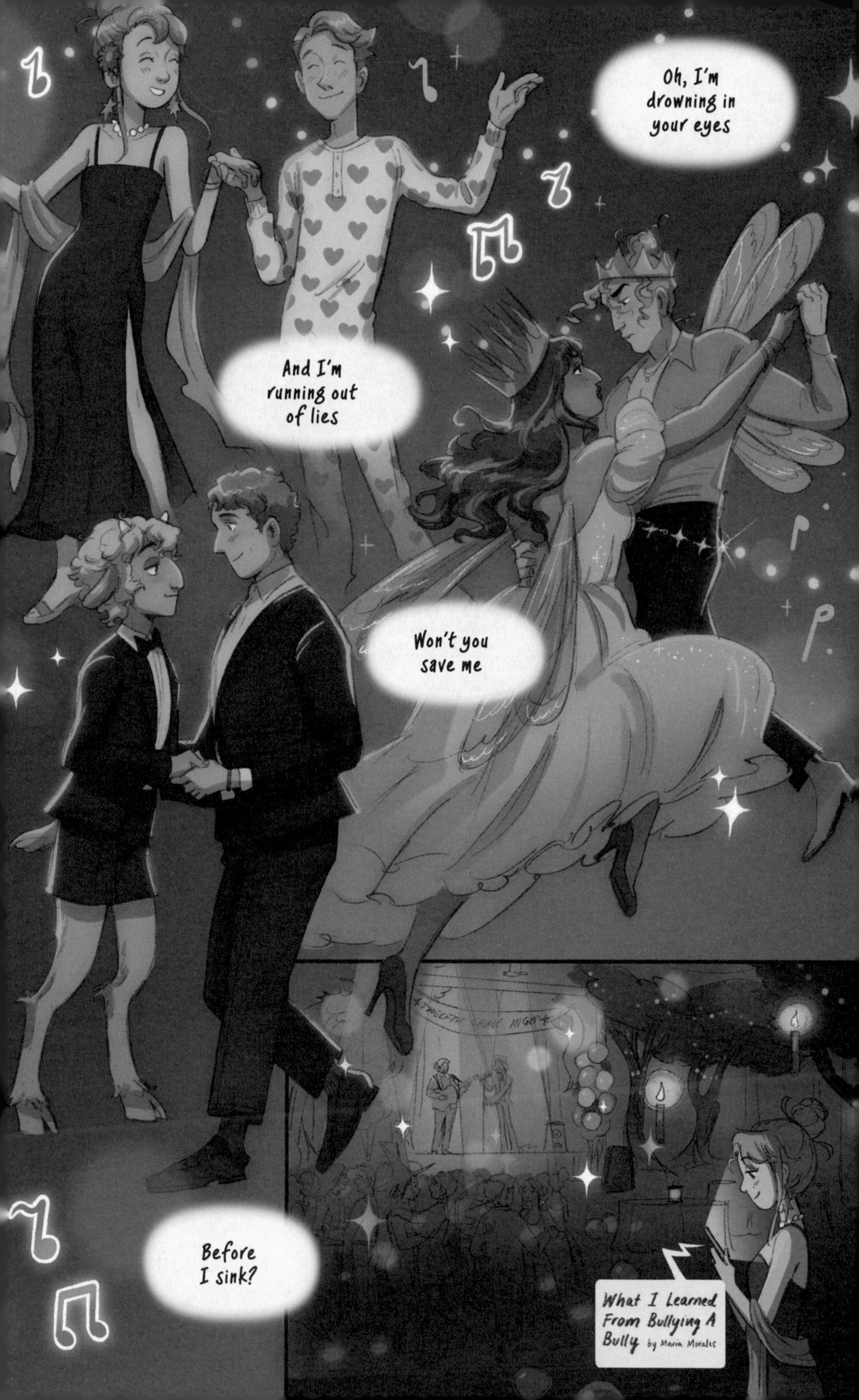
Oh, I'm drowning in your eyes
And I'm running out of lies
Won't you save me
Before I sink?
What I Learned From Bullying A Bully by Maria Morales

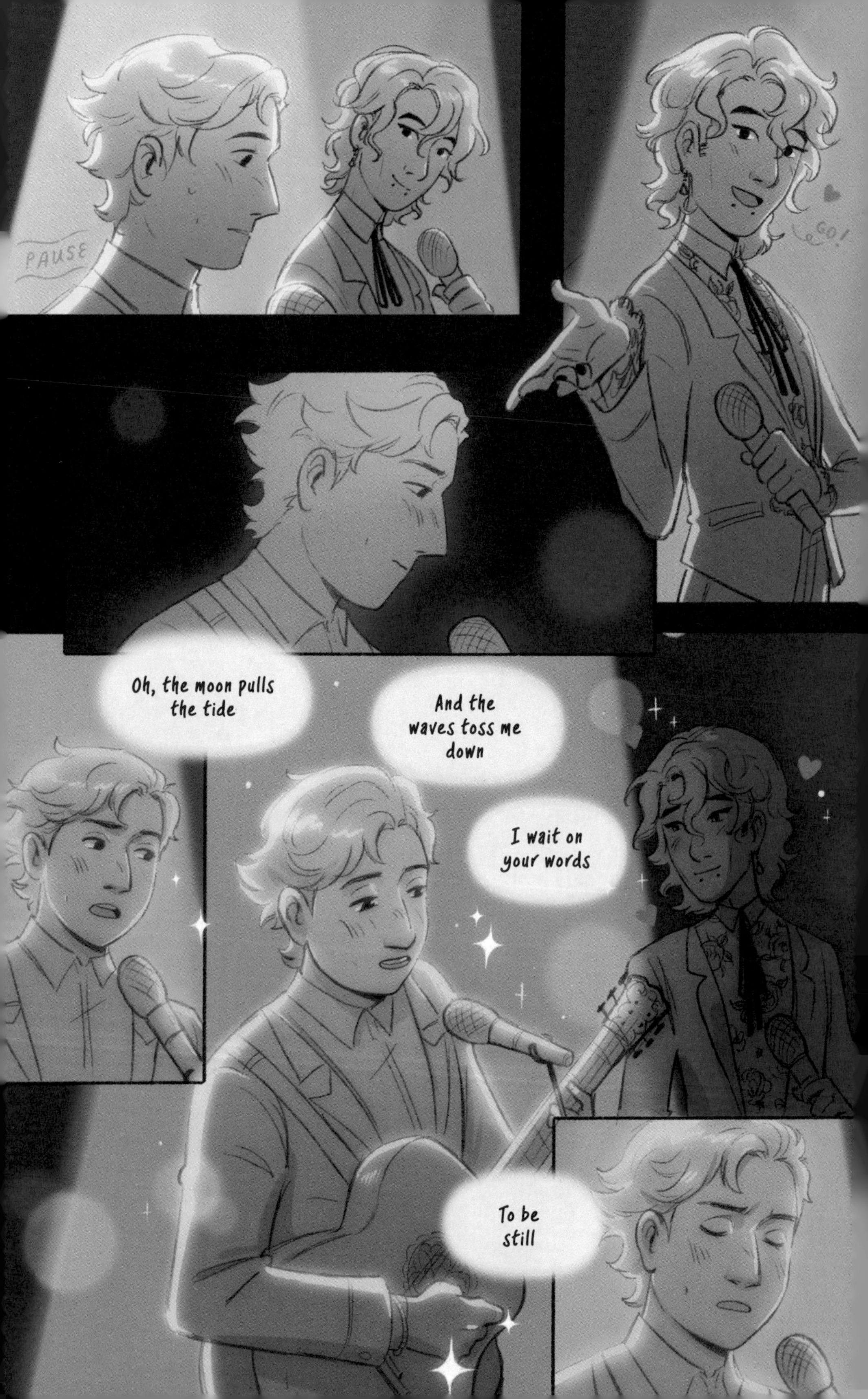
PAUSE
GO!
Oh, the moon pulls the tide
And the waves toss me down
I wait on your words
To be still

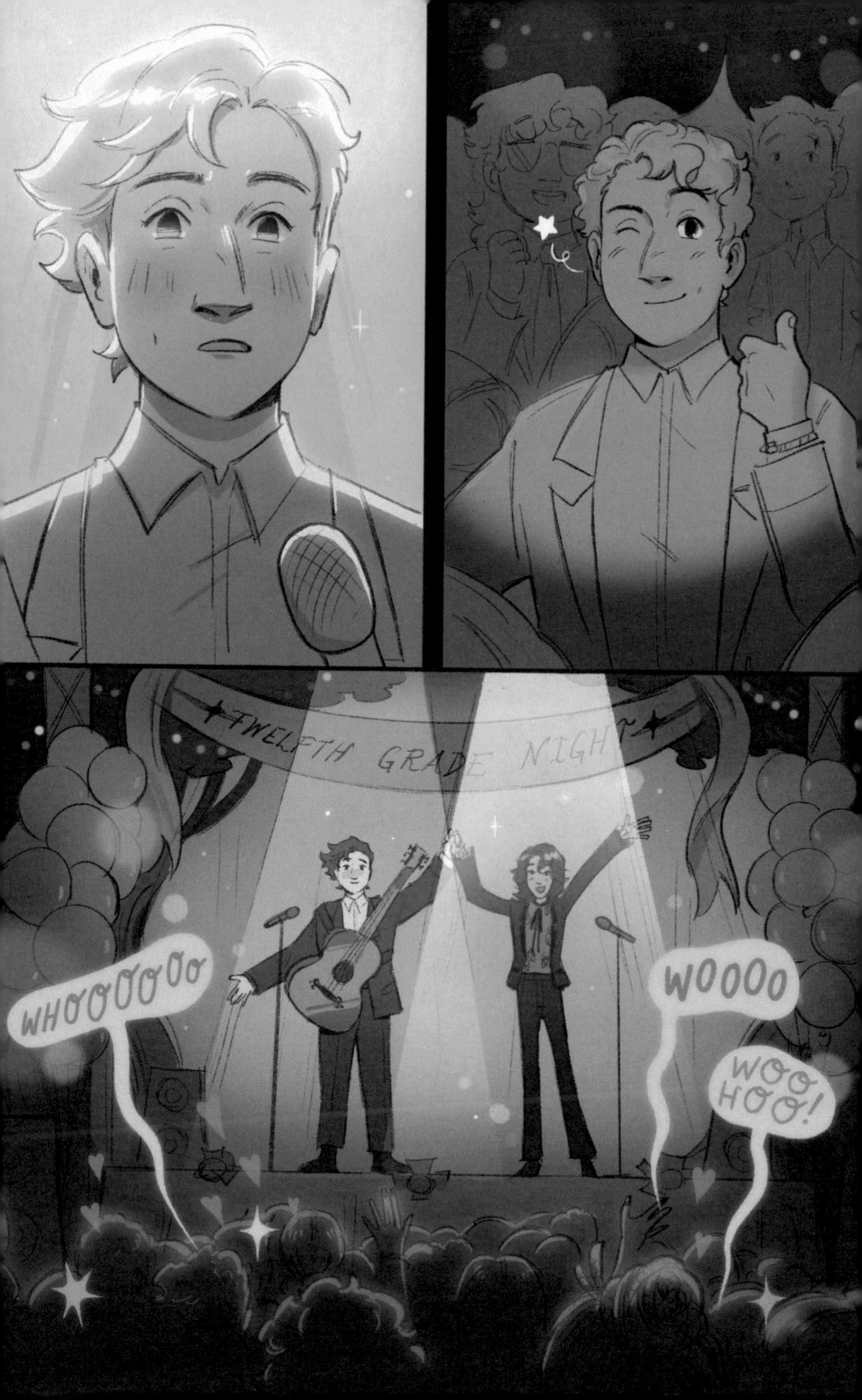
TWELFTH GRADE NIGHT
WHOOOOOO
WOOOO
WOO HOO!

SO, IT TURNS OUT HIGH SCHOOL CAN BE OKAY.
IT HELPS IF YOU FIND YOUR PEOPLE . . .
AND ROLL WITH THE PUNCHES . . .
eenMariaMorales
CountTakesQueen
TAP
TAP TAP
AND LET YOURSELF FEEL YOUR FEELS.

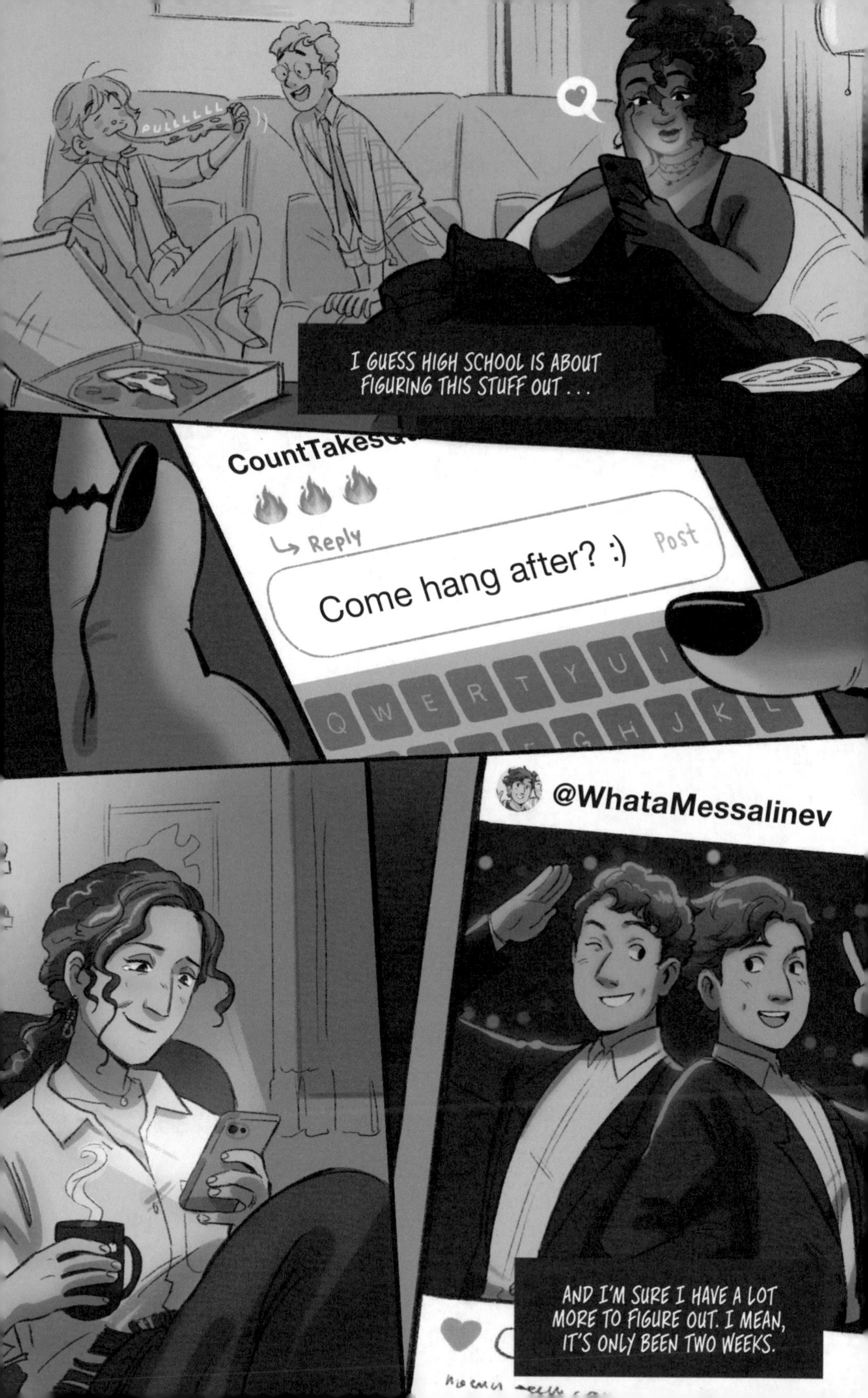
PULLLLLLL
I GUESS HIGH SCHOOL IS ABOUT FIGURING THIS STUFF OUT . . .
CountTakesQ
Reply
Post
Come hang after? :)
@WhataMessalinev
AND I'M SURE I HAVE A LOT MORE TO FIGURE OUT. I MEAN, IT'S ONLY BEEN TWO WEEKS.

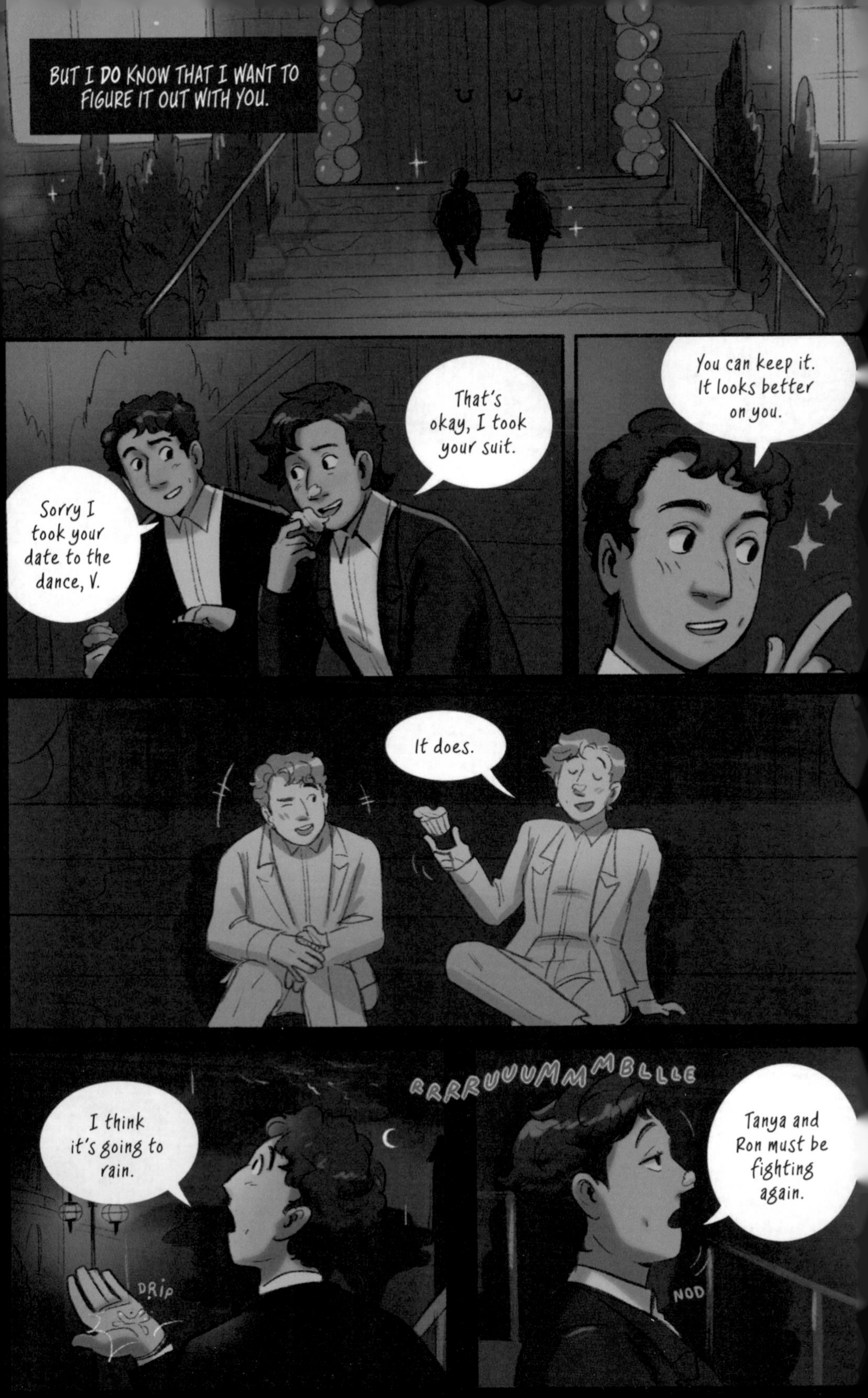

BUT I DO KNOW THAT I WANT TO FIGURE IT OUT WITH YOU.
Sorry I took your date to the dance, V.
That's okay, I took your suit.
You can keep it. It looks better on you.
It does.
I think it's going to rain.
DRIP
RRRRUUUMMMBLLLE
Tanya and Ron must be fighting again.
NOD